SOOTHSAYER

ALLISON SIPE

LIKE MAGIC
STUDIO

This book is a word of fiction. Names, characters, places and incidents are either the product of the author's imagination or are used fictitiously and any resemblance to actual persons, living or dead, events, or locales is entirely coincidental.

Text Copyright © 2015 Allison Sipe
All Right reserved

No part of this book may be reproduced, scanned, or distributed in any printed or electronic form without the explicit permission of the author.

Cover Art Copyright ©
<a href='http://www.123rf.com/profile_NejroN'> / 123RF Stock Photo</a>
Cover Designer: Alessio Varvarà

❀ Created with Vellum

ALSO BY ALLISON SIPE

SOOTHSAYER SERIES

Soothsayer

Avalon: A Soothsayer Novella

Trivium

Le Fay: A Soothsayer Novella

Elysium

REALMS SAGA

Realm of Flames & Steel

Realm of Stars & Shadows

BOOK PLAYLIST

If you like to listen to music while you read, then you're in luck! We've created a playlist just for Soothsayer on Spotify and you can listen here:

You and I are not the polite people that live in poems.
We are blessed and cursed by our times.
- Guinevere

PROLOGUE

ENGLAND, 1782

Utter darkness enveloped the world around us, the air thick with mist. I couldn't see anything beyond my own feet. The trees rose up out of the ground like hands of the dead, cold and lifeless. The fallen leaves and sticks crackled under my boots like bones being snapped in two. A chill ran through my spine, leaving goosebumps on my flesh as I continued on behind my companions.

No one said a word as we walked. The even breathing and footsteps of the men in front of me was the only indication I wasn't alone.

I didn't know why we were being led into the woods in the middle of the night. I only knew it was of grave importance that no one knew we were here. After what seemed like hours of trekking through fallen leaves and mud, we came to an abrupt stop. I looked around but found nothing of consequence in sight. A small tremor of panic rose inside me as we stood in silence. The fog was thicker here than when we first started our journey, and I could barely see Thomas Ainsworth standing next to me as we huddled together in the small clearing.

"What do you suppose we're here for?" I whispered as I leaned toward Thomas.

"Don't know, but I think we're about to find out." He pointed toward the darkness in front of us.

I couldn't see anything, but I could hear each footstep crackle in the heather. I felt my muscles spring to life and readied myself for whatever might be making its way toward us.

"*Inlíhtnes,*" a woman spoke the enchantment and stepped into the clearing. Illuminator Orbs like I'd never seen glided toward us and lit up the small patch of grass where our group had gathered.

Soft blue light fell on each of us, banishing all other colors to the shadows. My nerves calmed as I recognized the beautiful woman standing before us. Her name was Belinda Hughes and she was a gifted Soothsayer. Her dark hair swirled around her face and down her shoulders like seaweed as she glided toward us. Her cloak reached the ground and was pulled tight around her, shielding her from the cold.

Belinda was blessed with one of the most respected gifts in our community. She had the gift of Sight. Only a direct descendant of Merlin himself could be born with the gift of seeing the past, present and future.

We all bowed to her out of respect as she stopped in front of us.

"Thank you for meeting me on such short notice," Belinda's smooth voice purred.

I straightened up and attempted to relax, but knowing that it was Belinda who brought us out here had my nerves coiled and ready to spring at the first sign of a threat.

"Of course, Milady," Colin said, and inclined his head out of nervous habit.

"I'm sure you're all wondering why I had Colin gather you up and drag you all the way out here." She paused a moment, considering her words before she continued. "I've had a vision of the utmost importance that mustn't fall into the wrong hands. As you are all aware, your families are the most powerful and well respected in the Magical World." She paced as she spoke, barely rustling the leaves under her feet.

"Someday, many years from now, your influence will reach beyond this land and across the sea. Because of your families' influence, I've chosen to entrust my vision to the five of you," she paused and looked at each one of us. "But before I tell you anything, I must mark each of your bloodlines with a spell of secrecy. Should anyone belonging to your bloodline betray what I tell you this evening, all will know of your betrayal. Do you understand?" She asked with grave sincerity.

We all nodded in unison.

"Edric Patridge," Belinda called as she pulled a crude-looking dagger from inside her cloak.

Edric took a step toward her and waited for instruction.

"Give me your hand."

Edric pulled his leather gloves off, finger by finger, and extended his exposed hand to Belinda. She pricked the center of his palm three times and a pool of blood began to form.

"*Ligaveris sanguinum vitam verba haec,*" Belinda recited the blood-oath spell and the crimson pool on Edric's palm started to rise. "*Numquam undo hoc iuramento.*"

We all watched mesmerized as Edric's blood floated above his hand in a small, pebble-sized ball.

"*Vel omnes noverit proditio.*" As Belinda finished the spell, the blood sank back down into Edric's skin and the pinpricks on his palm vanished without a trace.

"Thomas Ainsworth," her voice chimed.

Thomas stepped forward and extended his hand and performed thw same spell.

"William Maxwell." Her eyes met mine when she finished with Thomas.

I stepped forward, inclined my head and extended my hand. My pulse quickened as she pricked my palm. The blood felt warm on my hand as she recited the spell. Moments later the blood was gone and my hand was cold once again.

She performed the same spell on Kyle Landon and Colin Deardon and then slipped the dagger back into the concealed pocket of her cloak.

"I have seen a great war," she began without preamble, "that will threaten to enslave the Magical World. The dead will rise and seek to take the throne that once belonged to Arthur."

"Who will rise from the dead?" Thomas' voice cracked as he spoke.

"Morgana."

The blood in my veins turned to ice, "But she can't, it's impossible. She's been dead for hundreds of years," I said in disbelief.

"She can and she will," Belinda said gravely.

"Is there nothing we can do to prevent her?" I asked, truly afraid of what it might mean for future generations if the Magical World was enslaved by Morgana.

"It cannot be prevented. She will rise with a vengeance. But there is a small glimmer of hope," she paused, mulling over her next words carefully. "There will be a woman named Violet. She's the key to waking the Lady of the Lake and bringing an end to Morgana's war once and for all."

"Lady of the Lake," Thomas exclaimed, near breathless, "I thought she entombed herself after Arthur's death."

"Violet will carry the mark of Merlin's bloodline, and she will be able to wake The Lady from her slumber. It's the only way to banish Morgana back to the land of the dead."

"After everything that happened with Arthur, do you really

think The Lady will want to help us again?" It was Colin who spoke, seizing our attention.

"He's right, besides there's no magic powerful enough to wake her from the slumber of a broken heart." Edric kicked at the dirt as he spoke.

"You're right, there isn't any magic powerful enough. But there will be, and that's why I need you to pass this prophecy down through your heirs," Belinda explained.

"How are they supposed to find this woman when the time comes?" Edric asked.

"She will find who she is meant to find."

I couldn't be sure, but I thought Belinda glanced in my direction.

"And how does this war come to be?" Kyle's voice was barely a whisper.

"Through betrayal. It's the reason I've marked your bloodline, to fish out the traitor when the time comes. You see, the future is not as simple as our time is now. This makes it difficult to be clear of the small details." She furrowed her brow like she was trying to see through a thick haze of fog. "I've been able to narrow it down to the five bloodlines gathered here, but that is all. Each one of your descendants will play a key role in what happens in the future. And as the time nears, a future Soothsayer will be able to see more clearly."

"How do you suggest we pass this information down through the generations?" Thomas asked, fiddling with the pocket watch in his hand.

"That will be up to you." Belinda took Thomas's hand in hers to stop his fidgeting. "Do you all understand?"

"Yes," we said in unison.

Belinda released Thomas and took a step backward.

It was rare for a Soothsayer to share their visions with anyone. The fact that she dragged us out here to reveal the future to us proved how important this prophecy was.

"Off with you then. If anything else comes up, I shall summon you for another meeting," Belinda announced. Her eyes met mine for a pregnant moment and a small smile touched her lips. "Just a moment, William." She stepped toward me and placed her hand on my shoulder. Her expression became unfocused and distant. I held my breath and waited for her to return to the present. As her eyes came back into focus, she made a quick glance toward the other men.

"What is it?" I asked, my nerves shaking my body even in her grasp.

She searched my eyes for a moment and then leaned in closer to me, her fingers digging into my shoulder. "Robert must find her before it's too late," she whispered against my ear.

Violent chills quaked up my spine as she released her hold on me and disappeared into the darkness. The small orbs of light followed behind her and then vanished as well. None of us moved. We stood watching as Belinda disappeared back into the forest. I rubbed my hands against my shoulders to fight off another shiver as her words echoed in my head.

After what seemed like an eternity of silence, Thomas turned to me, nodded, and disappeared into the fog. Edric, Colin, and Kyle each did the same, leaving me standing alone in the forest. I took a deep breath and started back to town as well. My mind raced over everything Belinda had said, and I couldn't help but wonder who Robert was. What could I possibly do to ensure he found Violet when the time came?

I walked inside, craving the comfort and warmth of my home. I pulled my journal out from the desk drawer, threw another log on the fire and poured myself a dram of whiskey. I sat before the hearth in my large armchair and recounted the evening in my journal. I spared no detail and hoped my account of tonight's events would be enough. I sipped at the rest of my drink and let the fire and whiskey warm my bones and soothe my nerves. Only when sleep threatened to overtake my energy and cloud my memory did I close my journal and drain my glass. I returned the leather-bound chronicle to the desk's bottom drawer and recited a spell to disguise it from prying eyes. With my duty done for the night, I headed upstairs to bed. The sun crept over the hills as I crawled under the covers and fell asleep.

CHAPTER ONE

PRESENT-DAY

 shot upright and awake, heart pounding and covered in sweat. I tried to remember what exactly I'd been dreaming about, but the images vanished like wisps of smoke on the wind. I shuffled my feet across the carpet and opened my bedroom window, letting the cool air refresh my sticky skin. It did little to slow my heart though, as the muscle battered against my chest, threatening to escape. I took a deep breath, closed my eyes and held onto the pendant I always wore around my neck. It was my grandmother's and even though she was gone, I could still feel her warm embrace every time I held the cool metal between my fingers.

Though I couldn't remember anything that had happened in my dream, my chest felt heavy with sorrow. Taking another shaking breath, I watched as the sun rose over the horizon and broke through the grey, patchy clouds. I looked toward my bed as my heart slowly returned to a normal pace. The sheets spilled onto the floor, looking like I'd just finished a wrestling match. I shivered as the dawn air brushed my skin and sent goosebumps crawling across my skin. Not wanting to return to bed, I decided to walk down to the shore and clear my head.

I reached the beach on my single speed bike as the sky changed from vibrant yellow and orange to robin's egg blue. The white caps on the water became more visible with each passing moment as the waves thrashed against the shore. The clouds rumbled on the horizon, promising rain today. Despite the rough water, a few people were paddling out in their wetsuits and as I watched the surfers, a wave crashed on the shore and threw a mist directly into the sunlight. The tiny drops of water sparkled like diamonds in the crisp morning air. I lifted my camera and took a picture of the sunrise and another of the bobbing heads in the water, sitting on their boards, waiting for the next set of waves.

The beach was my happy place, and it was never more beautiful than in the morning when the sun welcomed a new day. The unease of my nightmare lingered in my mind, but the tightness in my chest eased a bit as I breathed in the salty sea air. Once the sun was high in the sky above me, more people started making their way down to the sand. I adjusted the shutter speed and aperture on my camera and snapped a quick picture of a man running barefoot along the shore. I looked at the screen to make sure I'd achieved the desired effect and smiled as I reviewed the photo.

The man was a dark figure running along the pristine beach, salt water lapping at his feet. My candid photographs always turned out to be my favorite portraits of the day. There was just something special about capturing someone in their natural state. I walked up and down the beach, snapping pictures as I went, including one of a woman sitting on the sand sipping her coffee and feeding the seagulls. As I watched her toss a piece of her bagel to the squawking birds, the hairs on the back of my neck stood up.

I looked behind me and a tall gentleman adjusted his base-ball cap to cover his face as he looked in my direction. Trying not to draw attention to myself, I edged closer to the woman feeding the birds. When I looked back over my shoulder, the man had completely vanished. Great, I thought, my nightmares were starting to make me paranoid.

After an hour or so, people dotted the shoreline setting up tents, tables, and grills. As more people arrived, the beach morphed into a playground and I decided it was time to head back and get something to eat. My stomach rumbled with enthusiasm at the thought of being fed as I walked back to my bike, past a bakery that smelled of fresh baked bread and sugar.

Pismo was starting to wake up as I rode through the heart of town. There was already a line forming inside the coffee shop as I rode past and pedestrians filled the streets. I took a short detour by the farmers market in the hopes I would find some-thing yummy to nibble on before I passed out from hunger. Parking my bike, I walked along the stalls, already crowded with people. Each booth gave off an enchanting fragrance that made my stomach rumble with delight. The sweet smell of ripe fruit, the sharpness of fresh-cut flowers and the decadent aroma of crepes all hung in the air. I sampled a few bites of the local fare, ordered a crepe and picked up a bouquet of sunflowers. On the way back to my bike, my pocket vibrated the announcement of a phone call. Popping the last bite of my crepe into my mouth and licking my fingers clean, I pulled my phone out and answered.

"Hey Beck, you're up early!" Becky was my best friend, for all intents and purposes. She was the first person I met here in Pismo, and we hit it off instantly. She and her brother had taken me hostage and unofficially adopted me, which was nice since I didn't have a family of my own.

"Coffee, twenty minutes," she mumbled and hung up.

I laughed and returned my phone to my pocket. Becky really

had a flair for the dramatic sometimes. I tossed my bags into the basket on the front of my bike and leisurely made my way to our favorite coffee shop just a couple blocks away.

It was around nine o'clock when I pulled up to the Java Beach Café and Becky was already anxiously waiting for me outside.

"I got you your favorite." Becky held out a brown paper bag as I joined her at the take away counter.

"Thanks." I took the bag from her even though I was stuffed, I couldn't pass up my favorite pastry. We both started eating and made small talk by the counter while waiting for our drinks. "So what's so earth shattering that you're out of bed before noon?" I asked, nibbling on a warm and deliciously gooey piece of donut.

She gave me a heavy sigh and said, "I needed an excuse to get away from my date."

"I'm assuming he wanted to make you breakfast or perform some other heinous act of kindness the morning after." I rolled my eyes.

"He made, pancakes." She shook her head, mocking me.

"You know, some women would love to find a man who cooks her breakfast in the morning."

"Yeah well, I'm not some women. Besides, I needed to ask you something. Do you know a David Ainsworth?"

"No, I don't think so, why?" I asked, puzzled.

"I was telling David a story last night, and when I mentioned your name he got a little weird and…" she wouldn't meet my eye, which was never a good sign. "He knew your parents. He said he went to college with your mother."

"My parents?" I wasn't expecting that. They died when I was just a kid and I moved to Pismo, after college in the hopes of having a fresh start. "David Ainsworth." I rolled the name around in my head, but nothing clicked.

"Medium latte," the barista called out Becky's drink.

She grabbed her paper cup from the counter and we made

our way out of the café. We strolled along the sidewalk in silence for a few moments. I wondered if I could connect David to my parents, but I had never heard his name before.

"Did he say anything else?" A million questions zipped through my head before it dawned on me that Becky had just spent the night with this man. "Wait, back up. I'm assuming David is who you were trying to escape this morning after spending the night with him."

"Yes." She narrowed her eyes at me.

"And David went to college with my mother." I raised my eyebrows.

"Hey, I don't discriminate. He's damn good looking and to be honest he was very persistent." She said the last part under her breath.

"Right." I laughed and shook my head. "So did he say anything else about my parents?"

"No, not really. He sends his condolences. Do you want me to introduce you? Maybe he can tell you some stories or something." Her half smile was sincere, but anxiety rolled off her as she fidgeted with the lid of her coffee.

"No," I said and took a deep breath. It was tempting, but I didn't want to open old wounds and I didn't want to put Becky in the middle of my past. "No, I think I'm okay. Thanks, though."

"Thank God, I wasn't really planning on seeing him again." We both laughed as we walked around the corner and headed in the direction of the bookstore.

"Another book?" She asked as she noticed the direction we were walking in.

"I just want to pick up a collection of Walt Whitman's poems for a project," I noted.

I'd always loved poetry, and Whitman was one of my absolute favorites. For as long as I could remember, I'd wanted to put together a portfolio that paired pictures of my own work with his poems.

"I don't know why you need to have a physical book, when you can just look them up online," Becky remarked.

Becky lived for the digital age. I didn't think I'd ever seen her without her computer. Even now it was in the satchel hanging at her side. And don't get me wrong, I updated my camera gear and software fairly often, but I also had an appreciation for the way life was before technology took over our lives.

"You know that I like having the actual book. There's just something about the smell of the paper and having the pages in your hands that just makes the experience so much more exhilarating."

"I guess." Becky rolled her eyes. "Sometimes I worry about your sanity when you have your nose shoved in a book, sniffing the pages like a Bloodhound." She laughed and put her arm around my shoulders.

"Oh, please! I put up with you on a daily basis." I laughed and nudged her in the ribs.

"Don't you already have a copy you can use?"

"Yeah, but it was my dad's." I took a long gulp from my water bottle and tossed the empty container as we passed a trash can.

"Enough said," Becky replied. "Are you still in for the Yosemite trip at the end of August?" She deftly changed the subject.

"Of course, you know I love going on that trip every year."

"I was planning on booking the same cabin we had last year."

"That'd be perfect." I pushed open the door to the bookstore. A familiar jingle welcomed us as we entered.

"Good morning, ladies," Frank welcomed us from behind the counter. "How are you today, Miss Evans?"

Frank Murphy was an older man who owned the bookstore and the bait shop down by the pier. He stood slightly taller than my five foot five inches, and his hair had more salt than pepper.

"Morning Frank. How many times do I have to tell you to call me Violet?" I said with a smile.

"Oh I know, but a lady should be addressed properly," he said with a good-old-fashioned nod, his manners reminiscent of an older time.

"Even so, I prefer Violet. So how've you been?"

"Oh, can't complain. You ready for the big wedding?"

"You know I could shoot that wedding with one hand tied behind my back." I shrugged my shoulders confidently.

"That's true, you're very talented. But this is a Maxwell wedding. Everyone's been buzzing that it'll be the event of the decade."

"Well, I don't know about that." I shrugged. Everyone seemed to care so much about the Maxwells. Personally, I didn't get it. "I'm sure it'll be predictably over the top though."

"Now, Violet, you behave yourself. The Maxwell family has a long history here. They're good people," Frank insisted. His tone was reminiscent of a parent reprimanding a misbehaving child.

"I'll be on my best behavior, Scout's honor." I raised three fingers in salute.

Frank laughed and waved me off.

Knowing the shop by heart, I made my way back to the poetry section with Becky right behind me.

"That old man is so weird about the Maxwells," Becky said under her breath.

I gave her a reproachful look and changed the subject. "So aside from the pancake mishap, how was your date last night?" I asked.

"A lot of fun actually. There's something to be said about going out with an older man." Her eyes glazed over.

"Finally met someone who could teach you a thing or two?"

She gave me a coy smile. "Let's just say experience is the best teacher. You should really get back out there and have some fun."

"Don't start with me about dating," I huffed.

I turned down the American Poets aisle and started skimming the shelves.

"And why not? When was the last time you went on a date? You're never going to find someone hiding behind your camera," Becky pointed out.

"Yeah, yeah, I know. I'm just focused on my work right now. And besides, it's not like I've met anyone who lights a fire in me recently."

"Lights a fire in you?" Becky laughed. "Don't be ridiculous, just get some coffee with someone, anyone. You need to stop being so picky."

"I'm picky for a reason. You of all people know how bad things got with Nick."

"I still can't believe he was into all that voodoo magic stuff," Becky said, looking at me apologetically.

Finally, I reached the W's section and started flipping through the books.

I could feel Becky's eyes watching me carefully. "When I find someone worthwhile, then I'll give it a chance," I said to placate her.

"Whatever you say." Becky didn't sound convinced.

Taking one of the Whitman collections off the shelf, I skimmed through the cream colored pages.

Becky's phone went off and she pulled it out of her bag. "Shit, I totally forgot. Aaron's coming into town and I'm supposed to meet him at my place." She looked down at her watch. "Twenty minutes ago! Sorry, Violet, I've gotta run." Becky exited the store as briskly as she could without breaking into a run.

"See ya later. Tell Aaron I say hi!" I called after her.

Becky waved her hand in acknowledgment and answered the phone.

Aaron was Becky's older brother. He came down from San

Francisco every summer to visit, and I'd grown close to him over the last couple of years. He was a good friend and always there to give you an honest male opinion, whether you liked it or not.

I put the book back on the shelf and pulled another one down to look through.

"Violet?" a unfamiliar voice asked behind me in a soft, cautious tone.

Turning to see who had said my name, I saw a man sitting in a plump leather chair with a book in his lap. His light blue button-up shirt stretched across his broad shoulders and his well-muscled legs revealed him to be tall even though he was sitting. His hair was dark and wavy, parted to one side and styled like a suave Cary Grant. His warm eyes reminded me of melted dark chocolate as they stared into mine. He was the most handsome man I had ever seen outside of a magazine.

Taken off guard, I mumbled, "Err... hi. How do you know my name?"

He rose from the chair and walked toward me. His shirt was rolled up to his elbows, exposing his fair skin. *He's not from around here*, I thought. Even if you used sunscreen every day, you'd still have a golden tint to your skin.

"I overheard you and your friend talking. She said your name as she was leaving. I'm Robert." He extended his hand to shake mine.

I placed my hand in his and he gave it a firm grip. His touch was soft and warm. The feel of his skin sent chills up my arm and the closeness of his body heightened all my senses.

This is ridiculous, I thought. I don't even know this man, and I feel like I'm going to start hyperventilating any minute.

"Oh, well, can I help you with something?" I asked, feeling self-conscious.

"Stranger, if you passing meet me and desire to speak to me, why should you not speak to me? And why should I not speak to you?" He quoted and then smiled a crooked smile that I assumed undid most women.

"You know Walt Whitman?" I gave him a dubious look. Most people knew of the poet, but few could quote any of his work from memory.

"Who doesn't." He shrugged. "I noticed you were holding a compilation of his works." He grinned, amused by my expression, and pointed to the book in my hand.

"Oh yeah. I'm trying to find a good collection of his work." *Handsome and smart*, I thought, eying him.

"Might I suggest you get this one?" He reached around me, placing his body inches from mine. I inhaled at the closeness and caught the sweet smell of his cologne mixed with the cool ocean air. I smiled in spite of myself as he pulled away with a leather-bound book in hand.

I reached for the book, turning it over. I glanced up at him and his gaze caught mine. His eyes were warm and curious. The world seemed to slow and for the briefest moment, I felt like I already knew him. I opened my mouth to thank him when his phone went off, startling us both. He cleared his throat and stepped away.

"I'm sorry, will you excuse me a moment?" He gave me an apologetic smile.

"Sure, no problem." I waved him away and turned back to the shelf behind me, heart still pounding in my chest.

He walked away and answered his cell. "This better be important."

He stopped just out of earshot, but I could still see him with his back turned toward me.

I looked between him and the book he had picked out for me. I didn't remember seeing this particular volume on the shelf. I ran my fingers across the worn cover and its gold lettering. It felt smooth under my fingers and the corners had been worn down to a dull curve. I flipped the pages open and let them fan across my thumb. I took a deep breath and could almost smell the fresh ink on the pages mingled with a century of dust.

Turning the book over, I wondered how such an old, unique book could end up crammed on the shelves next to the ordinary mass-market paperbacks.

I looked over my shoulder to see if Robert was still close by and saw him a few aisles down, idly pulling books off the shelf and putting them back without looking at them. His eyes caught mine for a split second and he cocked his head like he was trying to decipher a code hidden in my features. I smiled and looked away as he continued his conversation.

Putting the book that I'd taken down back on the shelf, I held on to the one Robert suggested. I walked a few aisles down to the fiction section to see if there was anything else I wanted while I was there. I examined a book with an interesting-looking cover and started reading the back. It looked like a promising murder-mystery, so I stuck it under my arm alongside the leather-bound book.

"Sorry about that," Robert said, his voice deep and soft.

I turned around to see him leaning against one of the bookshelves across from me.

Why was he back? What did he want from me? A warning bell went off in the back of my mind. Being friendly to a stranger was one thing, but seeking them out was a little odd.

"Don't worry about it." I waved my hand at him. "I decided to go for the book you suggested." I tapped the leather cover under my arm.

"Good, you won't regret it," he said with a devilish smirk.

I regarded him with careful consideration. "So, do you spend a lot of time loitering around bookshops?" I wasn't sure why he was still standing there. He didn't seem to be interested in any of the paperbacks lining the shelves. In fact, his interest seemed to lie with me.

He laughed and uncrossed his arms as he stepped toward me. "Of course. You end up meeting the most interesting people that way."

"Is that right?" I moved away from him and down the aisle. My breath quickened and the warning bells in my head *dinged* louder. He seemed nice enough, but you just never knew these days.

"Only the best kind of people enjoy a good read." He plucked a book from the shelf nearest him and grinned at it before returning it to its rightful place.

I smiled at his unconscious fiddling before our eyes caught. For a split second, everything around us blurred once more. A raw, almost primal feeling overcame me and it felt as though all my secrets and scars were laid out in the open.

I broke our gaze and tucked my hair behind my ear.

"Listen, I wish I could stay and chat, but that was my brother on the phone and apparently he's having a crisis that needs my attention," he lamented, shrugging and rolling his eyes.

"Oh okay, well, it was nice meeting you... Robert," I said, breathing a sigh of relief.

"Maybe I'll see you around town."

"Maybe." I did my best to keep my voice even.

"It was a pleasure meeting you, Violet." He offered a slight bowing of his head, smiled and walked away.

He moved fluidly down the aisle and out of sight toward the front of the store. After a few moments, I heard the jingle of the door and knew he was gone. I slumped against the book-shelf, finally able to breathe with him no longer nearby. He seemed like a perfectly normal guy, but there was something about him left me feeling exposed and anxious. I took a deep breath and made my way to the front of the store to pay for my books.

"Just these today," I said, putting the murder mystery and Walt Whitman collection on the counter.

"It's already been taken care of, Miss Evans," Frank said, looking up at me with a frown.

"What do you mean, taken care of?"

"The gentleman who just left gave me fifty dollars and told me it was for any books you decided to buy, and then he just left."

"He what?"

My legs still shook from his gaze, but that anxiety quickly turned into anger. Truthfully, I didn't know why I was angry. I wasn't too keen on the idea of him paying for my things, but the anger building inside of me couldn't be justified by his dropping a Grant on my behalf.

"I'm sorry, I thought the two of you knew each other." Frank coughed into his hand to hide his embarrassment.

"That's okay, Frank. How much do I owe you?" I asked, still trying to decipher my emotions.

"But…"

I raised my hand to cut him off.

"I don't need some strange man paying for my books. You'll take my money and do whatever you want with the cash he gave you," I insisted.

Frank grumbled under his breath as he rang me up, "It was a nice gesture."

"Nice maybe, but all the same I'd rather pay for my own things."

As I walked back to where I had left my bike, I thought about my encounter with Robert, trying to figure out what had just happened. I thought about the way our eyes caught and how naked I'd felt in that moment. A feeling of unease seeped into my chest the more I thought about him standing there, looking at me like I was some sort of puzzle he couldn't quite figure out. There was definitely something different about him, something unique that I couldn't put my finger on.

Lost in my own head, I reached my bike in what felt like in a matter of seconds. I decided to write the whole thing off and move on. I'd probably never see him again anyway, so there was no use in letting a stranger consume my thoughts. I shook the image of him from my mind, but couldn't entirely shake off the feeling of vulnerability.

My ride to and from the coffee shop had renewed my strength. I felt like I could take on the world, or at least the bookkeeping I'd been neglecting. My studio was my second home, small but quaint, and I loved it. A few of my favorite pictures hung from the front office walls, two large desks easily filling the floor. The second desk was for my receptionist, Jessie, who would come in for a couple hours after school. It was nice having Jessie around to do some administrative tasks; it freed up a lot of my time so I could get out, take more pictures and spend more time in the dark room.

I sat down at my desk near the back of the room, put my iPod on shuffle, opened up the spreadsheet program on my computer and started working.

The studio phone rang and I turned down the music before answering. "Good afternoon, this is Violet," I said into the old-fashioned plastic receiver.

"Hi Violet, it's Annabel. Thank god, I reached you." Relief laced her voice as she paused to breathe. Annabel was Jake Maxwell's Fiancé. There was only one more week until the wedding, and we still needed to finalize the photo list.

"Hey, Annabel, what's up?"

"Are you going to be at the studio for a while?"

"Yeah, I'll be here most of the day. Is everything alright?"

"You're going to kill me," she laughed.

"We're changing the list again, aren't we?"

"My soon to be mother-in-law is driving me nuts. She wants to make a few changes to the group photos. Can I come by and go over the updated list with you?" she asked.

"Sure. You can e-mail it to me if you'd like."

"No, that's alright. I need to get out of the house for a bit. I'll be down in a few."

"Okay, see you in a bit," I said and hung up the phone.

I saved a few of the changes I had made to the accounts receivable and closed the program. I double-clicked on the file for Annabel's photo list and it popped open on the screen.

The Maxwell estate was only about ten minutes away and Annabel would arrive soon, so I decided to check my messages real quick while I waited. I pressed the voicemail button on the bulky desk phone and listened to the first message. It was from a telemarketer telling me the warranty on my car had expired. The message was in Spanish. I laughed to myself and hit delete. The next was a message from my girlfriend Christy. The elementary school was having picture day soon and they wanted to schedule a day with me.

I called Christy back real quick and her phone went straight to voicemail. I left her a quick message with a few dates I'd be available for picture day in the next couple months.

No more messages or immediate business concerns to occupy the next few minutes, I pulled up a game of solitaire and waited. I barely cycled through the deck once when the studio door opened. I closed the game and stood up to meet Annabel.

"That was fast," I said, giving her a quick hug. Stressed as she was, she always looked amazing. She wore her shoulder-length blonde hair with delicate curls pinned to perfection.

"I had to get out of there. You have no idea how frustrating they can be. That whole family is so stubborn," she said with a laugh, shaking her head.

"Do you want something to drink?" I asked as we walked back to my desk.

"No, I'm good. Thanks."

"So what changed this time?" I steepled my fingers on the desk as I sat down, offering Annabel a patient, understanding smile.

"Well, we finally have a best man." She sat across from me, plopping her wedding binder down on the desk inches from my fingers.

"Cutting it kinda close aren't you?" I cocked an eyebrow at the overflowing binder.

"We weren't sure if he was going to be able to make it, but I think getting Aniela involved solved that problem."

"She's a force to be reckoned with," I laughed. Aniela was Jake's mother and the matriarch of the Maxwell family. From everything I'd heard, she was not a woman you said no to.

"I'm sure he wouldn't have missed his own brother's wedding, but I don't think he wanted to be the best man," Annabel said with a shrug.

"Oh, the best man is Jake's brother?" My eyebrows shot up on my forehead.

"Yep. Even though he doesn't live here anymore, they've always stayed close."

"Oh, where does he live?"

"In Europe, mostly the UK. He decided to stay out there after he graduated from school."

"Okay, so what's his name?" I asked, placing my hands on the keyboard.

"Robert Maxwell," she replied.

My fingers froze over the 'enter' key. The man in the bookstore was also named Robert. He must be the mysterious Maxwell brother everyone's been talking about.

"We've met actually, I think," I said, fighting the lump in my throat.

"Really? He just got in last night." Annabel smiled.

"Yeah, I believe I ran into him while I was picking up a few books this morning." I bit my lips and began to type his name into the excel sheet.

"I know that look." She rolled her eyes and laughed. "He can be quite the charmer, can't he?"

"You could say that." I shook my head and tried to hide the smile forming on my lips. As annoyed as I was that he paid for my things, I did have to admit that he was charming and his love for Walt Whitman did win him at least one point.

"I promise he'll be on best behavior at the wedding." She touched my hand and gave me a sympathetic look.

I patted her hand in acknowledgment. "Alright, what else?" I asked, changing the subject. I brushed a strand of hair out of my eyes and got back down to business.

"We need to change a few of the family group photos around," Annabel explained, opening her binder and flipping to the section she needed without skipping a beat.

"No problem. How do you want to rearrange everything?" I settled in for a long meeting.

We went through each group picture and split out the different families on Annabel's side then went through the groom's side as well. At the end of the list, we re-grouped the families back together and made a few changes to the other group photos. When the list was finished, I hit 'save' and silently panicked. I didn't know how I was going to organize five hundred people and get through that whole list during the cocktail hour. One thing I knew for sure: Annabel's wedding was going to be a long day.

"So just one more week. Are you excited?" I asked, turning toward her and closing Excel.

"I can't wait. I just want to start my life with Jake," she said, beaming. "And it'll be nice to be done with all of this." She gestured toward her wedding binder. "I mean, it's fun and all but if we weren't getting married next week, I'd definitely be eloping. Both of our families are driving us crazy. They mean well, but you know how families can be." She gave me a nervous smile, looking for confirmation.

I nodded and smiled back, even though I didn't know how

families could be. My family was gone and I would never experience what Annabel was going through.

"Thanks for being so patient with us. I know this isn't what you signed up for. We'll pay you more for all the trouble we've put you through," Annabel offered.

"That's not necessary. Let's just try to *not* change the list again," I said, half joking.

She laughed and rose from her chair. "I'll try my best. I'll see you Saturday, thanks again." She picked up her giant, over-stuffed wedding binder and headed for the door.

"See you next week," I called after her.

I watched her go, lost in thought about family. Even though she claimed her family was driving her over the edge she seemed so full of light and forgiveness. I wondered if I would have had the same grace dealing with my family as she did. I doubted it. As much as I loved them and missed them, even as a child I didn't have the patience Annabel had.

I turned back to my desk to finish the dreaded accounts receivable, but my cell phone went off before I could login back in.

"Hey Christy."

"Hey, just got your voicemail. I'll pass along the info, you up for a girl's night tonight?"

"Yeah, that sounds great." I logged into the A/R program as Christy talked.

"Same place, same time."

"Alright, see you there." I clicked the 'end' button and tossed my phone on the desk.

I spent most Saturday nights with a few of my single girl-friends at the local watering hole. There were always at least a few of us who didn't have any other plans for Saturday night, and it had kind of become tradition. I always looked forward to our girl's night out. It gave me a chance to unwind from the week and Christy was never short on gossip.

I input a pile of new invoices and recorded the payments I'd received over the last few weeks, including the Maxwell wedding check, which was going to get me through the next couple months without having to do another stitch of work. Of course I had a few things lined up, but this was probably the biggest check I'd ever received.

I locked up the studio around a quarter after six and hurried home on my bike. As I pulled up to my condo, I noticed a familiar looking guy snooping around the front of the complex. Before I could ask him what he was looking for, he took off down the street and disappeared around the corner. That was odd, I thought as I navigated my bike down the narrow pathway. I looked back toward the front gate before I unlocked the front door and a pang of nervous energy filled my chest. I really needed to get a grip and stop being so paranoid.

I propped my bike up on the front porch, grabbed my things from the basket and went inside. Warm stale air hit me like a brick wall the moment I stepped over the threshold. I peeled my shirt off as I padded down the hall to the bedroom and turned the shower on. If there were any pitfalls of living in Pismo, it was how warm and sticky the summers could be. I rinsed off with cool water and took my time getting ready for the evening.

CHAPTER TWO

The next week was fairly busy. Annabel of course changed the photo list one more time, and I spent a good majority of my days taking some beautiful landscape photos. A new developer saw some of my work and wanted me to do a collection of landscapes for his new hotel in Santa Barbara. Even if I was excruciatingly busy, I was always thankful when a new job came in.

As the wedding drew closer, the whole town buzzed with an odd sort of excitement. It was a mixture of awe at the new faces showing up every day and what seemed to be respect.

Finally, the big day arrived. Becky and I pulled up to the Maxwell estate around eleven in the morning. It was rare that I asked Becky to assist me, but this wedding was going to take more than one person to get the job done.

The Maxwell estate was one of the largest in Pismo Beach, with a wonderful view overlooking the Pacific Ocean. I had never seen the house up close before, but it more than lived up to its reputation.

The house was two stories tall with large arched windows on each floor. Ivy-covered the exterior of the stone house, adding to the perfectly manicured landscape. Large, sweeping trees had been planted all around the house, creating plenty of much-needed shade. White and blue flowers lined the large stone walkway to the front door, complementing the blue trim around the windows that were barely visible under the ivy.

The front door loomed large before us. It was made of a dark wood, almost black and had the most intricate Celtic carvings weaving in and out of each other creating a beautiful design across the entire surface of the door.

"Holy Seven Dwarfs!" Becky exclaimed, staring up at the house. "This place looks like it came right out of a fairytale."

I laughed and lifted the large, dark and rusted metal knocker hanging a little more than halfway up the door. When I let it fall, it echoed with a heavy *clonk-clonk* that sounded less like I was knocking and more like I was hitting the wood with a battering ram. We heard people bustling around the house and within seconds someone opened the door.

"Can I help you?" a short, plump woman asked.

"Yeah, hi. I'm Violet, the photographer..."

"Yes, yes. They're expecting you. Go straight upstairs, to the right, second door on the left." The woman pointed to the grand staircase and hurried away.

Becky and I stepped inside and closed the door behind us. The floors were a dark, polished wood and the grand staircase in front of us curved upwards that would allow at least four people to walk up and downside by side with each other. A circular skylight cast bright morning sun onto the staircase beneath it, and more sunlight poured through the windows behind us. Little dust motes danced in the beams, giving the entryway a mystical quality. Despite the dark wood that seemed to flow throughout the entire house, everything seemed very light. There were large windows everywhere you looked and all the shades had been pulled back. To the left of the staircase, French doors lined the back of the house and opened up into the backyard. All the doors had been pushed open and I spotted several people setting up chairs and hanging what looked like lanterns. One man stood in the middle of the yard giving orders to everyone around him.

"Could this place *be* any nicer?" Becky whispered, leaning into me.

"It sure beats a one-bedroom condo." I started for the stairs.

Everything had been decorated for the wedding, including the staircase. White chiffon ran the length of the banisters with lilies and roses spaced evenly apart. Long strands of ribbon hung from every other post beneath the banister, all the way to the top of the staircase. The ribbons rustled like blades of grass swaying in a summer breeze as we made our way up the stairs.

I reached the second level with Becky right behind me and turned to the right, making my way down the hall to the second door on the left. I knocked and readjusted the camera gear on my shoulder.

"Come in." Annabel's cheerful voice came through the door. "Hey Violet," she said as I walked into the room. "We're just starting to get ready." She smiled the kind of smile you only ever saw on a bride: pure bliss.

"Perfect, this is my assistant Becky." I motioned toward Becky as she stretched out her hand to shake Annabel's.

"Nice to meet you and congratulations."

"Thank you." Annabel beaming with excitement.

There were six bridesmaids in the room, still in their pajamas and bathrobes, three hairdressers and two makeup artists.

"I think this room might be bigger than my entire condo," I laughed.

The room really was one of the biggest bedrooms I'd ever seen. The four-poster king size bed sat on the far left side of the room. Along the walls, stations had been set up for each girl to get ready. Each vanity had its own giant mirror. Makeup and hair accessories were laid out on each of the vanity counters. The girls' long red bridesmaid dresses hung from the top of each mirror. The silk of the dresses flowed smoothly like crimson water, pooling on the vanity counters. The cream carpet offset the ocean blue walls and the open doors to the balcony let fresh air and sunshine into the room.

Out on the balcony, a small breakfast buffet and iced champagne had been set up for the bridal party. The excitement in the bedroom was almost tangible. It filled the room with an overwhelming sense of happiness. Some of the bridesmaids sat on the balcony eating and chatting while another girl with curlers in her hair fished through an overnight bag. The bride was talking to one of the hairdressers and a couple girls were already at their stations, one plucking her eyebrows and another painting her nails.

I turned toward Becky and whispered, "Can you start taking candid's of the girls while they get ready? I'm going to head downstairs and capture the setup."

"Sure," Becky said, setting the bulk of her gear down and preparing her camera.

"Oh, and don't forget to get a few shots of the dress before it goes on the bride," I instructed as I walked toward the door.

"Ok, no problem." Becky raised her camera at the girls on the balcony, capturing their laughter as they relaxed and ate.

I walked out of the room and back down the hall to the staircase. As I started to descend the front door flew open with a bang, startling me and stopping me in my tracks. Two guys carrying a wood box twice the size of either of them walked in.

"Need any help?" I asked as I skipped down the rest of the stairs, holding my camera to my chest as it bounced around my neck.

"Could you show us to the backyard?" One of the guys asked, huffing with effort.

"Yeah just head straight back. I'll make sure you don't hit

anything." I walked ahead and led them toward the French doors, then showed them over to an unoccupied piece of the patio. They stopped and slowly lowered the box.

"So, what do you have in there?" I asked when they stood up.

"It's the gazebo for the ceremony. We're the lucky ones that get to put it together," one of them said with a deep, sarcastic exhale.

"I'm Alex, by the way," he said, reaching for my hand and then pulling it back and wiping it on his pant leg. "And that's Eric." He pointed to the other guy. He was just an inch or so shorter than his friend and had shoulder-length, wavy blond hair that was tied back into a messy ponytail.

Eric raised his hand and wiped the sweat from his brow. I had to suppress a laugh at his casual outfit: flip flops, board shorts, and a t-shirt did not belong in the Maxwell estate.

"I'm the photographer for today, Violet," I said with a little nod toward my camera.

I couldn't be sure, but it looked like Eric and Alex shared a nervous glance between them.

"Right, the photographer. I guess we'll be seeing you around then," Alex said, plastering a friendly smile across his face. "We're both groomsmen." He pointed between himself and Eric.

"Right, well you better get ready soon if you're going to make it on time for pictures." Everything needed to stay on schedule if I was going to get through the photo list, and two late groomsmen were not a part of the schedule.

Alex grinned at me. "Oh don't worry, we'll be ready in plenty of time."

"Good. I should get back to work." I lifted my camera off of my chest. I couldn't quite put my finger on it, but there was definitely something odd about Alex and Eric.

The chairs for the guests had been set up in perfect little rows on the grass facing the ocean. I snapped a couple pictures of all the chairs from different angles and then turned my sights to the dining area.

Several tables had already been set up around the pool, but only a few were covered with tablecloths, the delicate material swaying in the breeze. They'd turned the pool into the dance floor by placing something that looked like bulletproof glass over the water. When Annabel told me about it weeks ago, I looked at her like she was crazy. As I eyed the dance floor, a very large man walked right across the pool without falling in. I still wasn't sure if it was strong enough to hold all the guests, but it was impressive.

Long wires had been tethered above the pool in a crisscross pattern, with the lanterns I saw earlier hanging from them. I took a few pictures of the lanterns swinging in the Pacific breeze and a few more of the lanterns all grouped together on the grass. I looked up the length of the house opposite the pool and saw a balcony that would have a great view of everything happening below.

I stepped back through the French doors into the house and went up the staircase. Instead of turning right as before, I turned left. I knocked on the first door on my right and when no one answered I walked in. This room was somewhat smaller than the bridal bedroom, but it was still bigger than my bedroom at home. All the shades were shut and hardly any light made it through the cracks. There was something eerie about this room, so big and dark. It smelled musty and stale like it had been in disuse for some time now and I suddenly had the oddest feeling I was being watched. I looked around the room, searching for a pair of suspicious eyes, and the thought was enough to get me moving toward the balcony doors to open the shades.

The sun burst through the windows and I squinted against the brightness. I looked over my shoulder, half expecting someone to be standing behind me, but of course, there wasn't.

The room, however, looked a lot less menacing with the light shining through the windows. I laughed at myself and shook my head. What had gotten into me lately? I was never this easily spooked. In fact, I liked scary movies and things that went bump in the night.

I looked back out the window and it took a second for my vision to adjust to the burning sunlight. This room had a wonderful view of the ocean, but the top of the patio blocked the view below. Disappointed, I closed the blinds and hurried out of the room, closing the door behind me.

I was going to go into the next room I came across, but I had a feeling the view would still be partially blocked by the patio, so I continued a little further down the hall. When I reached the third door on my right, I knocked and waited for a response. After a couple of seconds with no answer, I walked in.

This room was completely different from the first. The double doors leading to the balcony were already open and lit up the room. The bed looked like a California king, with white sheets crumpled into a heap in the middle of the bed. At the foot of the bed was a large black suitcase sitting on an oversized wooden chest. *Hmm,* I thought. Maybe one of the bridesmaids had slept here last night. I felt a little intrusive walking into an occupied room, but I figured if anyone came in I could easily explain what I was doing up here.

I stepped onto the balcony and sure enough, it was the one I was looking for. I could see the tables set up around the pool/dance floor as well as all the chairs for the ceremony. The backyard had seemed smaller downstairs with everyone bustling about and setting up, but from up here I could see how enormous it really was.

Ten by ten rows of chairs had been set up on each side of the runner, which was just now being placed down. I took a couple quick pictures as they rolled it up to the altar. The two groomsmen still hammered away at the gazebo, but it was at least standing now. Snapping a few more pictures, I lowered my camera. I noticed a large swing bench on the far right side of the yard, and I made a mental note of it for later.

All the candle lanterns had been hung, and it looked absolutely beautiful. I idly wondered how they were going to light all the candles in the lanterns that were hanging at least twenty feet off the ground now, but quickly decided it wasn't my problem.

I turned to walk back into the bedroom while scrolling through the pictures I'd just taken, making sure I got everything I wanted, when I noticed something out of the corner of my eye. I looked up to see a dripping wet, half-naked man wearing only a towel around his waist.

"Oh, I'm so sorry. I didn't realize anyone was in here," I said, looking down. "I knocked, but no one..." I peeked another glance at him while trying to apologize, when I realized I recognized the half-naked man. "Robert?" I abandoned modesty and looked up, staring at him.

"Violet! What a pleasant surprise." He ruffled his hair with another towel.

"I didn't mean to barge in on you, I was just trying to get a few pictures." I blushed. He looked even better than I remembered, although he did have clothes on the last time we'd met. I noticed his eyebrows were raised when I met his face, and I thought back to what I just said.

"Oh, no. Not pictures of you. Pictures of the wedding being set up downstairs," I quickly clarified.

He laughed. "I'm not accusing you of anything."

"What are you doing up here?" I tried to maintain a casual tone, even though the expression on my face was anything but casual. I knew I'd be seeing him at some point today, I just didn't expect to see him so naked.

"Showering." He smirked and looking down at the towel around his waist.

"Obviously, but what are you doing *here*, showering?" No

matter how hard I tried, I couldn't keep from looking him up and down. His torso was perfectly sculpted and his bare shoulders were broad. Droplets of water coasted down his long sides, landing on the towel around his waist. I followed one of the droplets all the way down until it disappeared into the towel. Immediately I looked away, embarrassed at where my thoughts had so quickly gone. It felt like I had been watching that drop of water for an immeasurable amount of time when I finally looked back up at his face.

"I'm staying here for the wedding," Robert said, not looking at me as he threw the smaller towel into the hamper.

"Right," I pointed at him and tried my best to avert my eyes, "best man."

"Is that a problem?" he asked

"That means you're Jake's brother?" I still couldn't believe this was happening. The man I had often found myself thinking about since the bookstore was standing in front of me wrapped in nothing but a towel.

"Slightly younger, more charming brother, yes."

I moved closer to the door and did my best to keep my eyes on the ceiling, but failed miserably.

"So, you're the photographer for today, I see." He crossed his arms and leaned against the wall.

"Yes I am! I mean, yep, I'll be here all day." Why did he have to be so handsome? It really wasn't fair.

"Wedding photography, huh? I didn't take you as the mushy love type," he said with a smile.

"I'm not." A nervous laugh escaped my throat. "I do weddings and portraits on the side to pay the bills."

"What company do you work for?" He raised his eyebrows. Usually, people didn't act this interested in my work.

"I actually work for myself."

"Your own business, well, that's impressive." He nodded his head. "So you like poetry and photography."

"What are you compiling a list?" I asked, embarrassed.

"Not exactly." He smiled, making my breath catch in my throat.

"I… I should get back to work." Slowly, probably a bit too slowly, I turned and walked toward the door.

"Violet?"

I turned back to look at him.

"It's nice to see you again," he said and walked toward me.

"Yeah… umm, you too," I stuttered.

"We'll talk later." He assured me. He opened the door and I stepped over the threshold.

I left Robert in all his naked glory. It took a few moments of deep breathing, leaning against the wall outside that door to calm myself down, before I could walk without stumbling. With my nerves returned, I decided I should check on Becky and the bride. The girls were starting to change into their dresses and Annabel was almost done with her hair.

The rest of the afternoon went by pretty quick and without further incident. I took pictures of the groom and the grooms-men, which Robert didn't exactly make easy. He kept a playful gaze on me the whole time, and I found it almost impossible to keep the camera steady. Becky couldn't stop commenting on how unbelievably sexy he was and how he couldn't keep his eyes off me, which didn't help either. I was already having a hard enough time not thinking about him in that towel without her mentioning, how did she put it, how "impressive" he looked. She had no idea how much better it got.

The bride and bridesmaids' pictures were a breeze and a lot of fun to shoot. You could feel the electricity in the air beaming from the bride. It must have been contagious because I was in an unusually good mood for standing on my feet all day. Weddings were always exhausting, but this one was different and I found myself gliding from one photo to the next without needing a break. Soon after the pictures with the bride were finished, the ceremony started. It didn't drag on like other weddings I had done, which was nice.

The sunset over the ocean just as the bride and groom looked lovingly into each other's eyes and exchanged their vows. It made the ceremony all the more charming. Annabel and Jake's left hand were bound together by a piece of cloth and the officiant chanted over their joined hands. The guests didn't seem confused by the prayer, so it must be a family custom or something.

After the ceremony, I took a few pictures of the bride and groom on the large swing bench I had seen earlier. The pictures looked even better than I had imagined. Becky and I finished taking pictures of the happy couple with family and friends, checking them off the list as we went. Shortly after we finished, it was time for the grand entrance and for the reception to begin.

The dance floor looked amazing. Red and white rose petals floated on the water beneath the glass, and the pool lights flittered through the flowers, making the dance floor look otherworldly. Once the grand entrance was over and the first dance out of the way, I grabbed Becky, deciding it was time to take a break for a few minutes.

"Man, it's been a long day." Becky stretched her neck from side to side.

"And it's not over yet," I beamed. "They left out food for us in the kitchen if you wanna go grab a bite real quick. I'll hold down the fort." I nudged her off the wall. I knew she had to be hungry because my stomach protested loudly against Becky eating before me.

"You sure? I can wait if you want."

"No, it's alright. I'll grab a bite when you get back." I raised my camera and looked in the direction of the dance floor, indicating there was still work to do. Except I couldn't help but look at Robert.

"He's unbelievable, isn't he?" Following my gaze, she saw Robert dancing with the flower girl. "You should go talk to him! He's been eying you all day." Becky raised her eyebrows with implication.

"Oh, shut up and go eat," I laughed and pushed her in the direction of the kitchen.

"If he was interested in me, I wouldn't hesitate," she noted, biting her lip.

"He's not interested in me. Guys who look like that are just looking for their next conquest."

"Yeah, and he wants to conquer you!" She gave me a knowing look as a small smile played at her lips.

"Knock it off, it's not going to happen."

"Alright, alright." Becky raised her hands in surrender. "I still say you should think about it. It's been a long time for you," she said over her shoulder as she walked away to get her food.

After she got back, I went to the kitchen to have a quick bite myself. When I walked back out Becky was talking to Alex, one of the groomsmen who had built the gazebo earlier, so I walked around the dance floor taking candid pictures of the dancing guests.

It was starting to get late and most of the photos had been taken already. Once the cake was cut and the toasts made, you could only have so many pictures of champagne-crazed people doing the *Electric Slide* before things got repetitive. All we needed now was the bouquet toss and garter toss.

Becky had been flirting with Alex off and on all night. I knew she wouldn't be of any more use to me now that the wedding was winding down. All she had on her mind now was getting back to her place, or his. When Becky finally came up for air and glanced in my direction, I waved her over.

"You can get out of here if you want." I nodded in Alex's direction.

"I can't leave you empty-handed," she insisted, though not too strongly.

"Honestly, Beck. I'm going to wrap it up soon, anyway. I can finish without you."

"You sure?"

"Of course. Go enjoy yourself," I said, knowing she would. "Just leave your gear by the front door before you head out."

"Okay, will do. Thanks, Violet." She headed over to Alex, letting him know they could leave.

"Aren't you a nice boss," a voice said from behind me.

I turned around to see Robert standing just a few feet away. He had a drink in one hand, his tie loosely undone and his jacket unbuttoned. I sighed internally at the sight of him. Even with his suit somewhat disheveled from being worn all day, he still looked too good to be true.

"She wasn't any use to me anymore, anyway. Becky tends to have a one-track mind," I chuckled under my breath.

"And what about you? Does your mind have more than one track?" he asked with a wicked smile.

"In fact, it does. I'm not ruled by my hormones." I returned his smile. And it was true. Normally I was in complete control of myself, but Robert had a way of affecting me with just his presence. It unnerved me, but I couldn't focus on it.

"I thought as much. You seem to be a much more reserved person." He adjusted his disheveled tie as he took a measured step toward me.

"I wouldn't say I'm reserved, just cautious." I swallowed hard, taking half a step back.

He continued making his way closer to me, narrowing the gap between us.

"What I meant was, you seem to be more of an intimate person. Unlike your assistant Becky, who shares the wealth so to speak," Robert explained.

I opened my mouth to defend Becky, but Robert raised his hand to silence me.

"I mean no offense to your friend, to each his or her own," he clarified, taking one last step.

Unconsciously, I leaned closer, inhaling the sweet mixture of cologne and liquor.

"I must say that I admire that quality in someone," Robert continued as he stared down at me. His eyes shimmered in the soft light, glazed over with excitement and whiskey.

"What quality?" I asked, almost whispering. He was so close that even with the music and chattering party-goers, I didn't need to speak at a normal volume anymore.

"Wholesomeness. It's something that's not easily found." His eyes pierced through me as he spoke, and my mind went completely blank.

"And now, it's time for all the single ladies to come onto the dance floor to catch the bouquet!" the D.J.'s voice boomed over the music and Beyonce's, *Single Ladies* blasted through the speakers.

"That's my cue," I said, turning and walking away before he could object. I breathed a sigh of relief, feeling like I'd been held underwater and could finally get air into my lungs.

I spent the remainder of the evening avoiding Robert's charms. I couldn't afford to lose myself to him. He was exactly the type of guy that would sweep you off your feet and then break your heart beyond repair. The smarter side of my brain kept me from walking over to him while the other side of my brain allowed me to watch him through my camera's viewfinder, justifying that I only wanted to keep tabs on him so I would know where not to be.

With the night winding down, I packed up my equipment and got ready for the evening to end. It was just after midnight and I was exhausted. Time didn't seem to matter to the bride and groom;

they floated around the dance floor to the light melody, even though only a few guests joined them. I smiled at the couple one last time and headed toward my car. I grabbed the gear Becky had left at the main entrance and headed out the front of the house. I could feel the happiness surrounding the bride and groom wrap itself around me. Being in their presence was truly intoxicating.

It was pitch black and impossible to see anything when I reached my car. A thick ocean mist had rolled in and clung to the air. I put my camera bag down on the street and struggled to open the trunk. I finally got the key in the hole and clicked it over when I felt something slither around my waist and brush against my hair. My first thought was of Robert.

"Not a word," a husky male voice breathed into my ear. It wasn't Robert. The voice was much too raspy and cold.

"What do you..." I started, near panicked. I felt every shred of happiness that had been wrapped around me all day vanish into the darkness of the night.

"I said not a word," he growled, pulling my head back by my hair with one hand and pressing a sharp object across my throat with the other hand. My heart started pounding and I tried not to shake with fear. He bent me over the trunk of the car and grabbed both of my hands, tying them behind my back. The rope cut into my wrists and made me yelp in pain.

I turned my head to look at my assailant, but at the slightest movement he grabbed my head and slammed it back down against the trunk. Everything went blurry. I felt my pulse in my head. I wasn't sure if it was sweat or blood that ran from my temple to my cheek until a drop of red splashed onto the trunk. I saw my blood glisten crimson in the moon's thin light and started to panic as my survival instincts kicked in. *Just do what he tells you and it'll be okay,* I said over and over again in my head.

"Move again and I'll slit your throat!" he snarled behind me. "Now come here." He wrenched me off the trunk and pressed me into his body with my back held tight against his chest.

He put a black hood over my head and everything went dark. I could feel the knife at my abdomen this time, the blade squeezing my side until it ripped through my shirt. I took shallow breaths in an effort to keep the knife from pushing further into me. The feel of the cool steel against my stomach sent a shiver down my spine and brought the taste of bile to the back of my throat.

Keep it together, I chanted in my head. I swallowed hard, trying to regain some control over my body. His other hand wrapped itself into my hair, keeping a tight grip on my skull. The pain brought tears to my eyes and panic welled up inside of my throat like I'd swallowed a boulder.

"Your name's Violet, is that right?" he asked with amusement in his voice.

I didn't say anything. I was too afraid to speak.

"Answer me!" he snarled, pressing the knife harder into my stomach and breaking the skin.

"Yes, yes it is." My voice cracked with fear.

"We've been searching for you for a long time. To think of all the trouble we've gone through and you don't even have any power," he seethed.

"Power?" I could barely whisper. What did he mean, I had no power?

"You mean, you don't know about the prophecy?" He laughed a sickly, throaty kind of laugh, the kind that made your skin crawl.

"No, you must have the wrong person."

"How dare you question me!" He pushed me to the ground.

The pavement was wet and cold. I struggled to straighten my legs and run away before he could grab me again, but I wasn't fast enough. He flipped me on my back and straddled me so I couldn't move. My arms dug into the asphalt behind me and I felt the gravel tearing into my skin.

"Someone, help!" I screamed as loud as I could. I had parked my car a good distance from everyone else, a polite thing for a vendor to do at a wedding, but it meant my efforts to get someone's attention were useless.

He hit me square across the face and then wrapped his fingers around my neck. I could barely breathe. My face stung from his blow and tears streamed down my face as I gasped for air.

"Why?" I rasped.

"Because you're the only one who can wake The Lady and we can't have that, now can we?" he said as he slid the knife down my chest and pressed it against my abdomen again. "It's a shame, really, to have to waste something so beautiful." He brushed his thumb up and down my throat.

Prophecy? Wake the Lady? What was he talking about? The guy was certifiably nuts. This all had to be a mistake, some kind of misunderstanding. I tried to wiggle free from his grasp, but it only seemed to entice him more. He slid his hand from my throat down to my right breast. The moment he released my neck, I let out a blood-curdling scream.

"You stupid bitch!" he fumed. "Have it your way." He shoved the knife into me, pushing and twisting as far as he could manage.

Air erupted out of my lungs. I couldn't breathe. I couldn't think. I only felt my blood bubbling out of the wound in my stomach. Everything went into slow motion, the blade twisting inside me and my blood pouring onto the pavement. This couldn't be happening, this couldn't be real.

"Goodbye, Violet," my attacker laughed. I felt his body shift above me as he plunged the knife into my chest. A flash of blue light filled my vision as pain exploded throughout my entire body. I felt the weight of my attacker lift off of me and I knew I was alone.

I rolled over onto my side and laid there in the middle of the street. Blood rushed from my wounds like I'd been keeping it prisoner. It soaked through my clothes and pooled beneath me. I struggled to get my hands free, but it was no use, the rope was too tight. Every little movement sent a jolt of pain through my body, paralyzing me. There was nothing I could do, I was losing too much blood too fast and had no way of putting pressure on the wounds.

My body felt heavy. It grew harder to thrash around, to move at all. I opened my mouth to scream again, but no sound came from my blood-soaked lips. My eyelids fluttered closed and the world disappeared around me as I took the last few breaths of my life.

This is it.

CHAPTER THREE

I felt a hand press firmly against my abdomen. Someone was trying to stop the bleeding, but I knew it was a futile effort. Even as my thoughts faded and darkness closed in, I heard a familiar, far-off voice calling my name. I could no longer feel the pain of my wound and knew it wouldn't be much longer. It was strange knowing I was on death's door and not afraid. Instead, I felt at peace. I thought of my parents' deaths and wondered if they felt the same comfort I felt now.

"Violet!" I heard someone call my name again. But I didn't want to try to answer anymore.

"Violet, can you hear me?" the voice asked, starting to panic. I fought my heavy eyelids if only to soothe him and tell him it was okay to let me go. But when my eyes finally opened and I saw the person hovering over me, I didn't want to go anymore.

I fought against the inevitability of my death like a shipwrecked sailor battling the waves, resisting the blackness that held onto me. But death felt like such a peaceful place, like being swaddled in a blanket.

"Violet!" he yelled again. There was an edge of anger behind the panic.

Forcing myself to look at him, I caught a clear glimpse of his face. His brow furrowed with worry and he clenched his jaw in determination. I fought the dark waters pulling me down and gasped to remain conscious.

He was so beautiful.

Realizing my hands were no longer tied around my back, I tried to lift my hand to his face and soothe the worry from his brow. It would be nice, I thought, to feel the touch of another human being, one last time, but I couldn't find the strength to move.

"Violet, I need you to look at me so I can connect." His voice was severe as I groaned and coughed up a mouthful of blood.

"Look at me!"

Startled back to attention, I looked up at him with the last bit of strength I had and held onto the image of his mahogany eyes. I tried to say his name, to ask him what he was doing here, but no sound passed my blood-drenched lips.

"It's going to be okay, I just need you to stay fixed on my eyes. Please, Violet." He swallowed hard, but his voice held a determined edge. I didn't know how he thought he was going to save me. I didn't have much time left, but something in his velvet voice kept the darkness at bay and lightened the weight drowning my soul. He held my gaze with an intensity that made me think he could see right into my soul, and as we stared at each other, I noticed a small fleck in his right eye that was a shade darker than the rest of his iris.

Suddenly, I felt a warmth spread through my body. It started where he touched my stomach and slowly moved to my chest and extremities. The warmth of his eyes burned into me and coursed through my body the way lava flowed down a hillside, slow and merciless. He gritted his teeth, squinted his eyes in focus, and strained every muscle in his body as he looked down at me.

How was he doing this? I thought. The warmth spread all over me and I could feel it pulling me to the surface, out of the darkness. The tingling heat wrapped around each blood vessel, engulfing every inch of my body and brought me back from the brink of death. His hand moved away from my stomach and the warmth instantly left my body.

Then I felt it. The cool breeze on my skin, the sticky smell of the ocean air. There was no darkness, no warmth, and no pain.

"You're alright now," he said, panting like he'd swam a mile.

"Robert?" I sat up and searched for his face. I thought it would hurt to move, but I didn't feel anything. I ran my hands along my stomach where the knife had gone in but found no wound, just two small scars that hadn't been there before. I was still covered in my blood and my shirt was torn to shreds. I turned my wrists over and saw the marks the rope had left. I felt the small lump on the side of my head where it had met the trunk, but this seemed to be the worst of my injuries. How was I still alive?

Robert sat on the pavement to the left of me, his knees bent with both arms folded over his legs and his head down, looking away from me.

"What happened? How am I alive?" I wiped the dried blood from my lips.

"You're fine now, that's all that matters," he said, eyes still facing the pavement.

"But that man stabbed me. What did you do?" My voice was barely a whisper. "I felt you touching my stomach and then I was warm all over. I thought I was dying and then..." I didn't know how to continue. I felt exposed and foolish. I mean, how could I be dying one minute and fine the next?

"Violet, I..." He finally turned and looked at me with those piercing brown eyes. They didn't hold the same warmth they had a minute ago.

I moved closer to him and saw that his hands were covered in my blood. My stomach did a perfect double tuck off the imaginary balance beam in my abdomen as I watched my blood drip off his fingers and onto the pavement. Against my better judgment, I moved closer, wanting to feel that warm comfort again.

"How did you… what did you… I mean, I'm okay now," I said, placing a hand on my woundless stomach and looking up at him. Robert showed no emotion, his face stern and cold. I could tell he was trying very hard to hide something from me.

"Please, just tell me," I pleaded.

He sighed. "It's not that simple. All that matters is you're okay."

"Robert, please. I just want to understand."

He got to his feet and reached down to help me up. Out of the corner of my eye, I saw him take a quick glance at my bare stomach, but his face remained hard and expressionless when his eyes finally met mine.

"We should get you changed. You don't happen to have any extra clothes in your car, do you?"

"Err… no," I said, looking down at my tattered, bloody shirt and blood-stained slacks. At least my pants were black, so it was hard to tell they looked like a costume piece for some slasher movie.

"Alright, I think Brett's about your size. We can get some clothes from her."

"The bridesmaid?"

"Yeah, she's my sister, now come with me." He pulled me by the arm back toward the house.

"I'm not going anywhere until you tell me what just happened!" I yelled and yanked my arm free from his grasp.

I crossed my arms and stared at him with as much authority

as I could muster. He turned around to look at me and I almost fell to the ground. The heat I longed for radiated off of him, and I had to lock my knees to stay upright. He took two steps toward me and closed the gap between us. His eyes never left mine as he reached up and put his hand on my arm. His hand felt warm and soon that warmth spread to my fingers. My arm relaxed.

"Violet," he said, his voice calm and soothing. "We need to get you inside. Please just trust me and we can talk once you get changed."

I looked over my shoulder at the pavement stained with my blood, then turned back to him. I nodded in submission and he slid his hand down my arm to my elbow. He never loosened his grip as he led me back to the house.

As we walked up the path I thought I heard him mumbling something. I was about to ask what he was saying when he suddenly turned to the left, leading us around the side of the house and away from the still-in-progress reception.

"Where are we going?" I asked, looking over my shoulder toward the front of the house.

He didn't answer. Instead, he stopped and reached into the thick, ivy-covered ground and opened a door, revealing several stone steps. He nudged me through the door, down the stairs, and the door slammed shut behind us. He followed behind me with his hand on my lower back, guiding the way. I could feel the warmth of his hand and tried not to focus on the way his touch made me anxious with anticipation. As I walked through the hall, I felt like I had walked back in time.

The corridor in front of me looked like it was a hundred years old. Plain, dark sconces spaced about ten feet apart on the walls lit the way. The corridor was about five feet wide and a foot or two taller than me. The floor was concrete and the walls were made of some sort of crude-looking stone. Our footsteps echoed against the walls, and my heavy breathing filled my ears as we continued briskly through the passageway.

"Where are we?" I whispered, my eyes wide as I swallowed back the dread my surroundings conjured.

"This corridor leads to the basement and up into the house."

"Why do you need an underground corridor to get in and out of the house?" I frowned. First, I'm miraculously healed and now I'm in an underground tunnel that's probably hundreds of years old. What was going on?

"Well, we can't have you traipsing around a wedding with the bloody mess you are." He shook his head at my disheveled appearance.

We rounded the corner and after about ten feet reached stone steps leading up to a door. We walked up the steps and through the door into a dark basement. The room was huge, from what I could see of it. There wasn't much light in there compared to the corridor we'd just come from. The floor still looked concrete, but the walls were no longer made of the crude stones that lined the corridor. The pillars holding up the house were massive and must have been at least ten, maybe fifteen feet tall.

Robert led me toward the stairs against the wall in front of us. As we walked by one of the pillars, I let my hand graze its smooth, wooden surface. We walked up the stairs and through another door leading into the back of the house. I could hear the music of the reception again and it brought me back to reality. It still surprised me how beautifully the house was furnished and how light and open everything seemed, despite the dark color palette running through the house. Everything was very modern looking and it was obvious the Maxwell's spared no expense.

"I still can't get over how beautiful everything is."

"It's over the top," Robert noted as he rushed me up the main staircase.

"Your house really is amazing."

"It's not my house."

"That's right, you don't live here normally. Why is that?"

He sighed. "Can we just get you changed before we play twenty questions?"

"Fine."

At the top of the staircase we turned to the right and he led me down the hall toward the bridal suite. The floor was carpeted up here, unlike downstairs. Family pictures hung all along the walls, but one photo caught my eye. It was a black and white of a young boy standing on a cliff and looking out over the water. The setting sun made the water glisten, giving the picture a sort of magical quality. I paused at the picture for just a moment before Robert guided me down the hall and through a door on the left side.

"I was eight in that picture," he whispered into my ear, noticing my interest.

I blushed slightly at the feel of his breath on my neck and opened my mouth to answer him, when I noticed there was someone else in the room, someone I recognized from the bridal party.

"What happened?" she asked, not looking at me. The tone of her voice was calm, but her bright blue eyes were wide as saucers as she stared at Robert.

He moved from behind me toward her and they walked over to the window at the far end of the room.

"I had to save her," he said under his breath.

"You used your ability on her?"

"Brett, she's The Waker."

"It's her? You're sure?" Her expression suddenly changed from annoyance to curiosity as she shot me a quick glance.

Their voices became almost inaudible whispers as they tried to conceal their conversation. I moved closer as quietly as possible, trying not to draw any attention to myself.

"Think about it, the prophecy said her name would be Violet and look at her necklace."

Brett looked in my direction, "her bloodline," she gasped.

"You think it's a coincidence she got involved with our family?" Robert gave his sister a meaningful look.

"You know I don't believe in coincidences. But we have to be sure before we move forward with this."

"It's her. I could feel it when I saved her, she's the one."

I was trying so hard to hear what they were saying that I didn't pay attention to where I was walking and bumped into the armoire. The dull *thump* of my body running into solid wood drew their attention back to me.

Brett uttered something to Robert in a language I didn't understand and then walked toward me. "Let me get you something to wear so you can get out of those clothes," she said, motioning with her hand for me to follow. Robert didn't move from the window and kept his gaze on the floor.

"Robert, why don't you leave us be, so that she can change?" Brett suggested.

"Right, I'll go talk to the rest of the family and make sure we don't have any other visitors." He walked across the room, carefully keeping his eyes averted from me.

"Please be discreet. There's a wedding going on downstairs," she called after him as Robert closed the door behind him.

"I'm Brett, by the way," she said, extending her hand.

"I remember from earlier," I replied, forcing a smile. "I'm, Violet." Brett stiffened and an odd sort of intensity rolled off of her as I introduced myself. "I'm sorry about the inconvenience." I rubbed my hands against my shoulders, self-conscious now that Robert was gone.

"It's no inconvenience at all," she said and walked me over to the closet.

Brett was absolutely beautiful. She had long, flowing hair that was the same dark brown as her brother's. She wore the red silk dress that all the bridesmaids wore. The dress accentuated her slender curves and smooth, tan skin. I think she was about my height, but she looked much taller in her black pumps.

I felt like a woodland creature standing next to her. My hair had been in a tight ponytail earlier, but now it was falling out, throwing strands in unnatural directions. Plus, it was matted with blood where my head hit the trunk. My shirt was torn to pieces and my clothes were soaked through with blood that was rapidly drying an ugly brown.

"I think this should do." She handed me a pair of jeans and a gray t-shirt.

"Thanks," I said as she placed the clothes in my hands.

"There's a bathroom just across the hall. You might want to wash up a little before you change." She looked me up and down, as if evaluating me. "Just leave your clothes in the bathroom and we'll take care of them. I'll wait here if you need anything else."

"Okay, thanks."

I just wanted out of her presence. I needed a moment to breathe, to take everything in without watchful eyes. Goosebumps appeared on my skin as I thought of the knife plunging repeatedly inside me. The physical damage may have disappeared, but it would be a long time before I ever forgot the feel of cold steel penetrating my flesh.

I walked across the hall and locked the door behind me. I felt like I was going out of my mind and looked like it too. I stared at my reflection, taking in everything that had just happened. My attacker knew my name and thought I should have some sort of power. Oh, and of course, I was supposedly going to wake The Lady, whoever that was. Then Brett scolded Robert for using his ability on me. What was he? What ability? I had so many questions racing through my mind and couldn't comprehend how any of this was possible. Robert had also called me The Waker. What on earth was a Waker?

I needed answers, but had a feeling that wasn't going to be easy. Brett seemed to be running the show in there, and she didn't want me to know anything without finding out more about me first.

I turned the faucet on and threw some water on my face. The warm water felt good on my cold, clammy skin. I quickly took my clothes off and threw them in the sink. My skin was stained red from blood, as was my necklace. I grabbed the washcloth on the counter and wet it under the faucet with warm water. I wiped the dried blood off my face and body and threw the towel in the sink with my clothes. Carefully, I slipped my necklace off over my head and turned the hot water nozzle on. I held my necklace under the steady stream of water and watched as the blood dripped off of the delicate links that held my grandmother's pendant. Patting the silver chain dry, I replaced the necklace around my neck.

With most of the blood gone, I could see the gash on the side of my head, just above my temple. It didn't look too bad considering all the blood caked in my hair, but I guess head wounds did bleed more than other injuries. There was already a little bruising around the cut and the whole side of my head had swollen. I knew I was in for one serious headache tomorrow when the shock wore off. I checked out the rest of my face: a little swollen but otherwise intact. Next, I held up my wrists, turning them over so I could see the damage the rope had inflicted. They were incredibly sore, the flesh rubbed raw from my frivolous attempt to escape. I ran my hands under cool water to try to soothe the burning pain. My shoulders relaxed the tiniest bit as the pain in my wrists subsided. Last, I traced the tiny scars across my stomach and chest. It was hard to believe they'd been gaping wounds less than an hour ago. How did Robert save me? That question repeated itself over and over in my head: *how did he save me?*

With my assessment done, I slipped into the jeans Brett had

generously loaned me and instantly felt a little more like myself. I threw on the t-shirt and turned to look at myself in the mirror. Robert was right, Brett and I were about the same size. I fixed my hair as best I could, pulling it back into a loose ponytail, careful not to touch the cut on my head, and rushed back across the hall. I needed to talk to Robert; I needed to make sense of everything that had happened tonight.

"You look better. How're you feeling?" Brett asked as I reentered the room.

"I'm okay, I think. A little confused."

"Here you go." Brett handed me a glass of water and two pills. "Aspirin. I thought you might be feeling a few of your injuries by now."

"Thank you." I tossed the pills into my mouth and took a sip of water. With a gulping sigh, I sat down on the edge of the bed to wait for Robert to come back.

"You must have been pretty bad off if some of your injuries are still showing. Normally, Robert can make it look as if nothing ever happened."

I nodded my head and touched my stomach.

A few minutes passed without either one of us talking, and I could feel the anxiety building inside me. "Err… Brett?"

"Yeah?"

"Do you know where Robert is?"

"He's making sure you stay safe. I'll see you out to your car when you're ready," she said coolly. "You've got a pretty serious gash on the side of your head there." I blinked with confusion at the sudden change in the subject as she walked over to the dresser.

"What do you mean see me out? He promised he would talk to me once I got changed," I said.

"I know he did, but he's making sure you stay safe. I'm sorry, but you're just going to have to talk to him some other time."

She spoke quickly, but she sounded genuinely apologetic as she walked back toward me with a box in her hands.

"But…" I started to contest, but she cut me off.

"Listen, Violet, I know this can't be easy for you, but you just have to trust that we're trying to do the right thing and keep us all as safe as possible."

"I don't even know what that means." I shook my head and took another sip of water.

"I know you don't. You just have to trust us," she said, touching my arm. "Do you mind?" She raised a bottle of disinfectant.

"No, go ahead, thank you."

She cleaned the wound on the side of my head and placed a bandage over the cut. I waited until she finished before continuing our conversation.

"How am I supposed to trust the both of you when I don't even know what's going on?"

"That's why it's called trust." Brett smiled.

"But he promised me. I thought he'd… I just want to know what was going on," I sighed. I was so frustrated and tired. I just wanted someone to explain what was happening.

"I'm sure this is all very confusing. I do understand how hard it must be for you, but you have to understand that this is much more complicated than you could imagine."

"How could you possibly understand how I'm feeling?"

"Violet." Brett's eyes tightened at the corners as she said my name. "Please don't make this any more difficult than it already is."

Neither of us said anything for a few minutes. So much had happened this evening and I was trying to take it all in. Almost dying, Robert saving my life, sneaking through secret corridors into the house and overhearing that I'm The Waker.

I found my thoughts wandering back to the searing heat in

Robert's eyes when he saved me. As he stared down at me, I could feel him in my heart and soul. It was as if he had access to the deepest, darkest parts of me. That warmth not only saved my life, it spread through me like the sun on a warm day every time his skin came in contact with mine. I couldn't help but wonder if he felt the same thing, if there was some sort of connection between us. Maybe everyone he saved felt the same thing I did; maybe the connection wasn't personal at all. *How many others had he saved?*

"Can I ask you something?" I stared at my glass of water.

"What is it?"

"Has this ever… I mean has Robert ever…" I didn't know how to finish the sentence. I couldn't bring myself to say the words out loud.

"No, he hasn't," she answered, understanding my question.

"Oh." I took a large gulp of water.

"Do you remember what happened before Robert was with you?"

I thought I remembered everything crystal clear, but when I tried to think back on the evening, it was all a little fuzzy.

"I remember walking out to my car to put away my equipment and then everything starts to get a little hazy," I admitted.

"Where does your memory start to come back in?"

"I remember my attacker telling me he had to kill me because of some prophecy, that he was surprised I didn't have any power." I carefully watched her reaction. The set of her mouth tightened slightly, but she kept her face calm and collected, as if I had just told her the sky was blue.

She didn't say anything, so I continued. "He said that I would wake The Lady and they couldn't let that happen. But I have no clue what he's talking about. How does this have anything to do with me?" I started tearing up. I took a deep breath that rattled on my lips and gathered my senses.

"The next thing I remember is hearing Robert's voice and then I was warm all over, from the inside out. I thought I was dying and then…" I explained, suddenly realizing I was telling a complete stranger about my miracle near-death experience when I didn't even know what had happened. I also had the distinct feeling that no one but Robert would quite understand the raw sensation that had passed between us.

"And then?" She offered a patient nod as she waited for me to continue.

"And then it goes fuzzy again," I lied.

"It's okay, try not to push yourself to remember. Your mind is trying to protect you." She placed her hand on my shoulder. "I'm going to get changed real quick. The wedding is mostly over, anyway. Just relax for a bit and when you're ready, I'll walk you out."

"Thanks again for the clothes."

"Of course." Brett stood up and walked across the room to her large walk-in closet.

I sat on the bed alone for a few minutes, thinking everything over. So it wasn't a habit of Robert's to save every damsel in distress, but what did that mean for me? He wasn't even going to come back up and talk to me. I might not ever get to see him again. And then what, was I supposed to just forget him? Forget about him saving me and go on with my life like nothing ever happened?

I wasn't exactly sure how long I had been sitting alone. Time didn't seem to hold the same value, what with everything going on. I figured it hadn't been too long though because Brett still hadn't returned from the closet. I got the feeling she was trying to give us both some privacy, me with my thoughts and her to analyze every word I had just said.

I was too restless to sit still any longer, so I got up and walked over to the window. It overlooked the courtyard where the reception was taking place. Brett was right about the wedding being mostly over; it was almost one in the morning and nearly all the guests had departed. The gathering looked different from above: the white lights strung up everywhere twinkled like stars in the night sky. A light mist had blown in from the ocean and clung to the air, making the courtyard look utterly enchanting.

The bride and groom were tightly embraced on the dance floor along with a few other couples, completely oblivious to the time. The wait staff floated effortlessly from table to table collecting plates, cups, and silverware. I felt like I was watching something right off the silver screen, everything felt so surreal.

"Violet?"

I turned around. Brett had changed into jeans and a long sleeve, black V-neck shirt that had a pretty rhinestone design on the front. She was noticeably shorter in the ballet flats she now wore. Much closer to my height, like I'd originally thought.

"I think I'm ready to go home now," I said, though I bit my lip, unsure. I didn't want to leave if there was a chance I might get to talk to Robert, but nothing here felt real and I just wanted to be back home where everything was familiar.

"Alright." Brett took the glass of water from me and put it on the desk next to the window.

She walked me out of the room, down the staircase and out the front door. We walked in silence to my car. When we got about ten feet away, I saw no trace of a bloodstain. I blinked in wide-eyed confusion, finding no sign I'd been attacked at all.

"What happened to all the blood?" I asked, moving faster toward the car.

"It's been cleaned up," Brett said nonchalantly.

"Already? That was fast."

"We're very careful."

"Hmm." So this wasn't the first time they had to clean up a mess.

"Violet, I'm terribly sorry for everything that's happened to you tonight. I know you're confused and want answers, but for now, you're just going to have to trust us. We'll find out what we can but for your own safety, you can't say anything to anyone about what happened to you tonight," Brett informed me as politely as she could manage given the warning in her voice.

"And what am I supposed to say about all the cuts and bruises? People are going to notice?" My shoulders slumped in defeat as I realized I wouldn't be getting any answers tonight.

"Tell them you were mugged, but you didn't get a good look at the guy," she lied without skipping a beat.

"I guess you guys think of everything."

"Indeed we do."

Tired and hurt that they wouldn't trust me, I felt the tears welling up and blurring my vision. I refused to let Brett see me cry, so kept my eyes on the car as I unlocked the door.

"I'll keep Robert's secret. Not for you or for him, but because I owe him that much for saving my life," I said, buckling my seat belt and drowning out whatever response she might have made with the flaring of the ignition.

I drove off without looking back. I felt a little guilty for being so rude when Brett had been so nice and helpful. But I wanted answers, and one way or another, I was going to get them.

CHAPTER FOUR

I sat at my desk replaying everything in my head over and over again. My unanswered questions gnawing at me as I thought about Robert. How could he just leave without so much as a word?

After I drove off, leaving Brett in the street, everything turned into a blur. It was like my mind shut down after I left the Maxwell estate, overwhelmed by the shock of what had happened. I vaguely remembered making it to my bed that night and Harriet, my next-door neighbor and adopted grandmother, waking me up the next morning. She made me the most awful-tasting tea and applied a balm to my wounds, including the scars on my torso. At the time, I didn't have the energy to ask her what she was doing in my house or how she knew that I was hurt. I convinced myself she must have seen me come in on Saturday night. I was in and out of sleep the rest of the day and each time I woke up Harriet gave me more tea.

"Oh, Violet," Becky's voice chimed, bringing me back to reality. I blinked for a moment, remembering I was in my office and not still living through that terrible night. "Man, do I have a story for you." She walked up to my desk and sat on the corner.

"What's up?" I asked, not looking at her and trying to keep my hair across my face so she wouldn't see the cuts and bruises.

"So, you know that guy I met at the wedding?"

"Yeah what about him?" I started rifling through my desk drawers as another reason not to look up at her.

"Well, I ended up hanging out with him the rest of the weekend."

"Hung out?" I spared a glance at Becky to furrow my brow at her. She wasn't the type of girl to just 'hang out' with a guy.

"Yes," she shot back, her irritation apparently blinding her to my appearance. I returned my glance to the drawers. "Just because we hung out in bed all weekend doesn't mean we didn't spend quality time together." She giggled.

"Uh huh and are you going to see him again then?" I asked, standing up and walking over to Jessie's desk, pretending to look for something.

"I don't know. I mean he's nice and all and we had a good time, but I don't think I can see it going anywhere. Violet, are you listening to me?" Becky asked with a hint of irritation in her voice.

"Of course I'm listening. So you don't think it'll go anywhere."

"What's with you? What's so important that you can't take five minutes to look at me and have a conversation?" She hopped off my desk and made her way to where I stood. I kept my head down and started opening Jessie's file drawers.

"Violet, seriously, what's going on?" Becky demanded. She grabbed my arm and spun me around. Her expression transformed to a look of pure shock.

"Before you freak out, it's nothing, I'm fine," I said, trying to pull away from her, but my body was too tired and sore to put up much of a fight.

"What happened to you? Who did this?" Becky asked, gently

pushing my hair behind my ear so she could get a better look at the damage.

"It happened at the Maxwells, after you left." I sighed, defeated. I was hoping I could bypass seeing Becky until I looked a little better; I didn't want to lie to her.

"Did that Robert guy do this to you? I saw the way he was looking at you all night, I swear if he-"

"Would you calm down? Of course he didn't do this to me. Stop jumping to conclusions, I was just mugged," I interrupted, stopping her train of thought before it ran off the rails. Once she got going, it was hard to stop her.

"Just mugged?" Becky yelled.

"Yeah, come here, sit down." I motioned her toward the chairs at the front of the studio. "It was the end of the night and I walked out to my car to put my gear away. When I went to open the trunk someone came up behind me and attacked me."

"Oh my god," Becky gasped.

"I yelled for help and Robert and his sister were able to run the guy off before he could do anything more than this." I pointed to the cuts and bruises on my face.

"What do you think he was after?"

"Not sure." I suppressed a shudder as I thought about what my attacker did want: *me*.

"Have you gone to the police?"

"No, there's nothing to say to the police."

"Nothing to say," Becky yelled, standing up.

"I didn't get a look at the guy and he didn't take anything. What exactly would I tell the police?"

"Still, Violet. I think you should at least go talk to them."

"There's no point, so just drop it," I yelled back at her.

"Fine." Becky crossed her arms and looked out the window. I followed her stubborn gaze to a man standing across the street who appeared to be staring right at us. My heart jumped in my chest like a child on a trampoline and I gripped the edge of my chair. Leaning forward to get a better look, a woman came bouncing toward him, smiling and pointing up the street. She wrapped her arm around his and they walked out of sight. *Get a grip, Violet*. I thought.

I let out a heavy sigh. "Becky, I'm sorry. I'm just exhausted and on edge with everything that's happened."

"Don't worry about it." She shrugged. "Are you okay though?" She turned toward me and grabbed my hand. Becky always stroked the back of my hand when she was concerned, and I smiled at the small comfort.

"Yeah, I think so." I kept my eyes averted from hers.

"Why didn't you call me?" Becky asked.

"And ruin all your fun with what's his name?" I laughed, trying to lighten the situation.

"Don't do that."

"Do what?"

"Don't try to blow this off like it's no big deal. You're hurt and you have every reason to be totally freaked out. Do you know how lucky you are that Robert and his sister heard you yelling for help?"

She had no idea how right she was. If anyone other than Robert had come out to help me, Becky would be planning my funeral right about now. I suppressed a shudder at the thought of how close I'd come to dying that night.

"Why don't you go home and relax?"

"I can't, I have work to do," I said, standing up and heading back over to my desk.

"Oh please, what's the point of working for yourself if you don't take a little time off when you need it? Have you even gone to the doctor to get checked out?"

"No, but I told you I'm fine." I sat back down at my desk and grimaced after hitting the chair too hard. I really wasn't making a good case for myself.

"Are you? Are you really fine?"

I looked at her for a long moment, trying to decide what I could tell her without giving too much away. "Physically yes," I admitted. I sighed and put my head in my palms. My skull felt like a twenty-pound frozen turkey in my hands. I was so tired and hated not telling Becky the truth, hated being alone in this. "I was so scared, Becky. I thought he was going to kill me." I kept blinking to keep myself from crying as I spoke. The frustration and anxiety that had been building in me since Saturday night boiled over as a single tear escaped down my cheek.

Becky knelt down and put her arms around me. "It's okay, it's gonna be okay."

"What if it's not?" I whimpered through uneven breaths. "What if he comes after me again? What if someone's not there to stop him the next time?" I really was afraid my attacker would find out I hadn't died and come after me again. Especially since Robert had disappeared into the night. Even after all I'd seen it still felt crazy to think he had some kind of Magical ability, but I was too tired to think of a more rational explanation.

"Come on, I'm taking you home. You shouldn't be working today," Becky said in a stern voice as she stood and pulled me up with her.

"But…"

"I don't wanna hear it; I'm taking you home."

I took a deep breath and said, "Alright, just let me shut down." To be honest, my muscles cheered with relief. I hadn't slept well over the weekend. Every time I closed my eyes I saw myself lying in the street bleeding to death.

I shut down my computer and went into the back room to switch off the printing equipment.

"Ready?" Becky asked.

"Yeah."

Becky refused to let me ride my bicycle home, so I threw it in the back of her Jeep. When we pulled up to my place, she offered to stay and keep me company, but I told her I was just going to lie down. I got my bike from the back of the car and headed inside. The closer I got to opening the door, the harder it was to keep the exhaustion at bay. By the time I stumbled into my room, I could barely focus on anything other than getting into bed. One near death experience and two sleepless nights finally took their toll.

I woke up gasping for air, my heart pounding. It felt like I was drowning in my sleep. I tried to remember what I had been dreaming about, but nothing made sense. Only bits and pieces of the nightmare remained, I could still feel the cool rain on my face and the burning in my lungs. Rolling over, still gasping for air, I faced the clock: 5:27. I'd slept most of the day away, but at least I finally got some rest. Relaxing onto my back and staring at the ceiling, I stretched my arms and legs. My body ached all over, every muscle was sore from being thrown around like a rag doll.

I felt under my shirt for the larger of the two scars just under my right breast. I traced the scar back and forth, trying to remember exactly what happened when Robert saved me. *It just doesn't make sense,* I thought. The memory of that evening remained blurry, but Robert's voice was crystal clear in my mind. I closed my eyes and let the sound of his voice wash over me and calm my nerves.

With my breathing back to a normal tempo, I got up and walked to the bathroom to wash my face. The water splashed cold against the faded white porcelain sink, reminding me of how much I needed to clean my condo. While I waited for the water to heat up, I looked myself over in the mirror. The blood had dried in the cut across my temple, the edges pink and swollen. The bruising around the gash had faded to a dark blue and purple that measured from my hairline down to my eyebrow. It would be a few days before the bruise started to heal and even longer for the cut to heal. The tear in my lip wasn't very big to begin with and was now just a small slice on the left side of my bottom lip. Splashing warm water on my face, I was careful around the cut on my temple. After drying off with a nearby towel, I put some antibacterial cream on the cut, careful not to push too hard on the open wound.

As I changed into a baggy sweatshirt, my stomach rumbled in protest at not being fed since breakfast. Grabbing my cell off the nightstand, I ordered a small pizza and sat down at my computer in the living room.

I wished I could talk to Robert about what had happened. Not having any answers was driving me crazy, and it was clear Brett didn't want me asking questions. But why? Wasn't the cat already out of the bag once Robert healed me?

Frustrated, I pulled up a fresh internet window, I felt insane for what I was about to do, but what choice did they leave me?

The cursor blinked in the narrow search bar, taunting me as I tried to decide what to search.

Miraculous healing from a fatal wound. I typed hesitantly and pressed enter.

Spells for video games and bible links littered the front page of google. It's not like I was expecting to find a link titled, *So Robert Maxwell miraculously healed you and now you want answers,* but this wasn't getting me anywhere.

I clicked the next button, something I rarely did, and began to search through the depths of the internet.

The pizza arrived about twenty minutes into my search when I found something that looked promising.

Clicking on the link, titled *King Arthur and Magical Healing,* I braced myself.

There was a short story on the front page and as I skimmed it, I ate my pizza.

Arthur was born prematurely and they feared he wouldn't make it through the night. Three days after Arthur came into the world, a visitor arrived. It was Merlin.

Merlin was not only a Soothsayer, but he had the ability to heal fatal wounds. Arthur's parents let Merlin examine the premature babe and he told them he could save the child, but Arthur would be changed forever. They agreed wholeheartedly to give their son a fighting chance, and Merlin saved Arthur's life that night. From that day forward Arthur had a Magical soul.

I scrolled down the page a little further as I stuffed another piece of pizza into my mouth.

Merlin foresaw that Arthur would end the clan wars and bring everyone together under his rule. Without Arthur, the tribes of England would destroy each other and in turn destroy the future of Britain.

Interesting, it was at least a better story than the Disney version, I thought.

His parents didn't have the slightest clue how he was different. After all, he looked and acted like any other child. But when Arthur turned sixteen, Merlin return for him.

He explained to Arthur that Magic was real and that he had a destiny to fulfill, but in order to do so, he would have to leave his family behind and become Merlin's apprentice.

The words, magic was real, made the back of my brain tickle. I had never believed in Magic, but how else could I explain how Robert healed me.

Arthur grew into his Magic and became a fierce warrior under Merlin's guidance. Some say their Magic was linked and they moved as if they were an extension of one another.

Scrolling a little further, I continued reading.

Once Merlin deemed Arthur fit to rule, they returned to his home-town and he pulled the sword from the stone, becoming King and ruling over all of Britain until the day he died.

I sat back in my chair as I came to the bottom of the web

page. This wasn't exactly what I had been looking for, but I had to admit, something about it felt familiar.

A rustling noise outside made me sit up and look around the living room. My heart raced as I watched for movement. I heard another noise that sounded like someone was trying to unlock the front door. What if it was him and he was back to finish the job? I went to grab my cell off the desk and realized I must have left it on the nightstand. *Damn!* I jumped out of my chair, heart pounding and mind racing, and made my way as quietly as possible to the hall closet. Opened the closet door, I grabbed the baseball bat I kept as a crude alarm system.

I held my breath as I edged toward the front door. My hands were clammy as I gripped the bat, ready to strike. I waited for another sound but heard nothing. My knees locked in place as I stood frozen in my entryway, trying to listen for anything that might sound out of place. After a minute or two, I built up enough courage to take a quick look through the peephole. There was no one there. I kept one hand on the bat as I slowly unlocked the door and opened it. I peeked my head out the door - both hands back on the bat, ready to swing.

Everything seemed perfectly normal. The ocean breeze rustled the trees and a few crickets chirped from some dark corner.

"Violet, what are you doing?" Harriet asked, coming out of the shadows.

My heart leapt into my throat and I jumped backward at the sound of her voice. Harriet came into the light from my right side, looking at me as if I was crazy.

"Shit… I thought you were…" I sighed and tried to collect myself. "I thought I heard someone trying to… wait, what are you doing out this late?" I asked, confused. It wasn't like Harriet to lurk around in the dark.

"Couldn't sleep." She shrugged. "Thought I'd go for a walk."

She smiled and looked up the full length of me to the Louisville Slugger I still held above my head.

"You didn't see anything, did you? Anything that looked out of place?" I asked, looking around her into the darkness, still jittery and my fingers white on the bat.

"No, not at all." Her voice was light, but I noticed she kept her distance from me.

"I could've sworn I heard someone." I relaxed ever so slightly and lowered the bat a few inches.

"It was probably just one of the neighbor's cats. Why don't you go back inside and get some sleep? It's late."

"You're probably right." I lowered the bat to the ground and self-consciously rubbed the tiny scar on my stomach. "Night, Harriet." I turned to go back into the house.

"Goodnight, dear."

As I walked across the entryway, a cool breeze ruffled my hair. My feet froze and I looked in the direction the breeze had come from. The living room looked empty, so I edged forward with my bat once more ready to swing. The palms of my hands were sweaty and my stomach felt like it had bottomed out. Something was definitely off, but nothing looked out of place.

An ocean-scented breeze ruffled the drapes over my patio window, the cool air freezing me in place. I couldn't remember opening the window, but it was possible I just forgot to close it earlier. I moved cautiously toward the opening. With one hand still gripping the bat, I closed and locked it. I relaxed some, but I still had the feeling something wasn't right.

"Pull yourself together, Violet," I told myself.

Looking over at my computer, the King Arthur web page was still up and I immediately felt ridiculous. Glad that no one was around to make fun of me, I turned the computer off and threw the empty pizza box away.

I'd had enough crazy for one night and my full stomach was

sending me straight into a food coma. Bat cradled in my arm, I went to bed and fell asleep thinking about Arthur and his destiny to rule Britain.

CHAPTER FIVE

The next few weeks went by without incident. I did a little more research on King Arthur but came up empty-handed. If some sort of Magic was behind Robert healing me, the only way to confirm it would be to confront Robert, who had mysteriously vanished.

My cuts and bruises slowly started to heal so, on the outside, I looked more like myself every day. But on the inside, I had been forever altered. Nothing felt the same anymore. I didn't know how I was supposed to slip back into my life as if the attack and Robert had never happened.

Becky, on the other hand, thought she had the answer to all my problems: a double date. She told the guys to meet us at the Mexican restaurant, *Cantina,* at eight. True to form, Becky had made us about ten minutes late. She spent so much time fussing over what I was going to wear that she barely had any time to get herself ready. As we walked up to the restaurant, Becky pointed out the guys and informed me the tall blonde was my date. We stepped onto the curb and Becky gave her date a quick kiss before turning to introduce me.

"Violet, this is Daniel," she said, looking at her date and

patting him on the chest. It reminded me of a new owner scratching her freshly adopted mutt's belly.

"Nice to meet you." I extended my hand.

"You too. Beck never shuts up about you," Daniel said with a laugh as he shook my hand.

"And this is Ian. Ian, Violet. Violet, Ian." Becky waved her hand between us with a big smile.

"It's very nice to meet you." I extended my hand to Ian.

His cool blue eyes crawled over me and the corners of his mouth turned upwards.

"The pleasure's all mine," Ian cooed. He took my hand in his and raised it to his lips.

I smiled and politely removed my hand from his grasp. *This is going to be a long night,* I thought. I'd had my share of sweet-talking, suave types of guys and learned the hard way to stay far away from them.

I had to give it to Becky, though. She told me he'd be good looking and he was. In a very obvious way, but handsome, nonetheless. His dark jeans and white button-up clung to him in all the right places, accentuating his fit physique. It was a warm summer evening, so he'd rolled up the sleeves of his shirt just below the elbow, leaving the top few buttons undone to show off the hollow of his neck. He was tan, but the faded orange color of his skin betrayed it as a fake tan.

"Shall we?" Ian held out his arm for me to take.

I took a deep breath, grabbed his arm and we headed into the restaurant.

The *Cantina* was new in town and fairly busy. Daniel had called ahead for a table so we didn't have to wait long before being seated. The lights were kept low to help set the mood, and candles in tinted glass vases glowed in the center of each table. Mariachi music played through the audio system, bringing the restaurant to life. Beautiful portraits of Mexican dancers and landscapes decorated the walls. Ian pulled my chair out for me to sit down and then sat next to Daniel across from me.

"So, Violet. I hear you're a photographer," Ian said, leaning across the table with his chin barely a safe distance from the candle.

"Yes, I am," I replied, wondering if the evening would be improved if Ian accidentally set his shirt on fire.

"What kind of pictures do you take?" He sounded genuinely interested.

"Pretty much anything."

Becky stepped on my foot under the table and I had to bite my lip to keep myself from yelling out.

"What I mean is, I'll take any job to help pay the bills," I added, biting my lip to ignore my throbbing foot. "Portrait's, school photos, weddings." The word "weddings" brought on a hundred flashes of the night I was attacked. Robert's intensity, Brett dressed in red, my blood-soaked clothes. I had to suppress a shudder as I remembered the feel of the blade sliding into my stomach.

"I see," Ian said, bringing me back to the present, "but what kind of pictures do you actually enjoy taking?"

"Don't get me wrong, I do enjoy the odd jobs from time to time. It's just, there's something about a bare landscape, a part of the world untouched by human hands that I like to capture."

"You should go by her studio and see some of her work," Becky suggested, tearing her attention from Daniel for a brief moment.

I glared at her. How could she be doing this to me? She knew I didn't even want to be here, and now she was making additional plans for us.

"Your studio?" Ian asked, looking back at me.

"Yeah, I own my own studio."

"Wow, that's really great. I'd love to come by sometime and take a look."

"Yeah, sounds good." I kept my voice even, trying to be nice.

Before I could change the subject and ask what he did for a living our waiter came over to get our drink orders and drop off the complimentary chips and salsa. Both Ian and Daniel got beer and Becky and I ordered margaritas, blended for me, on the rocks for her. Plus an extra spike of tequila. I needed a strong drink and now.

"So, what is it you do for a living?" I asked while looking over the menu.

"I'm in film, mostly editing." He shrugged nonchalantly.

"Film, huh? So you're a Hollywood big shot?"

He laughed. "Not really a big shot, not yet at least. I'm still working my way up the ladder."

"He's being modest. This guy calls all the shots," Daniel said, laughing and pointing his thumb in Ian's direction.

Ian looked up at me from under his lashes, obviously a little embarrassed by his friend. He had a childlike innocence about him I hadn't noticed before. Maybe my first impression of him wasn't quite accurate.

"Have you worked on anything I might have heard of?" I asked, a little more interested in the conversation now.

"I mostly do indie films, but I've assisted on a few main-stream movies. I don't really like to talk about it too much. In LA, it's all about what you've done and who you know. That's all anyone ever talks about, so I don't really like to talk about work when I'm outside of the industry bubble."

"Oh, well, I'm sorry. I didn't mean to pry. I was just curious." My cheeks flushed and I shifted uncomfortably in my chair.

"It's nothing to be sorry for. Besides, I want to hear more about you." He put his hand on top of mine and looked up at me.

Pulling my hand from underneath Ian's, I reached up to grab my margarita before it could be placed down on the table and took a much-needed sip. Our orders were taken and before Ian could ask me anything else about myself, I turned my attention to Daniel.

"So Daniel, what do you do for a living?"

"I have an auto body shop. Mostly I restore older cars," he answered, scooping up some salsa and shoving the chip in his mouth.

"It's actually a nice shop," Becky clarified as she looked at Daniel with an admiring gaze. She really seemed to be taken with this guy. I was surprised; maybe she did have real feelings for him.

"You mean to tell me the shop is actually in good shape?" Ian laughed. "The last time I was there, it looked like a bomb went off."

"Screw you, I was just getting settled in," Daniel laughed, nudging his shoulder against Ian's.

"So Ian, how long are you in town for? Maybe Violet can show you around while you're here?" Becky suggested interrupting the guys' banter.

I almost choked on my margarita. I had to stifle a cough into my napkin and take a sip of water to wash down the tequila burning my throat.

"I'm just here for the long weekend, but I'd love to see the sights. It's been awhile since I was last in Pismo," Ian said and tossed me a look of equal parts concern and confusion.

I kicked Becky under the table but kept a smile on my face.

"Yeah, that sounds great," I lied. "I'll just have to make sure I don't have anything going on at the studio."

"She doesn't. She's free all weekend." Becky glanced at me out of the corner of her eye. Man, was she pushing it.

I just smiled and took a cautious sip of my drink. Ian actually looked a little uncomfortable at the obvious tension between Becky and me. He seemed like a pretty decent guy and in spite of myself I felt bad for being so rude, or maybe it was just the liquor talking.

"I'd be happy to show you around."

It seemed to work. He smiled and his eyes brightened. I was definitely going to have to give Becky a piece of my mind for doing this to me, but there was nothing I could do about it at the moment.

The food arrived quickly, despite the fact that the restaurant was packed tighter than a hipster in skinny jeans. Steak fajitas and warm flour tortillas were placed down in front of me. The *sizzling* of the meat on the cast iron pan and the smell of seasoned peppers had my mouth watering instantly. We all talked about work and Ian asked me about my other interests. It turned out that we had a little more in common than I would have thought. He asked about my family and I saw Becky tense out of the corner of my eye. Family was supposed to be a neutral topic, but when you didn't have any family to talk about, it could get a little awkward.

When we finished the meal, Ian picked up the check, noting he was honoring our hospitality and not just paying because he was obligated to. We all stood up once Ian got his card back. Becky and I headed to the restroom and told the guys to meet us outside.

"So what d'ya think?" Becky asked the second we were out of earshot.

"He's... nice." I bit my lip and stared at my reflection in the mirror. Ian did seem like a nice guy, but there was just something missing.

"Just nice?"

"I don't know, there's just something off about him."

"Oh no you don't, you're not going to nit-pick this guy to death until you find something wrong with him." She turned away from the mirror to look at me. "He's nice, smart, successful, and sexy as hell. What more are you looking for?"

"Warmth," I said under my breath.

"What the hell does that mean? Look, Violet, he seems to be

interested so just give it a shot. If it doesn't work out, then he'll be gone in a few days."

"Maybe you're right," I said, staring at the sink. She did have a point. Just because he didn't light me up like Robert did, didn't mean I should totally blow him off. And it really wouldn't hurt to distract myself from thinking about Robert either.

"Of course I'm right. Now get your sexy ass out there and work some magic." Becky smacked my backside and we both laughed as we walked out of the bathroom.

"Oh and just so you know, I'm leaving with Daniel so you'll have to get a ride from Ian," she whispered behind me as we walked outside to meet the guys.

"Thanks for the heads up," I said under my breath sarcastically.

"You ready to go, babe?" Daniel asked Becky.

"Always." She smiled and bounced into his arms.

"It was nice meeting you, Violet," Daniel said.

"Night, guys," Becky called, her voice thick with implication.

"Night," I sighed. "So, I guess it's just you and me then." I smiled at Ian.

"Come on, I'll give you a ride home," he said, holding out his arm for me.

I looped my arm through his and we walked up the street to his car. He paused and pulled out his keys in front of a Smart Car. Looking at the car hesitantly, I worried about its safety as I hopped in reluctantly.

"So, where to?"

"Umm, just head down the street and make a right at the light."

He started up the car and the engine was so quiet it sounded like a golf cart.

"Now that we're alone," he said as he pulled out of the spot. *Oh crap,* I thought. "I have to ask. How does a girl like you manage to stay single?" He grinned in my direction.

"Umm, well, for one thing, I'm really focused on my work and making a life for myself."

"I know how that is. I've been so focused on my own career for the past few years, I haven't had much time for a personal life." He paused and took a breath like he was going to say something else, but then stopped.

"What?"

"Can I ask you something?" His arm grazed mine in the tight space.

"Sure," I said, leaning toward the passenger window.

"Do you ever get lonely, not having anyone?"

I took a second to answer. I wasn't sure what he was getting at, but I had a gut feeling he hoped I was lonely enough to allow him to entertain me with his company.

"Sometimes, but I'm very happy with the life I've built for myself. I like the freedom of not having to answer to someone else," I answered, satisfied at the truth of my words. Even after everything I'd been through, I could honestly say I was pretty content with the way my life had turned out so far.

"You're different, you know."

I blinked. "How so?" I edged closer to the window.

"Most women I meet can't wait to find their next relationship. They're always looking for Mr. Right or Mr. Right-now in some cases. But you're secure. You're..." He hesitated, trying to find the right word, "Unique."

I laughed.

"What?" He gave me a confused smile.

"Oh, make a left up here. I'm just up the block on the right side."

"So what did I say that was so funny?" he asked.

"It's just, I've tried very hard not to be unique," I said and looked out the window. "I'm right here." My complex flashed by the window. Ian hit the brakes and put it in reverse, parking in a spot that was really only big enough for motorcycles and scooters.

"You can't change who you are." The tenacity in his expression had no effect on me.

"Thanks for the ride. And thanks for tonight. I had a really good time." I meant it. Ian might not give me butterflies or ignite a fire inside me, but he was still a nice guy and the evening had gone better than I'd thought possible.

"So did I. I'm glad I got to meet you."

"You too. Night," I said, opening the passenger door and stepping out.

I closed the door and started walking to the gate when I heard a window roll down behind me. I turned to look and Ian was leaning across the car, almost out the passenger window.

"What time should I pick you up tomorrow?"

"Tomorrow?"

"You didn't forget that you're supposed to show me around now, did you?" He smiled.

"Oh, that. Well, I normally get up around five in the morning on Saturdays to make it to the beach for sunrise." I hoped this news would discourage him from wanting to spend time with me. Ian was nice and all, but I didn't really want to spend an entire day with him.

"Sounds good. See you around five-thirty then. Sleep well," he said, rolling up the window before I could protest.

"You too," I said under my breath and turned to unlock the gate.

I sighed with relief as I locked the door behind me, nearly collapsing on the tiled entryway floor. I changed out of my dress and into sweats faster than Superman changing back into Clark Kent. I set my alarm and crawled into bed.

I yawned and rolled onto my side. As much as my brain wanted to over analyze the evening, a tequila-induced sleep forced my eyelids to close and I passed out.

~

I had hoped Ian wouldn't show up. Most people didn't like getting up before the sun, but he arrived just before five-thirty and we headed out for the day. He was quiet most of the morning, no doubt still feeling the effects of the sandman, but he didn't take his eyes off me the whole time. It felt like he was waiting for something to happen, like I would magically sprout wings and fly away. I tried to ignore him, but I couldn't help feeling exposed and vulnerable as he tracked my every movement.

I finished shooting a few photos and we watched the sunrise over the water. With any other guy, I might have thought it romantic to watch the fingers of dawn stretch across the sand, but with Ian, the sky couldn't brighten up fast enough.

"How about we get some coffee?" Ian suggested. He stood, dusting the sand off of his jeans.

"Coffee sounds great. I know just the place," I replied. Ian reached for my elbow and helped me to my feet. Robert's face flashed across my eyes and his voice echoed in my head, *"Violet, I need you to look at me."*

I pulled away from Ian and dusted myself off without looking at him. *What the hell was that?* I thought.

"Stand up too fast?"

His voice startled me. "Huh? Oh, yeah. Just a little light-headed." I lied. Ian's blue eyes flittered over me and a shiver ran down my spine. I couldn't quite put my finger on it, but something about Ian was off and I was ready to be rid of him.

We pulled up to the Java Beach Café and instantly I felt a sense of relief wash over me. It was packed with people and the familiar scent of fresh donuts and coffee filled my nose.

"This must be the place to be," Ian said with a smile as we walked inside.

"You betcha. Java has the best pastries within a hundred miles."

We put in our orders and found a place to sit outside.

"So does your family also live in Pismo?" he asked as we sat down.

"No, they don't." I fiddled with the napkin dispenser, avoiding eye contact and hoping he'd switch to a different subject.

"So you're not originally from around here, or did they move away and you stayed behind for the view?" He wiggled his eyebrows and a feeling of unease settled in the pit of my stomach.

A small, plump woman bustled over to our table and quickly distributed our coffee and breakfast.

"I moved here after college. My parents aren't around anymore and I needed a place to start over." I tore a piece of my donut off and popped it in my mouth as I waited for my coffee to cool a bit.

"Oh, I'm sorry, I didn't mean to pry." Ian sipped his coffee and for the first time today, took his eyes off of me.

"Yes you did," I said, calling him on his bullshit.

"I'm just trying to get to know you. Man, you're a hard nut to crack, aren't you?"

I sighed. "I just don't talk about my past much. I try to focus on the future."

"I understand. I lost my dad when I was ten and my mother was never the same after. It was like a piece of her died with him."

"I'm sorry, I didn't realize…"

"It's alright, it was a long time ago. Thankfully, I had my uncle. He took me under his wing and kind of became a surrogate father."

"Same with my aunt. She took care of me after my parents

died, but unfortunately we haven't stayed very close over the years."

"I'm sure she's always looking out for you, one way or another."

"Maybe," I mused. This conversation was making me feel uneasy. I was being too free with my past, something I never did. I could feel the unnatural desire to open up to him cling to my chest like a bird to its prey. The words he wanted to hear bubbled out of me without my consent. I felt compelled to answer him and tell him whatever he wanted to hear, and it terrified me.

"What about siblings?"

"Nope, it's just me." I tried not to answer, but the words just popped out. I took a sip of my coffee as panic gripped me.

"That's lonely."

"It's all I've ever known." I shrugged. "What about you? Any brothers and sisters?" I tried steering the conversation toward him to get the heat off of me.

"An older sister, but we don't stay in touch. After my father died, she went away to school and we took different paths in life."

"It must be hard to have family and not be close to them."

"Not really, my uncle is my family," he said, his voice cold and hard.

Whatever had happened between him and his sister must have been pretty bad. I couldn't imagine having a sibling and not being close to them. I let the topic of family drop as we quietly sipped our coffee. If it were me, I wouldn't want some stranger digging into my family history. Then again, a stranger was currently digging into my family history and I was letting him. I couldn't figure out why; even Becky had to work to get details out of me sometimes, and we'd been friends for years.

"So, no parents, no siblings, no husband, you're all alone.

That's kind of sad actually." Ian frowned and reached across the table to hold my hand.

"I'm not alone. Just because I don't have blood family doesn't mean I don't have people in my life that I care about." I pulled my hand back and placed it in my lap.

"I'm sorry, I didn't mean to upset you. New topic?" He leaned back in his chair and took a bite of his bagel.

"Sure." I took a sip of my coffee and let it warm me from the inside out. Despite it being a beautiful day, I felt cold to the bone.

"So, how well do you know the Maxwell family?"

I froze, my donut halfway to my mouth. Did he know something about what happened?

"The Maxwell family?" I managed to sputter out.

"Yeah, Becky said you two worked that wedding. I figured you had an in."

"Oh, well, no. Annabel hired me to photograph the wedding, but I'd never met them before that." I felt like I was walking on thin ice. He narrowed his eyes as if analyzing my every word.

"Interesting family, aren't they?"

"How so?" I sipped my coffee, playing it cool.

"Well you know how it is, wealthy families always have skeletons in their closet." He let out a low chuckle, but the set of his jaw was serious. He was definitely up to something, and the compulsion to tell him everything I knew about the Maxwells was taking over. The more I fought against the feeling, the stronger it got.

His phone rang, startling us both, and he excused himself from the table. I let out the breath I'd been holding and I could feel the compulsion to divulge any more information slowly fade as he walked away.

He stood out of earshot, but his face was serious. Whoever was on the other end of that phone meant business. He looked my way and the corner of his mouth turned up in a handsome smirk.

He hung up the phone and in a few long strides returned to our table. "I'm sorry to do this, but that was work and I have to run," he said.

"Oh okay, no problem." I tried to suppress my sigh of relief that this nightmare was almost over.

He grabbed my hand and pulled me to my feet. My heart kicked up a notch with the skin to skin contact and I tugged my arm to escape.

He leaned in close, whispered, "Until next time," and gently kissed my cheek before he walked away.

An overwhelming sense of dread filled me from head to toe.

The moment he was out of sight, I felt the tension in my body release and my head begin to clear. Never again was I going to let Becky set me up on a blind date.

With that thought, I made my way to her place to give her a piece of my mind. She may not like being alone, but I'd rather be alone any day than spend another moment with a guy like Ian.

I was still feeling uneasy when I pulled up to Becky's place and had to take a minute to gather my thoughts. I knew she would want a full report, and I didn't know how I was going to explain my strange morning with Ian.

Brett's warning sounded in my head about keeping everything a secret, and somehow this felt connected.

Bracing myself for the onslaught of questions, I walked up the brick pathway to her front door and knocked.

"Hey," Becky bounced with excitement when she opened the door. "So, how was the morning with Ian?"

I sighed. "Ugh, I would rather have had a root canal. Thankfully, he got a phone call and had to run off."

"I'm just glad you followed through and went out with him.

And see, the world didn't end," she laughed and threw herself down on the couch.

"Sure, but never again, you hear me? No more blind dates, no more Ian. Never again." I curled up on the loveseat across from her.

"We'll see. It really couldn't have been that bad." She rolled her eyes.

"Maybe, maybe not. I don't know, it was kinda weird. There's just something off about him." I stared at the ceiling.

"You always do this, you know. You have to find something wrong with every guy you go out with."

"No, I'm serious this time. He kept asking all these personal questions. It was like he was trying to find something out about me." I exhaled in a heavy sigh and let my head fall back against the couch.

"You don't think that maybe you're overreacting a bit?"

"No, I mean he was nice enough, but he really gave me the creeps today."

"What could he have possibly done to creep you out so much?"

"Like I said, he asked me a million questions about my family and how I ended up in Pismo," I retorted. I knew Becky wouldn't believe me right off the bat because she was right; I did find something wrong with every guy I went out with.

"He's just trying to get to know you." Becky waved her hand dismissively.

"That's what he said too, but it was all wrong. It's like he already knew me and was trying to confirm it. But the worst part was the way he looked at me."

Actually, the worst part was feeling like I had no control over my own words, but how was I going to explain that to her without sounding like a lunatic.

"The way he looked at you?" Her brow creased as she straightened up and leaned toward me.

"It was... intense," I said, sitting up. "It's like he was sizing me up, watching my every movement."

"So he just stared at you?" She raised an eyebrow.

"He never took his eyes off me the whole morning. It was like those National Geographic shows, where the lion stalks his prey."

"You really mean it, don't you?" she asked, leaning back in her chair.

I nodded. "Something was definitely not right."

"You're biting your lip. What is it?"

"What he said before he left, *'no parents, no siblings, no husband, you're all alone.'* It sounded like a threat."

"He said that to you?" She nearly shot out of her seat. Now she was concerned.

"And he asked me how well I knew the Maxwell family." I couldn't keep it in. I knew I couldn't tell her the whole truth about the Maxwells, but I needed someone to talk to.

"The Maxwells? What do they have to do with anything?"

"I don't know, he seemed to think I was close to them for some reason."

"Are you?"

"No, you know that," I snapped, surprised she'd even ask.

"I don't know, ever since the wedding you've had a wall up. If something happened with them, with Robert, you know you can tell me."

I frowned. I knew it was a bad idea to bring them up. "Nothing happened. They just..." I paused, unsure how to finish that sentence. I wasn't sure I wanted to tell Becky anything more.

"Violet, talk to me," my friend pleaded.

I let out a heavy sigh. "They helped me after I was attacked. That's all."

"And you think Ian knows something about that night, is that what you're getting at?"

"I think so. Why else would he pry into my life and ask about my connection to the Maxwells? It can't be a coincidence."

"I don't know, Violet. This all sounds crazy. I think you're still shaken up after everything and I'll admit, maybe pushing you to go out with Ian was a bad idea."

"We can agree on that. And maybe you're right, maybe I'm just making connections where there aren't any," I said and shook my head. I hated that I had become so paranoid and grunted with frustration, though the fear remained.

"And maybe you were right about me meddling in your love life." Becky's comforting smile returned. "I'll try not to push you too much anymore."

"Uh oh, are we talking about Violet's romantic endeavors?" Aaron announced as he walked into the living room, sat down next to me and turned on the TV.

"No, we're not," I said, stretching my legs across his lap.

"I just want to see you happy, you know that right?" Becky asked, ignoring my attempt to end the subject.

"I know." I smiled back. "When I'm ready I'll find someone, I will." A small part of me thought of Robert, but I pushed his image out of my mind.

"At the rate you're going, you'll end up a crazy cat lady," Aaron laughed, trying to ease the tension as he scrolled through the guide on the TV.

I tossed my head side to side in mock laughter and kicked him. "All I need is the bathrobe," I said.

"And curlers," Becky added, standing up, "Anything to drink?"

"I'll take some water."

Aaron selected a channel and the news blared to life, *"Four people were found dead in San Francisco this morning with what appeared to be some sort of markings on their foreheads."* I looked at the TV and a drawing of the marking they were referring to replaced the newscasters face. An underlined triangle came into focus first, then a fancy 'M' with a dash through the middle line sat below the triangle *"Anyone with information is asked to contact the San Francisco police."*

"I hate the news, it's always so depressing." Aaron changed the channel and familiar cartoon character bounced across the screen, "Much better. So tell me, Miss Evans, what are your plans for the rest of the day?" He gave me a hopeful grin.

"Depends, what did you have in mind?" I returned his mischievous smile, but the image of the triangle and 'M' made me feel uneasy. In the shadows of my mind, I felt like I'd seen it before but couldn't recall the memory. Nick, my ex, had shown me weird markings and symbols that he used in his 'group' to purify themselves, but this looked nothing like what he'd shown me.

"Well, seeing how this is technically my vacation, I thought we could go to the beach, maybe do some surfing."

"You know I can't surf," I laughed and tried to focus on the here and now. Whatever the marking was, it wasn't my job to figure it out. I had enough on my plate at the moment without worrying about some ritualistic murders.

Aaron had tried to teach me to surf a few years ago, and it was a disaster. I never stood up once and even took him out a couple times.

"Hah! This is true. It'll be nice to get out of the house though, and you and Becky can hang on the beach."

"As long as you don't try to get me on a board, I'm down."

"Deal."

Even though it was late in the day, Aaron was still able to get a few good waves in. Becky and I relaxed on the shore as I got some much-needed work done. I looked over my notes for the Caltome Vineyard shoot I had coming up as Becky sunbathed in a two piece that was more dental floss than a bathing suit. I was excited to have my next big photo shoot at a winery and it was nice that my life was getting back to normal. Being in the sun and breathing the fresh ocean air made me feel lighter. It was the perfect way to unwind after my morning with Ian. I almost felt normal again as I sipped some of Becky's famous home-made lemonade and enjoyed the warmth of the sun on my skin. Maybe my life could get back to normal after all.

CHAPTER SIX

I unlocked the front door of my studio, anxious to get some work done. I had a lot to catch up on and really needed a day without interruption. The mail had piled up on the floor beneath the little metal slot in the door, and I collected it onto my desk to sort through as I entered my office.

An envelope with just my name scrawled in perfect cursive made it to the top of the pile. I set everything else down on my desk and flipped it over. No return address, no stamps, weird.

I held it up to the light, peering at the contents and wary of white powder, but I couldn't see anything through the envelope. I shrugged and tore it open. Only one way to find out who it was from.

Violet-

Meet me at the end of the pier. 12 o'clock.

I think it's time we finally had that talk.

-Robert

My heart bottomed out somewhere in the pit of my stomach. So he was back. I wasn't sure this was a good thing or not. I had just started putting what happened behind me and getting back to a normal life; I wasn't sure I wanted to meet him.

I glanced at the clock. It was eleven, which meant I had an hour to drive myself crazy. To go or not to go?

I paced around the studio, trying to decide what to do. I desperately wanted answers to what happened that night, but couldn't decide if those answers were worth opening still-fresh wounds. Spending time with Becky and Aaron had lifted me out of the fog and back into my life before the attack. Did I really want to rehash everything and start the healing process all over again? I thought about calling Becky, but what would I say to her? I was keeping so much from her these days, she probably wouldn't be able to give me any advice.

Back and forth, back and forth. I wore a path in the wooden floors. I looked up at the clock again: eleven-thirty. Time seemed to be in fast-forward, closing in on me to make a decision. Every reason to blow him off I came up with felt foolish and immature. I knew I wanted answers, but deep down I was afraid of what those answers might be. I wish I had someone to talk to.

And with that, I made my decision. I needed to face this head on. Hiding from the truth would get me nowhere.

The pier was only half a mile away and I still had thirty minutes, so I decided to walk and try to catch my breath. A million questions floated in and out of my mind as I hurried down the street. Turning the corner, a fresh ocean breeze crashed into me and sent my hair flying in every direction. The musty aroma of salt-laden humidity filled my nose, clearing all the doubts from my head. I could do this. I was going to get answers and I was going to be okay. I'd been through hell and back when I lost my parents; nothing Robert would say could shake my resolve.

A newfound strength came over me when I reached the pier, stepping along the boards with purpose as I searched for Robert. A lone figure sitting on a bench facing the water soon came into view. I knew it was him. I took another breath to steel my nerves and made my way to the end of the pier. He stood as I approached and turned to face me.

"I see you got my note." A small smile pulled at the corner of his mouth. "I'm glad you came. I wasn't sure you would."

"I wasn't sure I would either," I remarked.

"Have a seat." He gestured to the bench and ran his hand through his hair, his smile turning into a nervous grin. What did he have to be nervous about?

"So, you wanted to talk." I sat down and looked out over the water. I needed to stay strong, but for some reason, my resolve always crumbled like stale pound cake around him.

"Straight and to the point, huh?" A slight chuckle escaped his throat.

"Yep."

"Well, I have some information on the man who attacked you. I don't know how helpful it is, though." He stared at the horizon.

"What kind of information?"

"I talked to the boys back home and they confirmed who sent your attacker."

"And?" My nails dug into my thigh.

"His name's Aiden Patridge." His jaw clenched into a hard line.

"Now that we have a name, we can go to the police."

"No, we can't. This isn't a problem they can solve. Aiden, he's different..." he hesitated and licked his lip, "like I'm different." His brow raised as he looked at me and I nodded in understanding.

"Okay, so what then?" I brushed the hair out of my eyes.

"It's complicated, Violet. Aiden's a dangerous man, and now that he knows I healed you-"

"Healed me?" My heart pounded like a battering ram against my chest as I interrupted him. This was it. He was going to tell me how he saved me.

"Yes, you see," Robert said, taking a deep breath before continuing. "He needed confirmation that you're The Waker. When I healed you, it was all they needed to know to move forward."

"Yeah, you've called me that before but I have no idea what you're talking about." Rolling my eyes I shook my head.

"That's not important right now." His eyes met mine. An anxious expression furrowed his brow as his lips formed a hard line.

"So let me get this straight. We don't know who attacked me, but we know who sent them. And they didn't kill me because they wanted you to heal me and confirm I'm The Waker?" I uncrossed my legs and counted on each finger the new pieces of information.

"Exactly." Robert smiled with relief.

"Robert, what the hell are you talking about?" I threw my arms in the air. Maybe I was wrong in coming here. Clearly, I wasn't going to get any real answers out of him.

"You're special and because of that, you're at risk. We both are now," Robert said as if that clarified anything.

"All the crazy aside, you're saying someone actually wants to hurt me?"

"No, they want to kill you."

"But why? I don't understand?" I pinched the bridge of my nose.

"You're meant to do great things, Violet." Robert gently pulled my hand from my face. "But some people, like Aiden, will stop at nothing to make sure you can't interfere with his plans."

Chills ran over my skin at the harshness of his voice. I sighed and tried to think rationally about everything he was telling me. "Alright, so how did they confirm that I'm The Waker," I rolled my eyes at the title, "just by you saving me?"

"Because if it wasn't you, I wouldn't have exposed myself." His shoulders stiffened and he fiddled with his fingers.

"You would have let an innocent person die?"

"Violet, you have to understand…"

I stood and took a few steps away from the bench. "Answer the question." My voice and body shook with anger.

"Yes." He stood and closed the gap between us. "Because you're all that matters. You're all that's mattered for hundreds of years." He wrapped his hand around my elbow and guided me back to the bench. "Now please sit down so we can talk."

"But how can you stand by and watch someone die when you have the ability to save them?"

He groaned and said, "I can't just go around stopping death. There are consequences for saving a life."

"What kind of consequences?"

"By saving you, someone else has to pay the price. The world has a way of balancing its self out, a life for a life."

"So, someone had to die so I could live?" My eyes widened in horror.

Silently, he nodded.

I didn't know what to say. I just stared at him, trying to make sense of everything. No matter how I turned it over in my head, it didn't make any logical sense that I was important enough to murder.

"Robert, I think you've got the wrong person," I tried to explain. The muscles in my body coiled like a snake ready to spring. "How can this have anything to do with me?"

"I'll explain everything in time. For now, all that matters is we found you and now we can keep you safe," Robert said, his voice calm once more.

"But how can you be sure I'm the person you've been looking for?"

"It's you, without a doubt." He sighed. "I'm sorry, I know this isn't easy for you."

We sat in silence for a long moment. I wasn't entirely sure I'd gotten any answers out of him. Nothing he said made sense, and I had even more questions than before. How was I supposed to cope with the fact that someone was actively trying to kill me?

"He's really still out there, isn't he?" I whispered.

Robert placed his hand on top of mine and squeezed. "We won't let anything happen to you," he vowed. His voice oozed with sincerity.

I didn't want to live in fear, always looking over my shoulder. I tried to think about every detail of that night, if maybe I had seen something that would help us identify my attacker. But just like every other time I thought about that night, I came up empty-handed. I glanced at Robert and could tell he was trying to let me sort things out for myself, but he grew more anxious with each passing second of silence.

"I can't live like this, we have to stop him before it's too late."

"Don't worry, he'll come to you," Robert said.

"So what, I'm bait? I'm just supposed to lie in wait until death knocks on my door?"

"Relax. We'll do everything we can to find him. But I have no doubt he will come after you again." He gave my knee a reassuring squeeze. "The only difference is that this time we'll be ready."

Tears filled my eyes, but I stared straight at the horizon, determined to not let them spill over.

"Violet," he said and put his hand on my cheek, "don't be afraid. We have a ton of people on this. We'll find out who he is and soon." He wiped a tear from my face.

"What do you mean you have a ton of people on this?" I asked, hating myself for letting Robert see me cry.

"There are a lot of people who don't want anything to happen to you."

I opened my mouth to say something, but he raised his finger to my mouth to stop me.

"I know you don't believe you're The Waker, but there are a lot of people who do, and they'll do anything to make sure you're safe," Robert explained. "So if nothing else, you can take comfort in the knowledge that you have a lot of people who are looking out for you."

"How many people?" I asked.

"That's not important," he said under his breath, turning away from me.

"Does everyone know who I'm supposed to be except me?" I started to pant, feeling like I was going to have a panic attack at any second.

Robert laughed. "Of course not. There's only a small group of people who know we found you and that you're not just some distant hope anymore. The Prophecy can be fulfilled now."

"Prophecy?"

"Right, you don't know about that either. Let's take it one step at a time." He looked at me and offered a hopeful smile.

"No, I want to know." I was tired of him doling out information at his discretion. I wanted to know everything, and I wanted to know it now.

The hope in his eyes faded as he realized dealing with me wasn't going to be as easy as he thought.

"Look, Violet. I'm sure this is a lot to handle and I don't want to put anything more on your plate until you're ready," he explained.

"And what, you think you get to decide when I'm ready to deal with more of this bullshit?" I yelled at him.

"No, that's not what I meant. I just...look, calm down, I

know how hard this must be and I don't want to put any more stress on you. Let's just take baby steps, okay?"

"Fine," I said, crossing my arms and looking out over the water.

I let the conversation drop for the moment. I needed to convince him to tell me everything about this prophecy and Waker nonsense, and it was clear he didn't want to divulge anything. But sooner or later, he'd have to explain.

I looked over at him as he took his hand off mine. How infuriating he was, sitting next to me all smug and playing the protector role. I was a grown woman. I didn't need him to protect me from the world. I'd made it through plenty without him by my side, and I would make it through this. Screw the prophecy. Screw being The Waker to a bunch of people I didn't know or care about. And screw Robert.

Working myself up into a blind frenzy, all I wanted was to get away from him, to get away from all of this. Without a word, I rose from the bench and headed back up the pier.

"Violet, wait," Robert called after me. I kept walking. "Violet!" His voice came closer, but I still didn't turn around. "Would you hold on a second?" He grabbed my arm.

I pulled out of his grasp and turned to face him.

"Just leave me alone." My voice was shaky and didn't sound as threatening as I would've liked.

"Just talk to me?"

"Why did you even bother coming back here?"

"I came back because I have to keep you safe. I didn't want to leave you that night without any explanation, but I didn't have any other choice." He lowered his head and his voice, the tired pain behind his eyes making me think he was sincere. I wanted to believe him, but this was all too much.

He took a tentative step toward me with his hand outstretched. "Please just take this slow. I know it's a lot, but I promise I'll explain everything."

"But why tell me anything at all if you're just going to keep me in the dark?" I asked.

"Because it's important that you believe what I tell you. I'm trying to earn your trust first." He took a step toward me and touched my arm with the tips of his fingers. Another step and his body was within an inch of mine. I felt the heat of his skin through both our shirts and my heart started pounding once more.

"You didn't tell anyone about the night I saved you," he whispered. His breath felt warm and sweet against my face. "I want you to trust me the same way I trust you." He traced the crook of my arm with his fingers and it happened again.

I felt the darkness surrounding me, pulling me under. I heard him calling my name and the warmth of his words on my skin. His touch, his fierce eyes. I could feel the warmth spreading through my body, from my head to my toes, pulling me to safety.

"Violet?" I heard Robert's velvet voice. "Are you okay?"

My head spun and Robert was staring at me, concern written in each line of his face.

"Err… I'm fine," I said. "I think."

"What happened? Your eyes just went blank and it was like you weren't here anymore."

"I don't think I was here." A nervous laugh escaped my throat.

"What do you mean?" His eyes widened from concern to curiosity.

"It's nothing. I just got dazed for a second."

"That wasn't nothing. Tell me what's wrong? Did you remember something?"

"No, I mean yes, but not what you mean," I said, trying and failing to explain the sensation.

"What was it?"

"It was just a flash, I mean, a memory of the night you saved me." I looked up at him, searching for recognition of what I'd felt that night. Instantly I saw a change in the set of his mouth. "Your touch made me remember what it felt like." I tucked my hair behind my ear, a little embarrassed, "When you healed me that night."

He stared back at me with a blank expression, only a hint of confusion hidden in his dark, guarded eyes.

He released me and put some distance between our bodies. "I should walk you back."

Seagulls hovered on the gentle winds of a beautiful summer afternoon as I led the way back to my studio. The breeze was only slightly cooler than the air temperature, and there wasn't a cloud in the sky.

"Robert, why didn't you come back that night?" I asked.

"I told you, I didn't have any other choice," he replied.

"You always have a choice."

"Look…" He sighed.

"Please, Robert. Just tell me, you owe me at least that much."

He didn't say anything, just looked at the ground and kept walking. He lifted his head after a moment and stared at me. I could tell he didn't want to tell me why he left that night, but his eyes betrayed him, threatening to spill over with the answers I sought. I didn't turn away from him, hoping whatever conflict raged inside his mind would bend in my favor. He abruptly looked at the sky, his decision made.

"I did come back, but you were still in the bathroom, freshening up."

Damn! I thought.

"Why didn't…" I began.

He raised his hand to cut me off. "I was going to wait for you to finish changing but Brett and I got into it. She can be insufferable sometimes. We decided I should handle the situation before it got out of control and she would make sure you got home safe. We were all at risk, and I did what was necessary to keep you and my family safe. The faster I found out what was going on, the better. So I packed a bag and headed to the airport."

"I guess I can respect that. I just wish you would have at least told me you were leaving."

"You wouldn't have let me leave without an explanation."

"You're right about that." I smiled.

I thought about everything Robert had told me as we continued toward my studio. If I felt confused before, I was utterly lost now. My mind buzzed like a beehive, stirring up more and more questions.

Robert followed me in as I unlocked the door to my studio. The summer sun had sent my body into hyper-drive, or at least I thought it was the heat and humidity. Every fiber of my being could sense him; I felt his eyes tracing the curve of my spine, the warmth of his breath in the air as he walked behind me.

"You really didn't have to walk me back." I tried to sound casual, but my emotions were all over the place.

"I've already saved your life once." A flirtatious chuckle escaped his throat. The walk seemed to have lightened his spirit's some. His shoulders relaxed and he carried himself in a more straightened, confident gait.

"Speaking of saving my life, did you want to explain that?" I asked. I stopped in front of my desk and turned to look at him.

"Not right now."

"But you said you wanted me to trust you. What better way to earn my trust than to tell me the truth about how... how you saved me." I stumbled over my words.

"I do want you to trust me, but baby steps remember." His eyes burned into mine, threatening to undo my resolve.

"Uh, huh."

"I should get going." He sighed and stepped away.

"Alright," I said in a soft voice.

I didn't want him to go. I wanted him to talk to me, wanted

him to let me in. But something hidden in his expression stopped me from saying or doing anything else. He might not want to talk now, but I'd get it out of him sooner or later.

"I'll come by your place later," he promised.

"Later?" My stomach leapt at his words.

"Yeah, I need to run by the house and talk with my family, but I'll come by later to check up on you."

"You don't need to do that." I didn't want to be treated like a damsel in distress.

"Yes, I do." He nodded, smiled and left.

Despite everything that had happened this afternoon, I still had a million questions. I leaned against my desk and threw my purse on the floor. So much for getting some work done today. I picked up the sandwich I had brought with me to work and tossed it in the trash. Normally I wasn't one to waste food, but the smell of sweaty meat and congealed cheese left me with the distinct reminder that someone wanted me dead.

CHAPTER SEVEN

Unable to think about anything other than my conversation with Robert, I decided to head home. The sun just started its fall over the horizon when I got home, and I desperately wished that I too could fall off the edge of the Earth and rise again to a new day. I still wasn't very hungry, but I knew I should eat something. I threw a boxed dinner into the microwave and leaned against the counter while my processed food revolved round and round. I thought I wanted to know everything, I thought I wanted to know how Robert saved me, but the more I found out, the more I wished I didn't know anything. Why couldn't I just let things be? Why couldn't I just be grateful I was alive and stop asking questions?

I closed my eyes and pinched the bridge of my nose in frustration. I took a deep breath, smelling the sweet aroma of boxed Kung Pao chicken. Chef Mike, also known as the microwave, announced my food had been transformed into something edible.

Using the tips of my fingers, I delicately removed the piping hot tray from Chef Mike and plopped it on a plate. I grabbed a

Stella from the refrigerator and headed to the living room to watch some TV while I ate.

The seven o'clock news sprang to life. An over-dressed woman behind a fake desk declared, "*A building collapsed today in Seattle...*" I changed the channel before the anchor could finish her sentence. The last thing I needed to watch was the sensationalized news.

I flipped through the channels until I found a harmless episode of *Friends* and went to work on my food. The spicy sauce and tender chicken gave a comforting warmth to my stomach. It felt good to return to the routine of eating a TV dinner, back to the ordinary and familiar, two things I'd been craving in my life lately. The tension in my back slowly eased with each bite as I sank into the couch. Unfortunately, I couldn't keep the thousands of thoughts from bouncing around in my head like Roger Rabbit on a sugar rush. I took a long swig of beer in the hopes it might relax me a bit more.

As I finished eating, I scooped up the last peanut covered in gooey Kung Pao sauce and popped it into my mouth. I had already seen this episode, the one where Phoebe tries to teach Joey how to play guitar, but it felt nice to relax, so I sat back, beer in hand, and tried to focus on the TV. I wasn't sure if it was the solid food or the beer, but the anxious feeling that had been eating a hole in my chest lessened a bit.

I took another sip of beer and wondered what Robert was up to. It pained me to think about him, but seeing him again had stirred something inside me, something ancient and primal. It wasn't just sexual attraction, although that was certainly a factor. I'd never felt anything like this before. It left me wondering what it was about him that affected me so much. I could understand if it was just a romantic or lustful pull toward him. No one could deny he was a good-looking man. But this was more than that. Something inside me called to him.

The episode of *Friends* ended, so I got up to change my

clothes. I threw on an old t-shirt and cotton shorts. As I walked into the bathroom, I took a long look at myself in the mirror. It was still me. The reflection didn't look any different, but I felt like I was changing. My whole world had been turned upside down and everything looked slightly askew. I shook my head, frustrated that I didn't feel in control of my life anymore, and pulled my hair into a ponytail.

Twirling my hair behind my head, I walked back to the kitchen to grab another beer. A knock echoed on the other side of the door, and I paused halfway to the refrigerator.

Quietly making my way to the front door, I grabbed the bat hidden in the closet. *I'm going to have to keep this thing by my side from now on*, I thought. I leaned up to the peephole when the person knocked again. It made me jump and step right into the stand next to the door.

"Violet, it's just me, open up," Robert's warm voice came through the door.

I breathed a sigh of relief but still checked the peephole.

"What are you doing here?" I asked as I opened the door.

"I told you I was going to come back and check on you tonight." He stepped inside, looking around.

"Right, but how did you get in here without buzzing me?" I closed the door, a little annoyed that he just assumed he could come in, but I decided it wasn't worth picking a fight over.

"I have my ways." He gave me a mischievous smile.

"A little warning would have been nice." I lifted the bat in my hand.

He looked me up and down and shrugged a little sheepishly. "You weren't already in bed, were you?"

I looked down at my attire. "No, just being comfortable in my own home." I pulled the corner of my shirt down to better cover myself.

"How was the rest of your afternoon?" he asked as he walked toward the living room.

I frowned, a little disoriented, and followed him. "It was fine, yours?"

"Productive. I caught up with my family and we think it would be best if you weren't alone." He perused the living room, picking up the magazines on the table and inspecting my book collection.

"Ok." I watched him, my brow furrowed. "So does that mean we're going to hire a bodyguard or something?"

"Or something." He smiled at me. "I'll be staying here and watching over you until this is over."

"You're what?" I asked in disbelief.

"I can crash on the couch," he said, fluffing a pillow.

"Excuse me, but you are *not* crashing on my couch." My voice sounded a little squeaky and I bit my lip, bewildered at the thought of him staying here.

"Be reasonable, Violet," he said, looking back at me. "You don't honestly think I'd leave you unprotected while you're in danger, do you?" He shook his head and turned toward the TV.

"You didn't seem to have a problem leaving me unprotected for the last few weeks. Why the sudden concern for my safety?"

"You think just because I wasn't here that we weren't watching over you?"

"Who's we?" I shivered, self-conscious at the thought of being watched without my knowledge.

"My family, and others we trust," he answered nonchalantly.

"If that's true, then why are you here now? Why can't you just continue the way you have been?" I bit back as he sat on the couch.

He sighed. "Will you have a seat?" He gestured to the spot next to him, but I didn't move. "Look, I know you're struggling with all of this, but…"

"But nothing, Robert. If you want to protect me, then do it from a distance." I turned away and walked toward the sliding back door. "I've been fine this whole time without you, so I don't see the point in you staying here now." My reflection looked pained in the glass, my eyes red from holding back tears.

"Violet, please. You don't understand how important you are," he said.

I could see him stand up and walk toward me in the reflection, but I did nothing to acknowledge his presence. His words reminded me of my Aunt Beth and how she always said how talented and special I was. His voice rang with the same sort of intensity. The thought of my sweet, loving aunt broke down some of my defenses.

I sighed and covered my eyes with my hand. "Then help me understand," I said, turning to face him.

"Come here." He placed his hand on my arm and guided me back to the couch. "We'll start with the prophecy where it all began."

I sat beside him without saying anything. I felt my heart accelerate and my palms begin to sweat. I knew I wanted answers but wasn't sure I was prepared to hear the answers Robert had.

"In England, back in the late seventeen-hundreds, there were five very powerful families in our community: the Deardons, the Ainsworths, the Landons, the Patridges, and the Maxwells. In the middle of the night, one member of each family was summoned to meet with Belinda, a very gifted Soothsayer," Robert began.

"Soothsayer?" I interrupted.

"It means speaker of truth. It's a person who can see the past, present, and future. You would call her a psychic."

"A psychic." My eyes practically bulged out of my head. I couldn't believe this mess stemmed from some lady who claimed to be a psychic hundreds of years ago. Robert couldn't believe in that stuff, could he? I felt like I was reliving the past all over again and Robert was about to tell me he was a part of some 'group' just like my ex. Why did I always attract the crazy ones?

"It's not what you think. The world has taken a sacred tradition and corrupted it into a money-making machine that feeds on the desperate and insecure. Now just the word psychic means cheap parlor tricks and lies, but a true Soothsayer would never use their gift in such a disgraceful way." He rubbed the back of his neck with his hand and looked at me, a little embarrassed. "Anyway, Belinda told those five men a war would come about in the Magical world and the only way to stop it..." He paused and looked at me, struggling to find the right words. "The key to peace would be a woman named Violet, who would wake The Lady and stop Morgana before it was too late." He blinked, looking at me with admiration. "Each person was instructed to pass this information down to their heirs, making sure that when the time came, you wouldn't fall into the wrong hands." His mouth formed into a hard line. "Which almost happened once already."

Robert looked at the palms of his hands as a shaky breath escaped his lungs.

"You said Magical world?" I asked, frowning in confusion.

"You're jumping the gun a little," he noted, looking back up at me. Not a trace of the sorrow gripping him a moment ago remained.

"I'm in charge of what I think I can handle. I want to know," I said as calmly as possible, but frustration laced my voice. I was really getting sick of only being told bits and pieces.

"I know you are, but like I told you this afternoon, I want to gain your trust first so you'll believe me when I tell you everything." He stared into my eyes, making that primal instinct hum deep in my core.

"Fine, but if I'm so important, how come I've never heard of this before?" I did my best to stay focused on the topic at hand, but the nervous energy inside me made it feel like I was standing on the edge of a cliff, ready to take some terrible leap.

"That troubled me too, at first. I would've thought your family would have told you about who you are," he reasoned, not looking at me.

"My parents died when I was young."

"I know that now. That's part of what I found out while I was in England." He paused and finally looked me in the eye.

"Oh, well, what else did you find out while you were there?" I asked, not wanting to talk about my parent's death.

He accepted my avoidance of the topic and continued, "My family needed me to make sure you were The Waker before we did anything else."

"And how did you find that out?"

"I spoke with a few people from the other families to make sure they didn't have any other prospects, and then I spoke to a Soothsayer who *happened* to be in town and she confirmed what I already knew." He chuckled.

"What?"

"It's not a coincidence she was there. Soothsayers can see the future, remember. So it was just further proof you were The Waker."

"But how can you be sure you have the right Violet? There have to be a million people with the same name as me." I fiddled with the necklace around my neck.

He moved his head to the side and studied me a moment. "Nice necklace." He nodded to the small pendant in my fingers and his eyes crinkled at the corners in satisfaction.

"Thanks, it's a family heirloom," I dropped my hand and looked away from him, "Stop trying to change the subject."

"Sorry, you asked how I could be so sure?" He paused and I nodded my head. "When I healed you, I felt the essence of who you are. I knew without a doubt you were who we'd been waiting for." He smiled and placed his hand on mine.

His hand felt warm and comforting against my skin.

Suddenly I was standing on my front porch with the sun overhead, watching myself and Robert. "It'll be okay," he said, pulling me against his chest and wrapping his arms around me. I couldn't believe what I was seeing. *"It'll be okay," I repeated his words under my breath.*

As I watched myself in his arms, he slowly leaned toward me. Closing the distance between us, I wrapped my arms around his neck and pulled him closer. He held me tight against his chest, his hand in my hair, and slowly bent to kiss me.

Just like that, it was over. I was back in my living room with Robert sitting beside me.

I pulled my hand from his and leaned away. My heart pounded in my chest. I could still smell the crisp wetness of the rain. Man, my daydreams were starting to get really intense.

"You okay?" His eyes roamed over me, puzzled.

What was going on with me? It made me shiver, thinking how real everything had felt. It was the same as this afternoon. When he touched me, I could clearly see and feel everything that happened the night he saved me.

"Yeah, I'm fine. It's just, this is all a lot to take in," I lied. Something weird was definitely happening to me.

"If you want, we can talk more tomorrow."

"I'm too keyed up to do anything else. Besides, we still haven't resolved why you think you have to stay here." I cocked my head to the side, waiting for an explanation.

"You really are difficult, aren't you," he chuckled. "Look, I'm not leaving you unprotected so you're just going to have to get used to it. You almost died once under my watch. I won't let anything like that happen again."

"And what, I have no say in any of this?" I retorted.

He sighed, then looked up at me. "Violet, if you're really uncomfortable with me being here then I can send over Brett or Annabel but someone has to stay with you now that we know for sure. I'm sorry, but that's just the way it is." His eyes burned into mine, melting me from the inside out. My daydream had left me distracted and wanting to close the distance between us.

"It's not that I'm uncomfortable with you being here," I admitted as I finally exhaled.

"Then what?"

"I just don't like…" I paused. "I don't like feeling so helpless." I looked down, ashamed, as my fingers fiddled with the tie on my shorts.

"You're not helpless, quite the opposite." He smiled and his russet eyes burned with a quiet reverence that made my heart skip a beat. The way he looked at me proved how much he believed I was something special, that I was The Waker.

"So tell me more about this Belinda person," I asked, trying to refocus the conversation. "Why does everyone take everything she says at face value?" I still didn't buy the whole psychic thing.

"To start, she hasn't been the only one to name you as The Waker."

"Do you really have to keep calling me that?"

"What would you like me to call you?" An innocent looking smile spread across his face and I faltered at how gorgeous he looked.

"I don't know, I just don't like being referred to as The Waker. It's too weird for me." I shrugged, trying not to come off too harsh.

"Alright then. Belinda hasn't been the only one to see…" Robert paused. "How important you are." His voice sounded strained as he spoke the last few words. He was trying to keep things light for my sake, but I could tell by the tension in his shoulders how much it frustrated him that I wasn't taking him seriously.

"There have been others," I said and swallowed. "Like Belinda?"

"Of course. A few are born every generation and they've all seen you."

"But how do you know they just haven't heard it from someone else and then repeated it?" I frowned, starting to get a little uneasy. What if this was all true? *What if I was... The Waker?* I forced myself to think the words. Then what would I do?

"The vision is passed down from Soothsayer to Soothsayer, but each time the next generation discovers more information that wasn't known before," Robert explained.

"More information?"

"For instance, the very first vision contained your name and that you would carry the mark of your bloodline." He pointed to my necklace.

My fingers went to the pendant I always kept around my neck. As I looked at the three crescent moons placed back to back and held together by Celtic swirls, the metal felt heavier with the weight of his words.

"The next generation's vision showed that you would be born in America, and so on and so forth until the most recent vision told us exactly where to look for you."

"You knew where to find me?"

"It's not a coincidence my family was one of the founding residents here in Pismo. We knew you'd eventually end up here. It was just a matter of time."

"But why did you have to ask the families in England about other prospects if you knew I'd end up here?" I asked, hoping that maybe he did get it wrong and the real Waker was still out there.

"We knew you would be here in Pismo eventually but we didn't know when. You could have been the wrong Violet, though I knew otherwise," he said with an air of confidence. "I still had to make sure that no one had any other leads."

I let out a long breath. "So everything's just set in stone? I'm not sure I like not being in control of who I am and what my purpose is. Is there really no free will?"

"Of course there's free will. You can choose not to believe me. You can choose not to do anything with the information I give you."

"And what if that's what I do? What if I don't believe you?"

"Then that's your choice, but the world you're fighting so hard to hold on to, the world you knew before I came into your life, won't exist anymore. No matter what your choice is, nothing will ever be the same again. So it's up to you." His voice was light but his face was cold, hard and deadly serious.

"I just don't know what to do or what to believe. None of this seems possible; you shouldn't have been able to save me but you did and now all this talk about Soothsayers... How am I supposed to know what's real anymore?" I gaped at him, completely lost. "How?" I whispered.

"No one expects you to just jump right in. As much as I'm here to protect you, I'm also here to help you through all of this." He put his hand on my knee. A jolt of emotion ran through me, the same emotion I felt when he kissed me. Well, kissed me in my fantasy.

I took a deep breath and pulled his hand off.

"I'm sorry, I was just trying to comfort you. I didn't mean to make you uncomfortable," he said and shifted on the couch to move away from me.

"It's not that, it's just..." I broke off, not knowing how to finish the sentence. What was I supposed to say, *it's just that I keep having these intense visions every time you touch me?* I laughed a short, humorless laugh and shook my head. No, I couldn't say that.

"What's so funny?" Robert asked, half smiling.

"It's nothing. You don't make me uncomfortable." I tried to reassure him. I actually felt very comfortable and at ease with him. "It's just been a long day. I think maybe I'll head to bed." I smiled, trying to hide the knowledge that I wasn't going to get any sleep with him in the other room.

"That's probably a good idea."

We stared at each other for a few seconds, the question of him staying here tonight lingering between us.

"You can stay, for *now*," I said, rising from the couch. "But this isn't going to be a permanent situation." I didn't want to give in, but he wasn't going to give up and I was done arguing with him for one night.

Even though I didn't know any of the Maxwells all that well, I felt the most comfortable with Robert. I knew that if anything happened to me, he would be able to save me. Which made me wonder what Brett and Annabel were capable of if he was willing to let them protect me instead of himself. I suppressed the thought; I had enough to worry about without adding more questions to the overflowing pile at hand.

"Thank you, Violet. I promise I won't be in your way."

"I'll get you some blankets and a pillow." I moved around the couch and opened the linen closet.

Even though I still didn't have many answers, I felt oddly comforted that I wasn't alone in this anymore. If there was one thing I could believe out of everything Robert had told me today, I believed he really was here to help me.

I walked back to the living room where I found Robert rearranging the throw pillows on the couch.

"Here you go." I handed him a couple blankets and a real pillow.

"Thank you."

"The bathroom is down the hall, first door on the right. Extra towels are under the sink."

"I appreciate it. Night, Violet."

"Night."

As I passed the front door, habit forced me to make sure it was locked. Unease settled in my chest at the realization that a locked door probably couldn't stop whoever was coming after me. With that thought fresh in my mind, I picked up the baseball bat and carried it off to bed.

<h1 style="text-align:center">CHAPTER EIGHT</h1>

My alarm exploded into a frenzy of angry buzzing, announcing my seven-thirty wake-up call. I groaned and rolled over, turning the alarm off. Sitting up, I stretched my arms over my head and my stomach growled at the scent of bacon and cinnamon wafting through the room.

I threw myself back down on the bed. How did I get myself into this mess? I barely knew Robert and already he was staying in my house, making breakfast and telling me stories about psychics and prophecies.

My life had really taken a sharp left turn to crazy town. Reluctantly, I mustered the strength to get up and hop in the shower. I needed to be in Santa Barbara by eleven for The Caltome Vineyard shoot and if I was going to stop by the studio first I couldn't delay any longer. While I waited for the water to heat up, I went back to my closet to pick out something comfortable for the long day ahead.

The owner of the winery where I'd be shooting was a friend of a friend of Harriet's. After seeing some of my work, the owner hired me to take some editorial pictures he could use on his website and brochure. I was thrilled at the prospect of my work being the face of this new winery and wanted to make sure my photos were everything they wanted and more.

Hopping in the shower and drowning my worries, I let the hot water relax my already tight shoulders. As I lathered my hair with shampoo, I made a mental list of things I needed to pick up from the studio for today's shoot.

I probably took a little longer than I should have in the shower so I rushed to dry my hair then threw on a pair of jeans and a casual white button up. Not being able to put it off any longer, I left the haven of my bedroom to face Robert.

As I turned the corner into the main room, the smell of cinnamon and salty bacon assaulted my senses. The dining table was piled high with pancakes, giant slices of French toast, scrambled eggs, a pile of bacon, hash browns and a bowl of fresh fruit. Everything smelled and looked wonderful. My stomach grumbled again, excited at the prospect of a real break- fast for once.

"Good morning." Robert looked up at me from the table where he was reading the newspaper.

"You made all this?" I asked in disbelief. I took my seat at the head of the table where a plate had been set for me, along with a fresh cup of coffee and a carafe of orange juice.

"It really wasn't any trouble, and I wanted to show you how nice it can be having me around." His eyes washed over me and a quiet smile played on his lips. "I wasn't sure what you liked, so I made sure there was a little of everything." He returned his gaze to the paper in front of him.

I ate my breakfast in silence, sampling all the savory treats on the table. I tried to remember the last time I'd had a real honest to goodness breakfast like this and realized it must have been when my parents were still alive. The memory of my mom bustling around the kitchen brought a smile to my face and a lump in my throat that made it hard to swallow a mouthful of scrambled eggs.

I looked over at Robert several times as I washed the meal down with coffee, wondering if I should try to make conversation, but he never looked up and he seemed perfectly at ease to just sit and read the paper.

I took one last bite of French toast, then took my plate to the kitchen. I was expecting there to be a complete mess, but it looked like no one had even toasted a slice of bread, let alone made an entire feast. I was about to ask where all the food had come from when I saw the clock on the microwave and realized I was already running late. I poured some coffee into a thermos and headed out the door with a quick "thank you" tossed in Robert's direction.

I made it to my studio in no time, staying off the busy streets and parking my car with several minutes recovered from my late start. I unlocked the front door and headed straight for the back room. The message light blinked on Jessie's phone, but I didn't have time to check it. If it was important, Jessie would give me a call when she got in. I quickly unlocked the back door leading to all my equipment and flipped on the lights.

Walking over to the storage cabinet, I pulled out my large camera bag. I hadn't looked at the bag since stuffing it in here after the wedding. The black canvas felt cool against my fingers, like it contained a piece of that night. I could almost smell the cold, sticky air wafting off of it as I pulled the zipper open. I stuffed it full of gear, then threw the bag over my shoulder and heading for the dark room.

I kept a medium-sized stepladder and my light diffusers in here, both of which I needed for the day's shoot. Juggling everything out into the main office, I picked my laptop off my desk, shut the lights off, locked the front door and placed everything on the sidewalk next to my car. Out of habit I went to unlock the trunk but stopped just before I put the key in the lock. It was like being hit with a bolt of electricity, and the memory of my attack flashed before my eyes.

"Hey, watch where you're going!" a man crossing the street yelled and a horn blared. I looked toward the noise and for a brief moment, I thought the man behind the wheel was Ian. Doing a double take as the car passed, I tried to get a good look at the driver's face, but was unable to confirm my suspicion.

I turned away from the trunk and unlocked the car with the keyless entry. The small tremor of panic subsided back into the dark recesses of my mind as I piled everything into the backseat and slid behind the wheel. Now that I was on my way, I could relax a little.

I turned onto the 101 south, selected the *Beatles* playlist on my phone and settled in for the hour and a half drive down to Caltome Vineyards.

Now that I was free of Robert, I could think about everything he'd said a little more objectively. I'd never been someone who believed in psychics or anything having to do with the spiritual world. Although, the one thing I had to believe was that Robert was something different, something Magical maybe. I'd spent the last few weeks trying to come up with a reasonable explanation for how he saved my life, but the more I thought about it, the more I couldn't deny that reason and logic had nothing to do with how Robert healed me.

So what did that leave me with? I still wasn't sure, but what I did know for sure was that I trusted Robert with my life. And if I could trust him to never let anything happen to me, then maybe I could trust that he was telling the truth. The problem with that was even if I trusted him to *tell* me the truth, it didn't mean I could *believe* the truth. And what was I supposed to do, anyway? Step up and be The Waker? Or walk the other way and write this whole thing off as a bad dream? I let out a heavy sigh and leaned my head against the headrest. So much for having a boring, normal life.

Thinking about my predicament made the drive to Caltome Vineyards go by fairly quickly. I pulled off the freeway in just under an hour and fifteen minutes and parked in a dirt lot in front of the building marked 'Guest Relations.' As I got out of my car, the sweet fragrance of dirt and over ripe grapes hit me like a ton of bricks.

I walked into the antique-looking building and into an elaborately elegant reception area. A large front counter made of aged wood accentuated the romantic charm and feel as you walked in. The winery's name was burned into the wall behind the large counter. The cursive letters flowed into each other like smooth and flawless grapevines. To my left and around a slight corner, enormous bookshelves along the walls displayed hundreds of bottles of wine. Opposite the bookshelves was another counter that matched the one just ahead of me. This counter had tall barstools neatly tucked underneath the wood with more wine glasses than I could count hanging from the ceiling. Several displays had been set up to showcase particular bottles and a few crates were still strewn about the room waiting to be emptied. I approached the counter and pulled on the string attached to a small brass bell.

A tall, red-headed woman appeared from behind a false wine case. "Can I help you with something?" Her voice was warm and the laugh lines around her smile were welcoming.

"Yeah, my name's Violet. Scott hired me to photograph the winery," I answered, taking in the woman behind the door. The flannel she wore was a faded blue and cream, a glaring contrast to her wild, fiery red hair.

"Oh yes, that's right." She shook her head. "He told me you were coming by today. Come on back." She motioned with her arm for me to follow her and disappeared behind the case.

She was pretty, though not traditionally so. Her eyes were like bright blue crystals, and the faintest evidence of shadows around them indicated how little sleep she must be getting. She kept her curly, thick red hair pulled back into a loose ponytail and a few hairs had managed to escape and fall around her face.

I made my way around the counter and as I came to the door she held out her hand and said, "I'm Meredith Deardon, Scott's wife."

Why did her name sound so familiar? Deardon, Deardon, where had I heard that before?

"Nice to meet you," I said, shaking her hand. She returned the handshake with a firm, calloused grip. Apparently, she didn't just handle the winery's paperwork.

The room behind the case was completely different and took me a moment to adjust to. It was a plain office with boxes stacked high against the walls. The fluorescent lights cast a comparatively rude glow after being in the soft, elegant light filling the room just outside. Everything was simple, plain, save for a glass door to my right with a beautiful view of the sweeping grape fields outside.

"Excuse the mess. We're still trying to get everything together before our grand opening in two weeks and things are just everywhere right now," Meredith apologized as she sat behind one of the two desks. "Scott had to run a few errands, but I can tell you what we're looking for. Our assistant, Matthew, can show you around and help you with anything you need."

I sat in the folding chair across from her and she hit the speakerphone button and punched in a number. It rang twice and a young man's voice came through the speaker. "What's up?" he asked.

"Matthew, I need you to come to the office and show someone around."

"Alright, I'll be there in five." The phone line went dead and she clicked the round button on the keypad to end the call.

"Matthew's wonderful. Anything you need, don't hesitate to ask, he knows this place better than anyone."

"Sounds great." I smiled and sat up straight in the hard plastic chair.

Discussing the finer details of the job, she showed me an old family photo that was taken in Italy that was meant to be the inspiration for my day's work. A small house sat quietly among rolling hills as sunlight illuminated the fog that hung over the sprawling landscape. The mysterious romanticism of the photo was the feel they were going for. I had to admit, the desire to jump into the image and explore all its hidden secrets was almost overwhelming.

"I think I know what you're looking for." I stood and handed the picture back to her.

"Wonderful, I'll be here when you're done. I'm always here." She muttered the last part under her breath.

I walked back through the false wine case and headed to my car. Placing all of my gear on the ground, I fished my camera out of my bag. With deft hands, I switched out the lens for a wide-angle one. Looking through the viewfinder, I adjusted some settings.

A loud rumbling noise came toward me as I popped a fresh battery in place. When I looked up, I saw a handsome man driving an open-air, four-wheel-drive vehicle toward me. I assumed this must be Matthew.

"Sorry, I know the Gator's a bit loud," Matthew said as he turned the key and cut the engine. "But it'll get you anywhere you need to go." He smiled and walked around the vehicle to meet me. "I'm Matthew. Anything you need, I'm here to help."

We shook hands as I said, "Violet." His callused hand nearly crushed mine with his grip, making it clear he wasn't an indoors kind of guy.

He wore a black t-shirt, dark jeans and work boots, which all showed signs of needing a good wash. His hair was dirty blond and tied into a short ponytail at the back of his neck. A few strands of hair had escaped and fell around his bronzed face. He wasn't overly muscular, but instead looked very lean. I had no doubt he was much stronger than he looked.

"I'm almost done getting everything together and then we can head out," I said, walking back to my car.

"No problem. I'm just gonna run inside real quick and check in with Meredith," he said, grabbing a binder from the Gator and jogging inside.

I turned on the camera to make sure everything was charged and ready to go, then switched it off and put it in my bag. Picking up the stepladder and the rest of my gear, I turned toward the Gator. The vehicle had only two seats in the front and a small bed in the rear, like a tiny open-air pickup truck. I put the stepladder on the wooden bed and the rest of my equipment on the front seat. Matthew came back through the guest entrance carrying a case of water with a binder balanced on top.

"Do you need help?" I asked out of courtesy. He clearly didn't need any.

"Naw, I've got it. Thought maybe we might get thirsty being out in the sun all day."

"And that warranted a whole case of water?" My eyebrows rose on my forehead as I looked at him.

"You can never have too much." Matthew smiled as he put the case in the back beside my stepladder and climbed into the driver's seat. I moved my bag off the seat so I could hop on as well.

"Alright." He flipped open his binder. "Here's a map of the grounds. Where would you like to start?"

I looked at the map, noticing the estate pressed up against a pretty large hill that might give me a great view of the whole winery from above.

"I want to start down here in the fields, but I want to make our way up to the top of this hill. Is that possible?"

"Anything's possible." He chuckled and snapped the binder closed with one hand.

"Alright, then let's get to it."

The engine revved to life and my body vibrated as we set off. The day progressed pretty smoothly. Matthew helped me with my stepladder and held the light diffusers whenever I asked. I could see why the Deardons kept him around. He really helped a lot and was an absolute pleasure to spend time with. His carefree attitude was infectious and I soon found myself joking and laughing along with him. Ever since Robert saved me, I'd been afraid and cautious, but being with Matthew eased that fear a little. We zipped through the fields, stopping here and there when I asked. I snapped pictures of everything, knowing I would go back through them later and edit out the ones that weren't that great. In my business, more was always better.

We were slowly making our way to the top of the hill when Matthew stopped the Gator under a large tree. We'd been out in the sun for a few hours and both of us were beginning to feel its effects. My shirt clung to my shoulders and stomach with sweat, and I had already gone through three bottles of water. Matthew looked like he had just gotten out of the shower. His ponytail looked dipped in grease from all the sweat pinning his hair to his head.

"Do you want to get out of the sun for a bit?" Matthew asked. I couldn't be sure, but it looked like there was excitement in his eyes.

"Sure, what d'you have in mind?"

"What makes you think I have something in mind?" He put his hand to his chest, feigning shock and surprise.

"Let's just say its instinct." I eyed him but couldn't keep a smile from forming.

"You must have good instincts," he said, grabbing another bottle of water. "Come on, it's just up here." He nodded.

"What is?" I asked and followed him out of the shade of the tree and back into the sun.

"You'll see." He gave me a playful look over his shoulder.

We soon approached a small shack just ahead of us. It looked like it had been restored recently, but still showed signs of being exposed to the elements. Ivy crawled up the sides and over a small, square window on the right wall. It was very quaint, but something about it instantly made my guard go up. Matthew seemed nice and all, but I really didn't know anything about him. Could this be a trap, a way to lure me to a hidden place after spending the day sedating me? I took another hesitant step in the direction of the shack.

"Seriously, where are you taking me?" I tried to keep my voice light.

"Just trust me." He turned to face me. "This is something you'll definitely want to get a few pictures of."

"I hardly think the Deardons hired me to take pictures of a shack, or what's in it."

"It's not the shack itself." His eyes twinkled with sweetness. "It's what's underneath it."

"Underneath?"

"Just come on." He stepped toward me and grabbed my hand.

"Hey!" I yelled as he jerked me forward.

Matthew just laughed and pulled me inside the shack. It was empty except for a few garden tools and a large crate in the corner. He released my hand before he reached for a hook in the floor and pulled. The hatch door creaked as he lifted it open. I stepped to the edge of the opening and froze.

CHAPTER NINE

"You okay? You're not claustrophobic, are you?" Matthew asked, seeing my reaction.

"What… oh, um, no."

A set of stone stairs below me led into what looked like a tunnel. Lights hanging on either side of the rough stone walls illuminated the narrow passageway. It looked just like the corridor Robert had led me through after he healed me.

I finally looked up at Matthew, who was watching me with curiosity. "Where exactly do these stairs lead?" I tried to mask the apprehension building inside me.

He looked me over, all the playfulness gone from his face. "It leads to the cellar where we age the wine." He frowned. I could tell he was trying to understand the sudden change in my demeanor.

"Oh, perfect." My voice squeaked with relief.

"You sure you're okay? You seem a little off."

A nervous laughed escaped my throat. "Can you blame a girl for being reluctant when a man she hardly knows drags her into a shack and opens up a creepy looking door in the floor?"

"I think I might actually be offended," he said and smiled back before heading down the stairs.

I breathed a sigh of relief and followed close behind.

We descended the stairs, going deeper and deeper underground. Neither one of us spoke while we walked. I was too focused on putting one foot in front of the other while trying to stifle the memory of traversing a similar corridor with Robert. We reached the bottom of the stairs and entered a short tunnel that opened up into a fairly large room.

"This is my favorite place on the property."

"It's beautiful," I said, taking a look around.

My voice echoed against the crude, high ceiling. The walls didn't look like they had been man made either. The whole room resembled a cave, like someone had dug out all the dirt and rocks and left a big empty space behind. Our shadows danced in the thin light from bulbs spaced evenly apart, making the room glow with a soft, yellow aura. Each breath filled my lungs with the faint smell of wood and freshly turned earth. Racks upon racks of bottled wine had been stacked against the walls, and I shivered a moment with the noticeably cooler temperature.

I quickly adjusted the shutter speed, white balance, and ISO ratio on my camera so I could capture the cellar just as it was without a flash.

Matthew sat down on a large crate against the wall and started telling me all about the cellar and how it was built. Pride and affection laced his every word.

I roamed the cavern, taking pictures of every nook and cranny. I let my hand graze over a few bottles of wine when suddenly everything shifted.

Matthew stood next to me, placing bottles on a shelf. I waved my hand in front of his face, but he didn't see me. I walked around the shelf to where he'd been sitting just a moment ago, but the crate was empty. When I returned he was still stacking bottles and whistling to himself.

"Hey stranger," a familiar voice said behind me.

Matthew looked up and a knowing smile spread across his face. "Fancy meeting you here." He walked past me.

I turned around to see who had caught Matthew's attention.

"Brett?" I blurted, my eyes bulging out of my head.

Neither one of them acknowledged me as Matthew picked Brett up and kissed her.

"You'll never guess what's happened," she said as he placed her back on her feet. "We found her, we found The Waker."

And just like that, I was once more standing with my hand frozen on a bottle of wine, camera half raised. Matthew was still chattering away about the cellar's history, when I walked around the corner to see him still sitting on the crate.

What the hell just happened? And was Matthew like Robert? Did he know something about this whole Waker business?

I looked back at the rack of bottles and then where Matthew and Brett had been standing just a moment ago.

"Hey, you okay?" Matthew asked, hopping off the crate and walking toward me.

"Nothing, I just thought…" What did I think? This wasn't the first time I spaced and saw something strange. Seemingly every time Robert touched me, my imagination went into hyperdrive. But this, this was different. It wasn't a memory or a daydream. So what gives? What was happening to me?

"Violet?" Matthew asked, placing his hand on my shoulder.

"Yeah, I just thought I saw something." I shook off the image of him and Brett.

Matthew's brow creased and he looked down at me with those big green eyes. His expression was serious, but there was a calmness that radiated off of him. As I looked up at him, I heard Brett's words echo in my head, 'We found her, we found The

Waker.' My lungs contracted and an overwhelming need for fresh air gripped me.

"I got everything I need down here. Why don't we head back up," I suggested, looking toward the exit.

"Right, let's head back up then." He gave me a tight-lipped smile that didn't reach his eyes.

I didn't say another word as I followed him back the way we'd come. I couldn't shake off the image of him and Brett together. I wanted to ask if he knew the Maxwells but was too afraid of what his answer might be, and in turn what that would mean for me.

As we walked up the stairs, I studied Matthew in front of me. Was it possible he was like Robert? Nothing about him indicated he had any special abilities, but I hadn't noticed anything different about Robert the first time we met either.

"Just crazy," I said under my breath.

"What's that?" Matthew asked as he extended his hand to help pull me up the last few steps.

"Nothing, just talking to myself."

"Self-talker." He chuckled. "Me too, keeps me from going crazy."

A shaky laugh escaped my throat and I took a deep breath as the fresh air hit me, "I think all the talking to myself might actually be making me crazy."

"You seem pretty normal to me." He looked back at me with his playful grin firmly in place.

"Great, I must really be nuts then." I laughed off the jitters and we hopped back in the Gator. If Matthew was like Robert and he did know something about The Waker, I sure as hell wasn't going to bring it up while I was alone with him. He may be close to Brett, but that didn't mean I could trust him.

It was late afternoon by the time we parked, and a soft glow of light sat over the whole winery. I walked around the top of the hill, getting pictures at different angles. The fields looked like long, elegant fingers splayed across the grounds. The staggering size of the estate played out before us. Matthew had talked about how large this place was, but seeing it from above was magnificent.

"Alright, I think I've got everything," I said, heading to Matthew, who waited patiently by the Gator. He looked so at ease, leaning back, sipping on a bottle of water, that I couldn't help myself. I lifted my camera and took a quick picture. "Okay, now I have everything."

"Hey, I wasn't ready for my close up." He sat up, spilling water down the front of his shirt.

"You'll never be more ready than you are when you're unprepared."

"That's actually kinda deep." He raised an eyebrow and nodded.

"Not just a pretty face," I laughed. He turned the key over and we headed back down the hill.

We made much better time coming down than we did going up. I hadn't realized how many stops we'd made along the way.

It was just after five-thirty when we arrived back at my car. Matthew helped me put all my gear in the backseat. I held onto my camera so I could get a few shots of the interior and grabbed my laptop off the front seat so I could put everything together for Mrs. Deardon.

"Thank you so much for all your help today."

"It was my pleasure, Violet."

"The pleasure was all mine. I haven't had that much fun in a long time. And you have no idea how much I needed it." I waved as he walked back to the Gator. A feeling of ease and calmness washed over me. Despite my reservations toward Matthew after the cellar, I had to admit, he was a nice guy and it was really nice spending the day with him.

I walked inside, set my computer on the bar and pressed the power button. While it booted up, I walked around taking pictures of the interior. I made sure to get a few pictures of the beautifully intricate sign hanging above the front desk as well as pictures of the wine bottles, labeled and ready for purchase.

Once I got everything I needed I sat down at the bar and popped the memory card in my computer. I went through the hundreds of pictures, quickly cropping and editing the ones I liked and passing over the ones I didn't. I paused when I got to the picture of Matthew. Cropping it a little, I saved it to my desktop so I could add it to my collection of candid's later. By the time I finished going through everything and doing my first round of editing, it was just after seven. Satisfied with what I had produced, I grabbed my computer and headed around the front desk to the back office.

"Mrs. Deardon, I have a selection for you to take a look at," I announced as I walked into the back room.

"Let's see what you've got." She motioned for me to have a seat.

I stepped into the office, and to my horror found Robert standing toward the back of the room, leaning against a stack of boxes. A jolt of emotions went through me, half furious to see him and the other half, the stupid half, delighted. I chastised myself for being excited; there was no reason for me to be happy to see him. And how did he know I was here, anyway?

"You? What are you doing here?"

"I needed to talk to Meredith about a few things," Robert said, perfectly innocent.

At the mention of Meredith's name, I realized she was watching us from her seat behind her desk. I took a deep breath and turned toward her, trying to regain control.

"I can come back when you're done with-"

"I'll let you ladies work," Robert interrupted me. "I'm going to see if I can find Matty." He stood and motioned for me to take the floor.

"Matty? You mean, Matthew?" I asked, sitting down.

"The one and only. I haven't seen him in a while. Thought I'd say hi and catch up while I wait for you."

"Wait for me?"

Robert cleared his throat. "Yeah, Annabel dropped me off. I figured I would just catch a ride back with you." He cocked his head to the side, waiting to see if I would argue with him in front of Meredith.

"I'll meet you out front." I leveled my eyes on him, making it clear I wasn't happy about this.

He gave me a charming smile in exchange for my glare and then turned his attention to Mrs. Deardon. "It's been good talking to you, Meredith. Please give Scott my best."

"I will. He'll be thrilled to hear the news."

"And I'll see you in a bit." Robert gave my shoulder a quick squeeze as he walked out the side door.

"Alright," Meredith said when Robert had left the room, "let's see what you've got."

I suppressed a huff of distaste and returned to my professional demeanor. I had work to do.

Putting my computer on her desk and we went through the pictures I'd selected for her review. Mrs. Deardon tagged the ones she wanted large prints of and asked for a few adjustments to the edits.

Overall she was thrilled and so was I. Some of the photos I had taken, especially the ones from the top of the hill, were so beautiful I planned on putting them in my portfolio.

"You really have a gift," Meredith said when we'd finished.

"Thank you, you have a beautiful winery."

"It's kind of wonderful, isn't it?" She sighed and a proud smile pulled at the corner of her lips.

I nodded in agreement.

"Well thank you so much for all your hard work."

"Of course. I'll set up a dropbox with all the pictures and email you the link once I get through all the editing in the next couple of days." I extended my hand to shake hers and she gripped my fingers tightly.

The sun hung low over the nearby hills as I walked outside. Robert and Matthew stood by my car chatting away. Neither one of them looked in my direction as I approached.

"Hey, Matty, I thought you'd be gone by now?"

"Hey, no way are you allowed to call me that."

"Oh, and he gets to?" I motioned toward Robert and kept a playful smile on my face as I approached them.

Robert eyed me but didn't say anything. Instead, he leaned against my car and watched the banter between Matthew and me.

"He's practically family. I barely know you."

Practically family? That's interesting. Maybe he did know something about The Waker.

"And I thought we bonded today," I said, pretending to pout.

"Bonding or not, you still can't call me Matty."

"We'll see about that." I stepped away from the boys and unlocked my car.

Robert walked around to the passenger side and said to Matthew, "We'll talk more later. Are you going to be around this weekend?"

"I was thinking about it, not sure yet though. We're pretty busy around here with the opening in a couple weeks."

"Alright, I'll be in contact." Without another word, Robert opened the passenger side door and climbed in.

"See you later, Matty," I said, laughing and waving as I got in the car.

He just stood there shaking his head at me as I started the engine.

"You two seem to get along," Robert finally said as I put the car in gear and backed out.

"Yeah, he's nice and he was really helpful today."

Robert didn't respond, so I looked over at him. He stared out the windshield with a thoughtful expression on his face.

"So, how do you know Matthew?" I asked. I couldn't bring myself to mock him when he wasn't around to defend himself.

"Old family friend."

"He doesn't happen to know Brett, does he?" Curiosity, apparently, had gotten the best of me.

"Yes, they know each other." Robert shifted in his seat and I had a feeling they knew a little more of each other than Robert was comfortable with.

"And what about the Deardons?" I asked.

"Same. Our families are close."

"What's wrong?"

"Why do you think something's wrong?" he asked, tearing his eyes from the dashboard.

"Because you're being short with me." I turned to face him as we approached a red light.

"I'm sorry, it's just been a long day." He let out a heavy sigh.

The light turned green and I stepped on the gas without saying anything else. Why did I even care that he was short with me? Who was I to question him? But I couldn't help myself; there was still so much I didn't know about Robert or about my situation, and I didn't know who else to ask.

"Robert?" I asked.

"Hmm."

"What did you need to talk to Meredith about?" I wasn't sure if he would answer my question, but it was worth a try.

He sighed and said, "You."

"Me?" I asked, frowning as I turned onto the highway.

"About who you are."

"Who I…Oh, you mean that I'm the…"

"The Waker, yes." His attitude surprised me, but I tried not to take it personally and pressed on with more questions.

"So Meredith's like you then?" I asked.

"Yes, both she and her husband are Magical."

"Is Matthew like you too?" I bit my lip.

A small smile played on his face. "No, he's not. He's a Promised One."

Great, I thought, he's not like Robert, but something else. When did this craziness end?

I swerved into the left lane to pass a slow-moving minivan and stepped on the gas, wanting to be home already.

"What's a Promised One?" I asked after a minute, suspending reality and just going with it for the moment. Robert seemed more willing to talk when I wasn't arguing against everything he believed in.

"Matty is human. He isn't like me or the Deardons, but he was born with the ability to sense Magic. His soul is promised to the Magical world," Robert explained.

"What does that mean?"

"There are some people in this world who are born to protect Magic but don't possess any Magic themselves. Matty is one of those people. There are many others just like him. For as long as anyone can remember, the Promised Ones have helped keep the Magical world a secret."

"So what do they do for you exactly? I asked.

"Anything they need to in order to protect our way of life. Promised Ones have infiltrated every facet of the economy and use their influence to hide our Magic in plain sight. Unfortunately, there are some people, both Promised Ones and Magical, who believe our world shouldn't be kept a secret. We think your attacker might be a human who works for someone against Magical secrecy."

The mention of my attacker made my stomach drop.

"But why would someone care if Magic was a secret or not?" I asked, balking at my casual use of the word *Magic*. I still wasn't even sure if I bought into any of this. The more I learned, the more I realized Robert probably wasn't making any of it up, but

I still hadn't written off my dream theory. Maybe, if I was lucky, I just might wake up from all of this. The thought made me pinch my leg, but nothing happened. I continued to cruise down the highway with Robert by my side as we discussed Magic.

"Could you imagine what people would do to us if they found out what we could do?" Robert asked, his voice breaking my train of thought.

I could feel his gaze on me, so I turned to look at him. The concern etched into the lines of his face was overpowering. He looked sullen, worn, like he had the world on his shoulders and he was crumbling under the enormity of what was at stake. I tore myself away from his heartbreaking expression and focused on the road. I could imagine what might happen if people discovered what Robert could do. My heart lurched at the thought of anyone hurting him. Regardless of what I might think about everything, one thing I knew for sure was Robert was a good person and he didn't deserve to be hurt in any way.

I looked back over at him, but he was staring out his window. I could almost hear the wheels turning in his head. I swallowed my own feelings and pushed forward with more questions.

"What does someone like Matthew gain by helping you?"

"Well someone in the know, like Matty, is a part of the Magical world and therefore reaps the benefits of Magic without having any himself," Robert explained after taking a breath to compose himself.

"But Matthew works at a winery. How is he helping the Magical world stay secret?" I asked, not sure how someone like Matthew was helping hide Magic from the rest of humanity.

"Do you remember what I told you last night about the first men who heard the prophecy about you?"

"Yeah, but what does that have to do… Deardon, that's where I'd heard that name before."

Robert let out a low chuckle. "Matty helps draw attention

away from them. His family is very influential and they are able to cover up any exposures that might occur."

Did Matthew sense something in me? Did Meredith already know who I was? Was that why she wanted Matthew to show me around all day? And why was Robert so quiet? What had happened today that changed his attitude so much? Was he giving up on me already? Did I care if he gave up on me? I did care, I suddenly realized.

"Ugh," I said with an audible sigh.

"What's wrong?"

"Nothing." I kept my eyes on the road, refusing to look at him.

"Violet, talk to me." His voice was soothing, but I could hear the frustration hidden behind his tone.

"I just don't know what to do with all this."

"I know," he said, placing his hand on my knee. "It's okay."

My knee tingled at his touch. I looked over at him, but he just stared out his window again. Something was clearly bothering him. I decided to let him be with his thoughts and not ask any more questions for now. I'd been so wrapped up in my life being turned upside down I never thought about what it must be like for him. His whole world had been wrapped up in finding me and now that he had, I became just a pain in the ass who never believed anything he said.

"I'm sorry."

"For what?" His hand remained on my knee and he gave it a reassuring squeeze.

"That I'm not what you expected to find."

"Violet, don't." He removed his hand and turned to face me.

"But, Robert..."

As I opened my mouth to speak he shook his head and said, "No." I turned my eyes back to the road and tried to make sense of everything I was feeling. Aside from being blindsided by the knowledge that Magic was real, I could feel myself falling for

Robert and that was just as terrifying as being called The Waker. Every time I let someone in, I ended up with my heart broken and I honestly didn't know if I could handle any more pain in my life.

We spent the rest of the ride in silence, both lost in our own thoughts. I turned onto my street a little over an hour later and found a parking spot along the curb. I realized I hadn't eaten anything since breakfast and put my hand over my stomach to muffle a growl. Robert grabbed my camera bag and computer for me, and I pulled my purse out from under the passenger seat. We walked inside and I headed straight for the kitchen.

"Where do you want me to put your stuff?" Robert yelled from the entryway.

I threw a square plastic tray into Chef Mike and punched in two minutes and thirty seconds.

"Sorry about that. Here, I'll take it." I reached for my bag and I walked into the living room to set everything down by my desk. "Are you hungry?"

"No, I ate before Annabel dropped me off at Caltome. Thank you though," he answered and followed me into the living room.

"Ok, well I'm gonna eat real quick and then I'll get out of your way."

"You're not in my way." Robert sat down on the couch.

"Still, I'm going to head to bed after I eat. It's been a long day." I wasn't tired, though. I would probably just read for a while, but I wanted to give him his privacy.

"Yes, it has." He gave me a small smile.

I ate the microwaved meatloaf and mashed potatoes alone in the kitchen to give us both some much-needed space. I didn't know what was bothering Robert and felt bad that I didn't know how to cheer him up. I couldn't help but think I was the reason for his melancholy attitude.

When I was finished eating, I walked back out to the living room to say goodnight. Robert was still sitting on the couch, but his head was bent over his lap. I tiptoed over to him and noticed he had a journal open on his lap. He didn't hear my approach, or if he did he was ignoring me, so I took a moment to drink him in. I knew I shouldn't, knew that letting even a piece of him in wasn't a good idea, but I couldn't help myself. There was this need somewhere deep inside me that ached to be close to him.

As I moved closer, I watched as his fingers traced the tiny handwritten words scrawled across the page.

"I've read this journal a million times," he said with a thoughtful sounding voice, like his mind was a million miles away.

I guess he did know I was there. I walked around the couch and sat down next to him. He took a deep breath and sat back, relaxing into the cushions.

"But it was just words until we found you." Robert angled his body, so we were facing each other and a melancholy smile tugged at the corner of his mouth.

His eyes pulled me in. I hadn't seen him this unguarded since he saved me. He wore every emotion written on his face: anger, sadness, awe. The control he always seemed to have shattered before me for the first time since that night.

"There was a part of me that never thought we'd find you." He placed his arm across the back of the couch and turned to face me. "That maybe they had already found you."

Without consciously telling my body to move, I shifted on the couch, bringing my leg up under me so I was facing him. My heart started to beat a little faster. His eyes never left mine and I felt a mix of emotions radiate off him.

"And then when we did find you, I almost lost you." He shook his head and looked back at the journal in his lap.

This must be what's been bothering him, I thought.

"But you saved me. Without you, I wouldn't be here." I leaned a little closer to him and placed my hand on his chest. He was so warm and my fingers itched to pull him closer.

"I shouldn't have needed to save you. I should have been keeping you out of harm's way in the first place."

I started to pull my hand back, but he caught it in his and kept it pressed against his chest. The steady beat of his heart pounded under my fingers and I wanted to comfort him.

"Maybe you were meant to save me," I said, shifting my shoulders with insecurity as the words left my lips. He was the one who believed in fate and prophecies, after all.

"But at what cost? Destroying your life?" He looked up at me and his thumb made little circles on the back of my hand, sending chills up my arm. "It'd be different if you were brought up with Magic, but you weren't and now..." He trailed off.

"You didn't destroy my life, you saved it," I said, trying to ease his pain and frustration. "You. Saved. Me." I leaned my body a little closer to him. I wanted him to see how much that meant to me, no matter how I might feel about everything else.

His eyes dropped from mine and his heart beat a little faster, making mine leap into my throat. The space between us was almost nonexistent. I could feel his breath on my face and the warmth of his body engulfing me. Something inside me stirred, pushing me closer to him.

"Robert," I breathed.

His eyes met mine and he placed his hand on my cheek. Any walls I still had in place shattered as we studied each other. I didn't care about not letting him in anymore. I didn't care about the prophecy or the Promised Ones.

Robert stared deep into my eyes and said, "Violet, I wish there was a way I could make this-" The sound of glass breaking had him on his feet in a split second.

"Follow me." He grabbed for my hand and pulled me after him. "Stay close." Startled, I did as he asked without question.

We slowly made our way in the direction the crash had come from. I could feel my pulse echo throughout my entire body as I crept behind Robert. Ever since the night I was attacked, I had been waiting for someone to come back and finish the job. At least this time, I wasn't alone.

As Robert reached for my bedroom door, he glanced back at me and motioned for me to wait in the hall. The door opened without a sound and Robert slipped into my bedroom. The darkness swallowed him whole. Only the hum of the refrigerator in the kitchen and my own ragged breathing broke the sudden silence in the house.

CHAPTER TEN

$\mathcal{U}$nable to sit in the hall and wait for something to happen, I took the few steps into my room, hoping to find nothing but Robert. The moment my foot crossed the threshold, something pushed me face first to the floor. The air in the room felt charged, like a summer storm, ready and waiting to unleash its fury. The thickness of the air made me feel deaf, and as I hit the floor, I heard not a sound. Panic flared through me like wildfire. Something Magical was happening in here, I could feel it deep in my bones. I tried to scurry away on my hands and knees deeper into the room, but someone caught my ankle and pulled me backward. I tried to scream, but no sound reached my ears. I could feel my vocal cords vibrating and I could hear my screams in my head, but my ears didn't pick up a single trace of noise. Kicking wildly, I pulled free as electricity moved all around me like floating rivers. I scurried away as a bolt of light struck the ground next to my head, momentarily stopping me in my tracks.

The assailant grabbed my leg again and dragged me toward the door. I flailed and my arm struck the nightstand and brought the whole thing down on top of me. The corner of the stand caught the side of my head and a bolt of pain shot through my body. Stunned by the blow, I stopped struggling and my attacker effortlessly pulled me into the hall.

"Robert," I screamed. This time my voice rang out and I prayed Robert wasn't still in my bedroom where sound ceased to exist.

"He can't hear you," a blonde woman said as she dragged me down the hall.

"Yes, actually, I can, Lila." Robert's voice was laced with venom.

The woman let go of my leg and turned her full attention to Robert. I pulled myself back down the hall away from both of them and watched as Robert lunged at the woman he called Lila.

They both fell to the floor and she was able to get the better of him, rolling on top of him. She pinned Robert to the floor with her knees and raised her hand over him in a way that sent a shiver of terror through me. In a split second, I realized she wasn't going to punch Robert, she was going to use Magic.

"No!" I screamed and charged her. Looking up just as my body crashed into her, we both rolled to the floor in a tangle of arms and legs. Lila pinned me in an instant and raised her hand again, this time directing it at me. Yellow sparks ignited the tips of her fingers and a sick smile splayed across her face.

Robert rushed her just as the sparks flew, the Magical attack striking the wall behind me and narrowly missing my head. The wall exploded and rained plaster down on all of us. I choked on the dust and wiggled away from the two of them, fighting for control next to me. Robert got a few quick punches in before she shook herself free from his grasp. She made a beeline for the door as Robert rolled onto his side, raised his hand and shot a ball of hot white light toward the intruder's back. She flew forward, crashing into the front entry table and taking it down in a heap beside her.

Robert rose to his feet, hand still raised in defense, and walked over to her. As he knelt down to check for her pulse, her eyes popped opened and she threw Robert across the room with an invisible force.

I watched in horror as she stood, dusted plaster off her jeans and came toward me. An orange electric looking ball formed in the palm of her hand as she towered over me. "Playtimes over." A menacing smile formed on her lips and her eyes narrowed.

Pushing myself helplessly against the wall, I closed my eyes and braced for the pain.

"Lila, please don't make me do this," Robert growled.

Opening my eyes, I noticed that Lila had turned to look at him. I wiggled away while her attention was otherwise engaged and then looked at Robert, horrified. He was holding a transparent, grapefruit-sized ball in his hand. Thick black smoke swirled inside the sphere as blue sparks crackled along the surface.

"You wouldn't," Lila dared him.

Robert's expressionless face cocked to the side. "Care to find out?"

Sparks flared on her fingers and she ran at him. Robert threw the smoky black sphere at her. As she dodged out of the way the sparks from her hand struck him in the shoulder. I followed the path of the black ball as it crashed into a photograph hanging on the wall above me. As the photo fell to the floor, it disintegrated into a pile of ash.

Another explosion pulled my attention back to the fight as smoke filled the room. Robert stood up from behind the kitchen table where he had landed. Searching through the smoke for another figure, I came up empty handed. She was gone.

"Are you okay?" Robert asked as he ran across the room and helped me to my feet.

"Yeah, I'm fine."

"You're bleeding." Robert touched just above my left

eyebrow. Warmth spread over my face and then his hand fell to his side. "There, good as new." I felt for the gash in my forehead, but it was gone.

"Thanks," I said, grimacing awkwardly. A lot of Magic had just gone down and I didn't know how to begin wrapping my head around everything. I couldn't deny what I'd just seen with my own two eyes, but that didn't mean I understood it.

"You shouldn't have attacked her, you know."

"She was trying to kill you."

"Violet, I'm supposed to be protecting you."

"But-"

"But nothing. Don't do that again," he warned, his voice hard and unforgiving. "I need to make a phone call. Are you going to be alright for a minute?"

I managed to nod.

He pulled his phone from his pocket and anxiously tapped his foot while he waited for the other party to answer.

"Hey, I need you here now."

I made my way to the kitchen in a daze. Without really thinking about what I was doing, I pulled a glass down from the cupboard and poured myself a healthy dose of whiskey. My hand shook as I raised the glass to my mouth and sipped the amber liquid. Robert had said they would come after me again, but it wasn't until now that I actually believed him.

I didn't know how many minutes passed as I stood in the kitchen drinking, but a knock at the door stirred me from my reverie and I walked out to see who had arrived.

Robert opened the door and Brett burst in. "What happened?"

"We had a visitor tonight." Robert pursed his lips, "It was Lila."

"Lila?" Brett turned at looked at her brother.

He closed his eyes and quietly nodded.

Clearly they had history with the woman, and neither of

them looked pleased by the fact that she had attacked us tonight.

"Damn, they're closer than they should be."

"I know." Robert frowned. I'd never seen him so serious before.

"Is she alright?" Brett asked Robert. "Are you alright?" She turned to me.

"Just fine." I tipped my glass toward her. "Although I can't say the same for my house."

"It's nothing that can't be fixed." Brett waved nonchalantly.

"Brett," Robert said and exhaled with frustration.

"Alright, geez. Someone's cranky tonight."

"Could you take this a little more seriously? What's gotten into you?"

"I am taking this seriously. I just don't have a giant stick up my ass," Brett spat back.

"I really don't need any of your shit tonight. Can you just help me get this place cleaned up?"

"You know, I don't know why you always call me when there's a mess to clean up. Why can't you ever call Jake?"

"Because I actually like Jake and I need him running perimeter tonight."

"Rude." They both smiled and got to work. It was nice seeing someone go tit for tat with Robert for a change.

Brett got to work right away and started cleaning things up, Magically. I would have helped, but the only thing in my arsenal was a dustpan and broom. By the time Robert and Brett were saying goodbye, everything looked as it did before the fight. The only indication that any altercation occurred was the missing picture that had turned to ash. I guess Magic couldn't fix everything.

"Fill everyone in, will you?" Robert asked his sister. I couldn't see them from where I stood in the hall, but I could hear them perfectly.

"Of course," Brett replied. "Do you think we should call on-"

"No, not yet. If there was something she could tell us, she would have sought us out already."

"Robert, are you okay?" Brett asked, her voice laced with concern.

"I'm fine, it's just been a long day."

"Do you want me to stay with her so you can get some rest?" My heart leapt into my throat. I didn't like the idea of Robert and I playing house, but after tonight I really didn't want him to leave.

"No, I'll stay with her."

A long pause followed.

"Don't look at me like that," Robert said. My interest peaked and I wondered how Brett was looking at him.

"Just be careful." I could hear the smile in her voice.

"Goodnight, sister."

"Goodnight, brother."

The door closed and I made my way out to him.

"So what exactly happened tonight?" I asked, propping myself against the back of the couch.

"Lila was sent here to kill you."

"And who's Lila?" I raised my eyebrows with interest.

"She's Aiden's daughter and someone I've run across in the past."

"Oh," I said and hiccupped. I slapped my hand over my mouth, embarrassed.

Robert chuckled. "Violet, are you alright? Honestly." He pulled my hand from my mouth and frowned down at me.

I nodded and another hiccup burst out. "What was-*hiccup*-that black thing that came out of your hand."

"It's called Cinder. It turns anything it touches to ash."

Hiccup. "And you were planning on hitting Lila," I said, mortified.

He nodded, "It's not something I ever like to summon, but

there was no way I was going to let her lay another finger on you."

Hiccup. I stared up at him, a dozen emotions running through me. Shock was at the top of the list as another hiccup erupted from my throat.

"Why don't we lay off the liquor." He took the almost empty glass out of my hand.

"Okay." I smiled sheepishly. "Robert?"

"Yeah?"

"What happened in my room?"

He brushed my hair behind my ear and said, "It was a silencing spell, meant to suspend sound so she could get to you without me noticing." He smirked. "It was an amateur move."

Hiccup.

Unable to process any of this and really starting to buzz, I decided it was time for bed. "I think I'm going to try to get some sleep," I said, rising from the couch.

"Wait, I want to give you something, if that's alright. I wanted to give it to you earlier, before we were interrupted. I think it will help you see the truth."

"Umm… sure." I furrowed my brows, hesitant.

He walked back over to the coffee table, picked up the journal and handed it to me.

"What is this exactly?" I finally asked. I had assumed it was his own personal journal when I saw it earlier.

"Just open it."

I opened the front cover and the binding crackled in protest. An inscription was scrawled on the inside cover in tiny, delicate letters:

To My William

With all my love, Constance

"Who's William?"

"He was the very first Maxwell to hear the prophecy about you."

"Maxwell, is he…"

"Yes, he's my relative."

"And Constance?"

"She was his wife. Although, when she gave him that journal, she was engaged to another man. It was quite the scandal, but it all worked out in the end."

"What's so special about it?"

"There is powerful Magic stored in that journal and only those who are meant to see it can have access to it." Robert smiled.

"So it's like a spell book?"

He laughed. "You watch too many movies."

"Don't laugh at me," I scoffed. *Hiccup.*

"I'm sorry." He rearranged the smile on his face. "What I mean is, this journal…" He touched the corner of the page. "It belonged to some very powerful people. Their words are meant to guide you."

"People? This belonged to more than one person?"

"It's been passed down through the generations. I'm able to access it because it belongs to my family."

"What exactly do you mean by accessing it?"

"It's different for me than it will be for you. My ancestors' blood runs through my body, so I feel and experience things when reading the journal, but I don't know what will happen to you when you read it."

"You said it's meant to guide me?"

"Every word in the journal carries the essence of the author. Their souls have lingered on the pages if you will. When you start reading, you'll feel a pull that will help guide you in the right direction."

"How do you know all this?" I asked, feeling overwhelmed.

"It's all in the journal."

My thumb held down the corner and let page by page flip by.

"Thanks, I guess." My emotions flew all over the map and I just wanted to crawl into bed.

"I'll let you get some sleep." His eyes caught mine for just a second and the heat coursing through me felt like a lightning bolt. Ugh, how could I want him right now? I'd nearly been killed, again, and one look from Robert made me what to forget all of it and jump into his arms. Maybe I did drink too much, I thought sheepishly.

"Right," I said, shaking him off. "Night then." I turned and headed straight for my bedroom.

I flipped on the light. The nightstand and its contents were strewn across the floor. I picked up the overturned piece of furniture and as I set the journal on top of it, the room turned upside down.

A field of lush green grass appeared under my bare feet. A woman stood in the distant with her back turned to me. Cautiously I took a step toward her, unsure of where I was or what was happening. The breeze ruffled her hair, but otherwise, she stood unnaturally still.

As I got closer, I noticed that she was holding a sword in her left hand and blood dripped from the fingers on her right hand.

"Violet," someone yelled from behind me.

I turned and Robert ran past me to the woman with the sword.

Following him, I got within a few feet of her, and realized she looked familiar. She looked like me.

"Violet, are you alright?" Robert asked the woman standing before us both. "Oh God." He hesitated and then reached a tentative hand toward her.

Her head, my head, moved like a bird inspecting a worm.

I circled around myself so that I was standing face to face with her. Neither of them noticed me or paid me any attention as I stared at myself in horror.

It was like looking in a mirror, except for the eyes. Her eyes, my eyes, were no longer green. The iris had been turned the color of amethyst and they glistened in the sunlight.

The field faded, but the image of my amethyst eyes staring back at me sent a shiver down my spine. What the hell was that? Was I actually starting to lose my mind?

I didn't have the energy nor was I in the mindset to deal with any more Magical phenomena tonight. I quickly changed my clothes, grabbed the comforter and a pillow off my bed and headed for the living room.

"You can have my bed if you want, but I'm not staying in there tonight," I said as I walked straight toward the soft carpet in front of the television.

Robert frowned. "Take the couch, I can sleep on the floor," he said. "I'll make sure your room gets cleaned up first thing tomorrow."

"Thank you," I said, dropping my blanket on the couch, "for everything." Tears stung my eyes, but I pushed them back as I crawled under my comforter.

"You're very welcome, Violet." Robert turned off the lights and I fell asleep to the sound of his even breathing.

CHAPTER ELEVEN

I stared at the ceiling when I woke up, unable to stop running through everything that had happened yesterday. The assault left me physically drained and I wasn't doing much better emotionally. Everything Robert had told me about the Promised Ones got me thinking about Matthew and how normal he seemed. A pang of sadness touched my heart. Was nothing what it seemed anymore?

Last night had definitely been an eye opener. I couldn't deny what had happened, but I couldn't bring myself to think about what that meant for me and the prophecy. My life was changing and no matter how hard I fought against it, change was inevitable. *Take it one day at a time*, I chanted to myself.

I swung my legs over the side of the couch and stretched my hands over my head. Robert lay fast asleep on the floor, one hand on his chest, the other above his head. My heart gave a gentle tug at the sight of him and the memory of how intimate our conversation had been the night before. What was going on between us was something my nerves couldn't deal with at the moment, so I got up and headed to the bathroom. Ignoring the disaster that was my bedroom, I shed my cotton shorts and t-shirt and hopped in the shower. The warm water washed over me and helped pull my head out of the fog.

I needed to choose a path. Would I... could I step up and be The Waker? Or would I turn my back on everything? There was no way I could keep living in limbo, not with the very real threat of death hanging over my head.

I ran down the list of things that had come to light since meeting Robert in the bookstore. I smiled to myself, thinking about that day. It felt like ages ago. The second time I'd met him, at his brother's wedding, he had stitched my fatal wounds back together with the touch of his palm. I decided I could accept that something beyond my realm of knowledge had saved me that night. And then there was last night to contend with. The firework show that exploded out of Robert and Lila was something I couldn't ignore. Magic, or whatever you wanted to call it, was real and if I could accept that then maybe I could accept the rest of it.

Turning the water off, my thoughts bounced around my head like an intense game of racquetball. Getting ready for the day, I threw on a black tank top and a floor-length white skirt I loved. I tossed my hair into a messy bun, not bothering to dry it, and dabbed some concealer under my eyes to cover the whiskey-induced shadows.

When I returned to the main room, I found Robert sitting at the kitchen table reading a newspaper with a coffee cup in his hand. He wore a white linen button-up shirt with the sleeves rolled up and dark jeans. *Damn, why did he have to be so good looking?*

"What, no big breakfast this morning?" I teased in an attempt to keep the mood light.

"We can't live like royalty every day." He did a quick inventory of me but was careful to avoid eye contact. Apparently, he was gauging the situation after last night too. "There's more coffee if you'd like." He set his paper down and got up from the table.

"Thanks." I stepped toward the kitchen.

"Do you have any plans for today?" he asked from the table as I pulled a mug with the Golden Gate Bridge stamped on the front from the cupboard and filled it to the brim.

"I was just going to head over to the studio and work on the Caltome pictures. Why?" I asked, sweetening my coffee with some raw sugar and joining him at the table.

"I thought we could do something fun today, maybe go to the beach and forget everything for a little while."

He folded his arms across his chest and leaned back in his chair. His muscled arms made his posture look intimidating, but his face was soft and friendly. He'd clearly put his walls back in place, and not a trace of the vulnerability from last night showed in his features.

"Really?" The suggestion surprised me. It didn't seem like he was the type to forget about duty and responsibility.

"After last night." Worry flashed across his eyes. "I just thought you might like to do something that didn't involve Magic." A tentative smile touched the corners of his mouth.

"I'd love to," I said, still skeptical. "Just let me get a little work done first. I can do it from here and then we can head out."

"Perfect." He lifted the paper back up, hiding his face behind the sports section.

I fished a granola bar from the cabinets and set to work at my command center in the living room. I called and left a message for Jessie, letting her know I wouldn't be in today and to call me if anything came up. As promised, I put together a dropbox with all the pictures I took yesterday and sent Mrs. Deardon an email with the link. I spent a little more time editing the photos Mrs. Deardon wanted prints of and put them on a flash drive so I could print them at the studio later.

After a couple hours of editing and getting as much done as I could at home, I was ready to head out. I walked through the glass sliding door to the patio where Robert sat writing on the first page of a fresh new journal. I guess his family really liked to keep a chronicle of their lives.

"Hey… I'm umm… ready when you are." I tried to catch a glimpse of what he was writing.

"Just a moment," he said over his shoulder.

"Sure." I walked back inside and decided to brush my teeth to get rid of my coffee breath. When I entered my room, everything had been set right. No more broken glass and everything had been put back where it belonged. It was like nothing had ever happened in here. I was thankful for that.

"Shall we?" Robert said as I came back into the living room

"Yep, all ready to go. I just need to stop by a mailbox on our way." I picked up a birthday card I'd been meaning to send to my Aunt Beth.

We headed out the door and started walking toward the beach. The weather was warm, but the breeze had picked up a little. A huge summer storm was in the forecast and the breeze likely brought it closer. Robert and I didn't say much on our walk down to the ocean.

We took a short detour past a mailbox and reached the sand in twenty minutes. Kicking off our sandals as we strode across the low dunes, I finally decided to break the tension. If I was going to be able to make a decision about all of this, then I couldn't just ignore him. I needed answers, I needed to know more about him and the Magical world. So much for a day without Magic, I thought.

"So are you ever going to tell me anything about you?" I asked, careful not to look up into his warm eyes.

"Me, huh?" Robert cocked his head in my direction, his mouth pulling up on one side to form a flirtatious smile.

"Yeah, I mean we always talk about me and how important I'm supposed to be but you've never really told me much about yourself. You want me to trust you, but I don't know anything about you." I blurted the words out with the sound of the waves breaking behind us. It was true, I didn't know much about him and maybe if I did, it would help me get a better grasp on how any of this was possible.

"Just because I won't tell you certain things about myself doesn't mean I'm hiding something from you. What you need to know and understand is much more important than anything about me," Robert explained.

"That's for me to decide." I crossed my arms, unyielding.

"No, it's not." The sides of his eyes tightened and I knew I was tap dancing on his patience.

"How can you say that? How can you be so sure about me?"

"Because it's what we've been taught our whole lives." He placed his hand on the small of my back, guiding me forward. I was sure he'd keep his distance after last night, but I was glad he didn't.

"The knowledge of your importance has been passed down through the generations. It's in my very blood. You will always be more important than me," he said, trying to make me see the serious nature of all this.

"But Robert, I want to know you. The only way I'm going to be able to understand all of this is through you," I pleaded and dug my feet into the sand, refusing to move forward until he opened up.

"If you won't tell me for my own sake, then tell me for the sake of the prophecy," I reasoned. "To help me believe." I searched his face, trying to get through to him. I knew it was a cheap shot, using the prophecy to get him to tell me about himself, but I didn't know what else to do. I was at a crossroads and needed to make a decision. I was tired of living in limbo, going back and forth between what path I should follow.

He looked out over the water, watching the foamy remnants of a wave wash along the smooth edges of the shore.

"How is knowing anything about me going to help you understand?"

"Because without you, I wouldn't even be standing here talking to you."

He sighed and turned, reaching his hand for me to grab onto. "Come on, let's take a walk." He smiled as I reached my hand toward his. The ever-present warmth of his skin made my fingers tingle as he tightened his grip on my palm and towed me down the beach.

"Is this really that important to you?" Robert asked after taking a few steps.

"Yes." I nodded with surety.

He glanced in my direction. "Alright, what would you like to know?"

I mentally flipped through the catalog of questions I had for him, searching for the one I most wanted him to answer. I took a deep breath, steadying my nerves. "Ok, how did you..." I hesitated. "I mean, how were you able to save me that night?"

"Why don't we have a seat," he suggested, motioning to the large rocks ahead of us.

As we walked over to the cluster of wind and sand-smoothed boulders to sit, I peeked a glance over at him. His eyebrows sat low on his forehead and he wore a nervous expression. I knew he didn't want to tell me how he was able to heal my wounds, but it never crossed my mind that he might be just as nervous to tell me as I was to hear it.

We sat side by side on the rocks and prepared for what was to come. Neither of us said anything at first. I wasn't sure who was more frazzled, me for finally getting the answers I desperately wanted, or him for having to divulge his secret. I fiddled with a loose string on the hem of my top and he idly kicked at the small rocks in the sand.

He took a deep breath and let it out in a huff. "Okay. This

isn't going to be easy for me to explain. You're going to have to be patient."

"Okay," I said a little too quickly, giving away my nerves.

He chuckled at my uneasiness and gave me an awkward smile.

"I've never told this to anyone who doesn't understand how Magic works."

I nodded, waiting for him to continue.

"While I am just like you on the outside, I'm very different on the inside," he began. "It's how I was able to heal you that night. I can do things most people can't even dream possible." He sighed, looking out across the beach. My heart raced beneath my ribcage and I couldn't help but feel apprehensive.

He looked as tense as I felt. He raised his shoulders in a defensive position and tensed every line of his body. He hunched his eyebrows low on his forehead, trying to hide the worry evident at the corners of his eyes and in the set of his full, pursed lips.

"I was born the way I am, with the ability to heal," Robert continued. He turned his powerful gaze on me, and the primal force that had been growing inside me churned. His hand moved to take mine again and he stroked the top of my knuckles with his thumb, distracting me and giving himself a chance to choose his next words.

I wondered if he had any idea the effect he had on me, if he knew that his touch awoke something powerful inside me.

"I was six the first time I was able to do it on command," he said, interrupting my thoughts. "We were all playing in the surf down at the beach, Brett, Jake and I, when we found a wounded baby seal. He was bleeding and had puncture wounds all over, like he'd gotten caught up in someone's propeller."

I stared up at Robert, catching his eye. He looked thoughtful as he recalled the memory.

"Brett was in tears, begging me to try to save the poor little thing. I was terrified and just as upset as Brett. I told both of them I didn't know how to save it, but Jake encouraged me." He chuckled at the memory.

Having met Robert's older brother and seeing him interact with his wife, Annabel, in a rough teasing manner, I had a pretty good idea of how he may have *convinced* Robert to help the seal.

"I didn't have the slightest clue how to help the animal. The few other times I had used my... ability," Robert said and paused, eying me uneasily, "I didn't do anything in particular. I'd find a squirrel or bird that got attacked by a hawk or something and just hold the animal and cry for my mother to come help. By the time she made it over to me, the bird was flying away, or the squirrel was jumping out of my hand and scurrying back up the tree." He shook his head and smiled.

"What is it?"

"It's just strange, saying it all out loud. I can't imagine how it must sound to you."

"Strange." I smiled.

He returned my smile with a heart-breaking grin and continued. "Anyway, the only thing I could think to do was to hold the animal like I'd done with the others. I couldn't exactly pick up the seal, since I was only six. I didn't have the upper body strength I do now." He jokingly nudged my shoulder with his. "So I sat down in the surf next to him and eased my hands onto his body. Brett sat silently watching me and it made me even more nervous. Jake stood by me and guided me through everything very slowly. The seal may have been injured, but you never know how a wild animal might react to a person being so close."

"You were a brave little boy, weren't you?"

"Not really. I was always a curious kid. I did plenty of stupid and dangerous things when I was young, always trying to satisfy my curiosity."

I smiled at the thought of Robert as a child chasing danger

and pushing boundaries. *His mother must have had her hands full with him*, I thought.

Robert hadn't noticed my thoughts had run away from me and continued, "I wasn't sure what to do, so I started running my hand up and down the seal's body. I can still remember the way his skin felt under my touch. The fine hairs were coarse and he was slick with ocean water. His breathing was very shallow and he only moved as the waves pushed and pulled his body. Nothing was happening and I felt so bad. I didn't know what else to do, so I started talking to him."

He looked away from me and back out at the water. He stayed quiet for a moment as he watched a wave crash onto the shore. His shoulders relaxed a little and I had a feeling he was seeing the whole scene unfold in the surf in front of us.

"My voice must have startled the little guy. He lifted his head slightly and looked up at me," Robert said, looking back at me and down at our joined hands, lacing his fingers through mine. My hand tingled as his grip fell into place and our palms lightly touched. I wondered if he was keeping our hands joined in case I decided to make a run for it.

"I'll never forget those eyes for as long as I live," he said. "They were never-ending pools of black coal that glistened like the sea. I could feel his pain as he stared at me. His nose wiggled with each breath and his whiskers danced back and forth on his face. I started to cry but didn't take my eyes off him and he kept staring at me. I felt something growing inside me. It was like a switch had been flipped and I could feel the pain of the animal subside. After a minute or two, the seal looked away from me and wiggled free from my hands and out into the water. Somehow, I'd done it. I'd saved him."

"But how?" I asked, amazed. I couldn't help but wonder what it felt like for the seal when Robert had healed him.

He merely shrugged. "It's just a part of who I am. Do you

remember when I saved you, I told you to keep your eyes on mine?"

"Yeah." I blushed. How could I forget the warmth flooding through me as he stared down at me?

"It helps me focus the energy if I can connect with you."

"Energy?" I looked at him, puzzled.

"How can I explain this?" he said under his breath. "It's like a hunger living inside me. I've learned how to control the energy so that when I touch someone, I don't heal any little scrape or paper cut. My ability only works when I want it to now."

"But why does eye contact help?"

He turned his body toward mine and brushed a stray hair behind my ear. "It creates a connection." He smiled and unleashed the full force of his gaze on me, erasing every last thought rattling around in my head. "It makes it easier for me to focus the energy." His fingers danced across my knuckles and my heart skipped a beat as warmth spread through my fingers and across my arm.

"I just don't understand how any of this is possible." I looked away from him and instantly the heat retreated from my skin.

"You can't try to understand it. It's just something you know and can feel," Robert explained, sighing as if suddenly deep in thought. "For instance, what did you feel when I healed you?"

"I felt warm, like you were pulling me into the sun." I glanced up at him.

"That's the Magic. You felt it inside you. That's the only way to know it's real, to feel it." He sounded full of hope, like he knew I was on the verge of understanding. But was I?

"Have you ever believed in something you had no way of explaining? Something that you just knew from the bottom of your heart it was true despite proof?" he asked when I didn't say anything.

"You're talking about faith." I shook my head. "Maybe I had that once, but I'm not so sure anymore. I learned the hard way that believing in something you can't see or touch just ends up causing pain." I sighed, remembering all the heartbreak I'd endured throughout my life. Everyone I'd ever loved had been ripped from me, leaving a hole in my heart I wasn't sure could ever be filled.

"Violet." His voice wrapped around my name like a gentle caress.

Something in my voice must have given me away. He looked at me with sympathy and understanding as the pieces fell into place for him.

"Just because they're gone doesn't mean the love between you is lost." His voice was like warm honey, sweet and soothing.

"You don't understand what it's like to lose everything, to be alone..." I trailed off, taking a deep breath to keep my emotions in check.

Robert just looked at me and squeezed my hand. I tried to read the emotions on his face, but he looked calm and collected.

"Anyway, we're not talking about me," I huffed and pulled my hand from his. I untied my hair and let it spill over my shoulders.

"Violet..." Robert tried.

"Just let it go, Robert." I didn't want to talk about this with him. He had a way of breaking down my defenses and I couldn't afford to let him in. Spending time with him and getting to know him was one thing, but being open to him and making myself vulnerable was something completely different.

"Okay, back to me then," he said, offering a nonchalant nod. "What else do you want to know?"

I thought for a moment and then decided to ask, "What's it feel like for you, the Magic I mean?"

"Well." He scratched his chin. "When I'm not using it, it's like a dull hum inside me. I can always feel it. And when I do use the Magic, especially for something big like healing you, it's this surge of energy that runs through every nerve in my body." He paused. "It's hard to put it into words."

"Can all Magical people heal like you?" I asked, glad the attention was off me.

"No, very few souls are born with the ability to heal."

"Really, why's that?"

"Well, some people are born with the ability to create profound music like Beethoven, some people are able to read the code of the universe like Steven Hawking. They're just born with an ability the average person doesn't possess. It's the same with Magical abilities; not everyone is created equal."

I guess that made sense. Not everyone could do the same things, regardless of what they told you in grade school. Everyone was created differently, whether it was from genetics, environment or our soul - we aren't all the same. For once, something finally made sense in all of this.

"It's the same in the Magical world," Robert continued. "Not all of us have special abilities, but we do all have the ability to learn how to use the Magic within us."

"So you're special." I looked up at him and fought a smile. He was special.

"I guess you could say that. I really don't like to think of myself that way, but healers are coveted." He smiled and reddened a bit.

"So you heal people all the time then, bring them back like you did with me?" I suddenly felt incredibly insignificant.

"I try not to. I'm not a God, Violet. It's not my place to choose who lives and who dies."

"Have you ever saved anyone else?"

"Not from death. At least, not anyone human," he said and shrugged, uncomfortable.

I stood up and took a few steps toward the water. "I just don't know." I looked out over the waves and wondered if Magic could really have a place in my life.

I heard Robert's footsteps shuffle through the sand as he walked up behind me. He placed his hands on my shoulders and just like that I was pulled into the fog.

Darkness surrounded me. I could barely see, but I was definitely standing in my living room. I looked around and saw my prone body lying asleep on the couch with Robert on the floor just below me. I started to mumble in my sleep and Robert sat up to check on me. He tightened the blanket around me and took my hand in his. At first, he didn't say anything, he just drew a pattern on the back of my palm.

"You have to believe me, Violet," he whispered. "You just have to."

The room swirled around me, making my head spin like I was on a 'Tilt-a-Whirl.' Unable to see which way was up or down, I reached out to grab hold of something solid.

Suddenly I was back on the beach with Robert.

"Violet, are you okay?" His voice sounded muffled as I blinked the sunlight back into my eyes. Robert knelt next to me on the ground with his arm behind me for support.

"How did I get down here?" I asked, putting my palm against my forehead to stop the world from spinning.

"Your face went blank and you just fell to the ground." Anxiety poured off of him.

I tried to put the pieces together. This wasn't the first time I'd had a daydream so real I couldn't tell the difference between reality and what I saw.

"Violet, what happened?" Robert asked as he helped me off the ground.

As I stood the blood rushed from my head and my vision blurred. I held onto Robert's arm for support as the fuzzy blackness disappeared.

"I don't know. The last thing I remember is you walking up behind me and placing your hands on my shoulders. You… your touch…" My heart began to race as dread set in.

"Did you do that to me?" I backed away from him.

"Do what to you?" He took a tentative step toward me.

I stepped further away. "Did you do something to make me see that?"

"See what, Violet, talk to me. Tell me what's wrong." He stopped and let his hand fall to his side.

Did he really not know what I was talking about? Was I really starting to lose my mind?

"You can't just ignore me," Robert said when I didn't answer. He took another slow step toward me, and this time I didn't back away.

"Why does this keep happening to me?" My voice trembled. Every nerve in my body felt stretched to the point of breaking. I couldn't comprehend what was going on, and I struggled to hold myself together. The tears that had been building up for days now finally spilled over onto my cheeks.

"What do you mean? What's happening to you?" He reached out to touch me but dropped his hands before he reached my side.

"These daydreams or visions or whatever," I said, placing my palm over my eyes.

Robert placed his hand on my shoulder, deciding it was safe to touch me again, and I let myself collapse into him. I placed my head against his chest and wrapped my arms around him. He wrapped one arm around me and pulled me close to him while smoothing my hair with the other, trying to coax me into relaxing.

"Visions?" he asked. Robert's voice was low and contemplative.

I didn't answer him but took a deep breath. His cologne barely lingered, letting me smell the sweet scent of the ocean clinging to his skin. He smelled of sweat and old wood, distinctly male and strong. It comforted me. I took a ragged breath and sighed. No matter what was happening to me, I knew I could find safety in Robert's arms. In that moment, I realized I'd already chosen my path. I couldn't have him in my life if I didn't believe in Magic. Knowing my path was one thing, though. Actually believing was another. But I was determined to try.

"Violet, this is important." He pulled away from me. "What exactly did you just see?"

"Umm… well," I said and blushed. "I saw you asking me to believe you while I slept."

He let go of me. "That was just last night."

"So that really happened, it wasn't just a daydream?" I asked, my eyes wide with hope.

"Have you seen things like this before?"

"Kinda."

"What do you mean, what else have you seen?"

"It's private," I frowned. I could feel the blood rush to my face and turn my cheeks a rosy shade of red.

"Private," he said, indignant. "Violet, this isn't a joke. What did you see?"

"Well, last night after you gave me the journal I saw…," I bit my lip, unsure of how to continue. What did I see exactly?

"What is it?"

"I saw myself, only it wasn't me. I was standing in a field, you were there and I was holding a sword. My hand was covered in blood, and my eyes…" I looked up at Robert, "They were amethyst."

"Was there anything else, any other details?"

I shook my head and looked down at the sand.

"Okay, I don't really know what to think about that one, but we'll deal with it," he said confidently. "Anything else?"

I felt like I was being interrogated.

"Why does it matter?" I looked away from him.

"Will you just trust me?" Though I wasn't looking at him, I could sense in his voice that he was rolling his eyes in frustration.

I hesitated to answer. I wanted to tell him, but I was afraid. I was afraid to admit what was happening to me. The vision, or whatever it was, of Robert kissing me flashed before my eyes and I instantly turned an even darker shade of red.

I sighed and looked out over the water. "I saw you," I finally admitted.

"What about me?"

I decided against telling him about the kiss, instead I would tell him about how I saw the night he healed me.

"Well, do you remember when we met at the pier when you first came back?" I snuck a glance in his direction.

"Yes."

"And do you remember when you touched me, it was like suddenly I was somewhere else?"

"Yes." He sounded apprehensive and that made me nervous.

"When you touched me, I saw you… healing me. It's like I was there all over again. I could smell the cool, sticky air. I could feel your hand on me and I could feel your eyes on mine." I cautiously looked at him, trying to read his expression. He gave me a reassuring smile. "And that's it, nothing else?"

"Nothing that matters." I blushed again, remembering his soft lips pressed against mine. That was either a vision or possibly just a fantasy. Whatever the case, I wasn't willing to share the details with him.

"Everything matters?" He furrowed his brow as he stared down at me.

"Well, this particular fantasy is none of your business."

"Fantasy?" There was humor in his voice and he stepped closer to me.

Shit.

"You know what I mean." The words struggled to escape my throat. I felt the heat of his body and couldn't help but be pulled in.

"Are you sure you don't want to tell me?" He brushed my

hair off my face. His hand lingered on my cheek before he pulled my chin up so my eyes were level with his.

"I'm sure." The words barely left my lips and I could feel myself leaning closer to him, yearning to feel the strength of his embrace.

"Suit yourself." He smiled and walked back to the small cropping of rocks.

I followed a few steps behind him. "Robert?" I asked tentatively, "do you know what's going on... I mean do you know what's happening to me?"

"I have a theory."

"Care to share what that theory might be?"

"I think your Magic is starting to manifest itself. The visions, they might be your ability."

"But what does this mean? What ability?"

"I think you might be a Soothsayer." His eyes lit up as he searched mine.

CHAPTER TWELVE

Robert rushed me off the beach. When I asked where we were going, all he said was that there was someone we needed to talk to. He called Brett on the brisk walk home from the beach and told her to expect company. We reached my car in record time and I tossed the keys to him. Still dizzy and a little shaken from the vision, I thought it best not to get behind the wheel.

As we drove up the coast, I wondered if my ability really was manifesting itself. *God, listen to me*, I scoffed internally. How any of this was possible, I had no idea. And why now? If I was The Waker, why hadn't I ever shown signs of an ability before?

"You coming?" Robert asked, opening my door. I was so deep in thought I hadn't even realized we'd stopped.

"Where are we?" I asked, looking around a large garage.

Before he could answer, Annabel, Robert's sister-in-law, shimmered into view right in front of us.

"What the..." I froze halfway out of the car. Where did she come from?

"I thought I heard someone in here," Annabel said. Her shoes *clacked* on the floor as she made her way around the front of the car. "Oh, I didn't realize you had someone with you." She glanced in my direction and came around to my side of the car.

"You really should be more careful, Anna," Robert noted. Disapproval radiated off of him. "What if it hadn't been Violet with me?" He reached his hand into the car for me to grab onto, but I hesitated.

"Oh please, Robert. When was the last time you ever brought someone home with you?" She rolled her eyes and snickered as she pushed him aside. "Why don't you try to unclench and relax?"

"Come on," he whispered to me and reached his hand a little closer.

I hesitated, then took his hand and got out of the car.

"It's so nice to see you again," Annabel said, giving me a quick hug. "Sorry about just *dropping* in." She winked with a playful grin on her face.

"Annabel," Robert warned. His voice was stern and carried an air of authority.

I knew Robert was special, that he could do things others couldn't, but Annabel too? When did it end? I felt the anxiety start to pick away at my insides the way a ravenous vulture picked at the bones of an animal carcass.

"Alright, alright." She raised her hands in surrender. "She's waiting for you in the living room. She arrived just a few minutes before you."

"Who's waiting?" I looked between the two of them.

"Bethany." Annabel motioned for me to follow her.

"Who's Bethany?" I looked all around with confusion and worry as I followed her into the house.

"She's a very *gifted* Soothsayer." Annabel exaggerated the word 'gifted,' her voice thick with adoration.

"A Soothsayer?" I looked over my shoulder for Robert as we made our way down a small, dark hallway. Somehow, through all this chaos, he had become the one person I could rely on.

"Don't worry," Robert whispered into my ear and placed his hand on my lower back. "She'll be able to tell if you have the gift or if they really are just fantasies." I could hear the smile in his voice and my face flushed at his words. I was glad that he was walking behind me and couldn't see the blood rush to my cheeks.

"I'll be with Jake upstairs if you need me," Annabel said, looking over her shoulder at Robert and then disappearing right in front of us. I stopped in my tracks. One second she was there, and the next she was gone. Seeing her disappear like that was the creepiest thing I'd ever seen. It was like a soft breeze came by and just whisked her away.

"How does she do that?" I asked now that she was gone. I didn't know how to react to anything anymore. Was it normal for people to just fade in and out of existence?

"I'll explain later." Robert nudged me along.

We rounded a corner and passed the grand staircase. The house looked just as beautiful as it had the day of the wedding. It seemed less festive without the flowers and ribbons, but beautiful, nonetheless. Their house gave off a very regal feel, like every piece of wood had its own secrets to keep.

"Aunt Beth?" I said, stunned as we walked into the living room. "What are you doing here?" I smiled and made my way over to her. I hadn't seen her in years. We'd stayed in touch for a while after I graduated college, but life got in the way and now we only exchanged cards on our birthdays and Christmas. I wrapped my arms around her, hardly able to believe she was actually here. Her floral perfume brought back so many memories and I couldn't help but feel like a little kid again. She reminded me of happier times, of the family I no longer had. I frowned, realizing how bittersweet it was seeing her again.

"Hello, sweetheart," Bethany said as she smiled and held me at arm's length, taking all of me in.

"Aunt Beth?" Robert asked, frowning at both of us.

"Yeah, she's… wait… that means you're…"

Realization set in. My Aunt Beth was Bethany, the Soothsayer we'd come here to see.

"Magical? Yes, I am," Aunt Beth chimed.

I looked at Robert, puzzled. "Did you know?"

"No," he said, walking over to me. He gave my shoulder a reassuring squeeze. "Go easy on her, Bethany. She's having a hard time handling everything, and it's already been a long day."

"Well, it's no wonder. If her parents had listened to me…" Aunt Beth sighed. "No matter. I'll fill you in, come along with me." She put her hand on my back and urging me to walk with her. Robert let his hand fall from my shoulder but followed us to the French doors.

"I'd like to talk to Violet in private," Bethany noted as she opened the door.

"But she…"

"I know it's your duty to protect her, but she's safe with me. She deserves to hear this from family, and I think a little privacy would be best. If she wants to share what I tell her with you, then it will be her choice to do so." She spoke with an air of authority I'd never heard in her voice before.

Robert bowed his head slightly, a gesture of submission I didn't expect, then looked at me. Concern dominated his face and without a word, he turned and walked away.

"Come along, dear," Aunt Beth said, holding open the door to the backyard.

We walked to the large swing bench overlooking the ocean and sat down. I smiled to myself, remembering Jake and Annabel on this very swing, her white dress flowing around them as they gently swayed back and forth. So much had happened since that day. I sighed.

The swing was old but well taken care of, and years of wear had smoothed the dark wood. Ivy covered the polished wooden frame holding up the swing. It was as if the swing was a part of the yard and had sprung up right out of the ground. The late afternoon sun hung low in the sky, making the nearby sea sparkle as it swayed to the beat of Mother Nature.

I pulled my legs up onto the swing and wrapped my arms around the rope, tying it to the frame. A small shiver made its way down my back. I wasn't sure if it was from nerves or the cool ocean breeze.

"I'm sorry I haven't been around for you," Bethany finally said, placing her hand on my knee.

"It's okay. I don't know if it would've made any of this easier if you were."

She smiled, but the expression didn't reach her eyes. She was worried and was trying to hide it.

"Robert said you weren't handling things very well?"

"How am I supposed to handle all this?" I shook my head. "I keep thinking I'm going to wake up and it'll all have been a bad dream."

"I'm afraid it's not a dream. Everything Robert's told you has been the truth."

I let out a long sigh. "I know." I'd known deep down Robert was telling the truth. It was simply difficult to accept that truth. "I just feel like my whole life has been a lie." I looked at my aunt for comfort. I may not have seen her in years, but she was still family and that in itself was comforting. There was at least one person in this world I was linked to in a irreversible way.

"Violet, this is just another chapter in your life, not the whole story. You're still you."

"Am I?"

"Of course you are," Aunt Beth said, caressing my hair.

"I don't know how to do this. I mean, I'm starting to accept everything that's happened, but..." I trailed off. The anxiety that had been building in me all afternoon nearly tore through my calm facade. I could almost feel my insides squirm as I fought to keep control.

"You will with time." She smiled and brushed a stray hair out of my face.

"How can you be so sure?"

"Because I know," she said with a sly smile.

"So you're a… Soothsayer?" I asked, remembering why she was here in the first place.

"Yes and so are you." She gave me a patient nod.

"And my parents, they had… I mean, they were…" I trailed off, unable to bring myself to ask if my parents had Magical powers too.

"Yes, they were Magical, and very gifted I might add." A calmness washed over her and I saw her body visibly relax into the swing. Something had changed her, made her less rigid than before.

"But why am I only hearing of this now?" I asked, feeling the tension leave my own body in response to her calm.

"We didn't tell you because your parents wanted you to have a normal life. I tried to tell them it was impossible, but they wouldn't listen."

"A normal life?"

"You were born a healthy *normal* child. You didn't have a Magical soul. It happens from time to time in Magical families." She waved her hand dismissively. "But you're different."

"Different how?"

"You're The Waker. The day you were born, I had a vision that showed me who you would become." Her lips turned up and her eyes softened as she looked at me. "It didn't matter how hard they tried to shelter you. You were always going to be a part of the Magical world. Albeit, I didn't quite know how it was going to happen."

"But if I wasn't born with a Magical soul, then how can I be The Waker?"

"Ah, that's exactly what your parents used to say. You may

not have been born with Magic, but you have a Magical soul now."

"I do? But... how?" I asked, looking down at myself. I searched my body for some sign I was different now.

Aunt Beth looked up behind her to see Robert standing on the balcony, looking out over the water. "Because of him," she said, turning back to me with a smile.

I turned toward the balcony. Robert leaned against the railing, staring out over the water. I let my gaze linger on him. He really was beautiful. I couldn't imagine not having him in my life anymore. He turned his head my direction before I could turn back to my aunt. His eyes caught mine and the corner of his mouth pulled up into a smile. I tore myself away from his gaze and bit my bottom lip in an effort to hide my own grin.

"But what does he have to do with my soul?" I asked and tried to compose myself.

"When he healed you, a piece of his soul infused with yours and vice versa," Aunt Beth explained, looking back up at Robert with a hint of a smile on her lips. Nothing got past her.

"How is that even possible?" I moved my hand to my chest. Was a piece of Robert really inside me? Is that why he has such an effect on me?

"The world is full of possibilities. You just have to know where to look for them." A small chuckle escaped her throat.

"Does that sort of thing happen a lot, souls infusing?" I asked, unsure of how it made me feel.

"No, it doesn't. But one of the most famous cases involved King Arthur." She raised her eyebrows and a secretive grin pulled at the corner of her mouth.

"You mean, that story about him being healed by Merlin is true?"

"So you've heard the story?"

"I may have done some googling after Robert healed me," I said sheepishly.

She laughed, "I'm surprised you were able to find anything."

"I thought it was just someone's fan fiction. I didn't actually think it was true."

"It's all true." The corner of her eyes crinkled as she smiled. "Which brings me back to you and Robert. You weren't born with a Magical soul because you were always meant to get your Magic from him. The same way Arthur got his magic from Merlin. It's why the visions didn't start until after he healed you." Her joy was almost tangible.

"You know about my visions?" A part of me was holding onto the hope that my imagination had just been getting the best of me lately.

"Of course I do. It's why Robert wanted to speak to me."

"How did you know? We were on the beach and-"

Aunt Beth raised her hand to interrupt me. "I always know." A wicked smile turned up the corner of her mouth.

"What do you mean?"

"I've been keeping tabs on the two of you. So when I saw you had left the beach to come talk to me, I made sure I was here." She smiled like it was perfectly normal to see things before they happened. But then again, I guess it was normal for her.

"Robert is very protective of you. He's worried about how you're handling everything, but you're a strong woman and it's time for you to step up and accept the Magical side of you," she said with as much love as she could, while still getting her point across.

"So that's it? I have a Magical soul now and I just have to live with these visions?"

"Yes, but you can learn to control them."

"I don't want to learn to control them, I want them to go away!" I yelled at her and stood from the swing, making the hinges creak as the bench swung back and forth.

"Violet, calm down."

"No, you don't get to tell me to calm down! You haven't been a part of my life for years and now, now you come back just to tell me to suck it up. Don't you get it? This is my life we're talking about!" I turned my back on my aunt and walked over to the railing lining the backyard.

"Exactly. This is your life and you need to start taking it seriously."

"I'm taking it as seriously as I can, given the circumstances."

"I know it's not fair to drop all of this on you and expect you to just accept it."

"You're damn right it isn't fair!"

"I know, but you do *need* to accept it."

"Are we finished?" I asked, turning back to look at her. She still sat on the swing, calmly waiting for me to return.

"Not quite. Please, come and sit down," she said, patting on the swing.

"What else is there to talk about?"

"Your parents."

"What about them?" I crossed my arms. She was the one person left alive who knew my parents and I wanted to hear anything she had to say about them, but I didn't want her to know how eager I was to talk. I was too frustrated about everything else.

"You need to know the truth about how they died."

Her words shot through me like ice water in my veins. I couldn't move, couldn't think. The truth... what truth?

"There was a car accident and-" my voice shook as I struggled for words.

"No, there wasn't," she interrupted me. "Come sit." She patted the seat next to her.

I walked back to the swing, slowly, feeling the weight of each step.

"What do you mean there wasn't a car accident?" I sat down next to her in shell shock.

"You're not going to like this." She pursed her lips.

"What really happened to them?"

"They were murdered."

I looked at my aunt in disbelief. Why was she doing this? My parents died in a car accident. They weren't murdered! There was a whole investigation and the police found no foul play. They'd just been in the wrong place at the wrong time.

"Let me show you," Aunt Beth sighed and reached for me.

"Show me?" I moved away from her grasp.

"You have to understand, I did what I thought was best for you. I was just trying to protect you."

"What on Earth are you talking about?"

"I altered your memory so you wouldn't be burdened with the truth."

"You what!" I yelled at her. I jumped off the swing and backed away from my aunt. I had never felt so betrayed in all my life.

"Violet, you hadn't talked in weeks, not a word to anyone. I had to do something. I couldn't stand seeing you in so much pain," she implored, begging me to understand. She stood up from the swing and took a step toward me.

"Wait, what do you mean I didn't talk for weeks? I spoke at their funeral."

"No, you didn't." She took another step toward me.

"Yes, I did," I said, stamping my foot and holding my ground. I remembered how hard it was for me to walk up to the podium and talk in front of all those people, the pain in my throat as I spoke.

"Just let me show you," she said, closing the gap between us and raising her hands to my temples.

"No, what're..." I pushed her hands away from me and backed away.

"Violet, please. You'll understand once you see. Please, let me show you."

I studied her face a moment and searched her eyes for any

sign she might be lying. My whole world had been turned upside down and I didn't know what or whom I could believe anymore.

"How could you?" The word barely escaped my lips.

"I was just trying to protect you."

"How were you able to erase what really happened?" I asked, trying to control my anger.

"With Magic." She exhaled and put her hands in her lap, composing herself. "Everyone in the Magical world has the ability to learn and strengthen the Magic within them. Changing someone's memory isn't easy, but with discipline, any Magical person can do it."

"Of course, more Magic." I huffed under my breath.

"Magic is a part of who you are now. It won't go away just because you wish it to." Her voice quivered with anger.

"So what happened to the real memory? You just ripped it out of my head and threw it away?" I fumed. How could she tell me my whole life wasn't a lie when I couldn't even be sure of what was and wasn't a real memory anymore?

"You can never really erase a memory. The brain is far too complex. All you can do is learn how to disguise it as something else."

"And you can do this to anybody?"

"It's not like that. You have to learn someone's mind first, all the little pathways and dark corners, so to speak. It takes a considerable amount of time to alter a memory. It was easier with you because you were so young, but still, it took a lot of power and concentration."

"And how do you learn someone's mind?"

"There's a spell you can cast that allows you to navigate through their mind while the person is unconscious."

"Does it hurt?"

"No, of course not!" she said, taken aback. "The person has no idea you've been inside their head."

"Did you change any more of my memories?"

"No." She pursed her lips and took a deep breath. "But your mother did."

"She did?" I felt like someone had sucker punched me. Never in a million years would I have thought that my parents were Magical people, but to find out my own mother had used Magic on me hurt more than I would have ever thought possible. "Why… why would she do that?"

"Your parents wanted you to have a normal life, but their Magic would slip every once in a while. It goes against our instincts to abstain from using Magic. It's nearly impossible to turn that part of ourselves off."

I sat, quiet, not knowing what to say. Their memory was the only thing I had left of my parents, and now she was telling me those memories might not even be real? My whole life, everything I ever believed to be true, was completely and utterly false. The anxiety festering inside me finally broke free. The sheer force of it sent a shiver through my entire body.

"How many times did she alter my memory?" I asked as a tear fell from my eye.

"Only a couple times that I know of. I can release those memories if you'd like," Aunt Beth suggested, though she blinked with hesitation.

"Can you?"

"It's hard to alter the mind, but once you have, it's fairly easy to connect once more."

"Okay," I said, overwhelmed with emotions. I wanted the truth. I was so sick of all the secrecy and lies.

"Come here," she said, once more motioning for me to follow her back to the swing. I sat down and she knelt in front of me. She reached up and placed her hands on the side of my head and closed her eyes.

"Mm, this is a good one to start with," she said, releasing me.

I felt a little strange, like a fog had been lifted, but I couldn't quite see what was on the other side yet.

"I don't..."

"Give it a minute."

As the fog slowly cleared I saw my mom standing at the kitchen sink, washing dishes in the house we lived in when I was a child. The six-year-old version of me sat at the table coloring. Without warning, a baseball came through the window in front of my mother. I looked up, scared by the noise, and in an instant, everything froze. The broken glass and the baseball hung suspended in the air, frozen in front of my mother. She plucked the baseball hovering in front of her and tossed it back out the broken window. Then she raised her hands to the shards of glass and the window reformed itself as if nothing had happened. The young version of me watched her in amazement. I remembered feeling like my mom was a real-life superhero. She walked over to me and asked if I was okay. I shook my head, yes, and then she placed her hands on the sides of my head just like my aunt had done a moment before.

"It's so real," I gasped. "But how am I supposed to know which memory is real?"

"Didn't you ever feel like something was off when you were younger? Like something was missing, but you couldn't put your finger on it?"

"Yeah." I shrugged.

"You were missing your memories, your real memories."

"What else is there?" I asked. My anger faded the second I saw my mother just the way I remembered her.

My aunt placed her hands on the sides of my face again. She let go after a few seconds and looked up at me.

Again I felt the fog lift. I closed my eyes and let the memory take me. This was different, though. It wasn't a memory I knew. My mom cradled me in her arms. I was just a baby. Both of my parents looked down at me, smiling. My dad pulled my mother closer to him with one arm and caressed my head with the other.

"She's perfect," my mother said, looking up at my father.

"Just like you," he said and smiled. "I love you. And I love you, Violet." My father gently placed his fingers on the side of my head.

"What was that?" I asked my aunt as the memory faded.

"Just like we can alter a memory, we can also mark a memory so that we can recall it at any time. That's a memory from the day you were born. They both loved you very much, Violet."

"I miss them so much." Tears fell down my face, leaving salty streaks in their wake.

Aunt Beth pulled herself up and sat down next to me, pulling me close to her. "I miss them too."

I let the tears fall freely from my eyes as I felt the pain of losing them. Fear and frustration bubbled inside me like a pot of hot water about to spill over.

"Will you show me what happened to them?" I sniffled.

"Are you sure? We can always do it another time."

"No, I want to know. I'm sick of being kept in the dark. I want to know the truth."

"Okay, but this isn't going to be pretty," she said and placed her hands against my temples again.

I thought for a moment about the car crash that had killed my parents, and then as the fog lifted it all changed. It was like a scene from a horror movie. There was so much blood, and my parents, my poor parents, lay still on the floor. I could barely stomach the image, but as I glanced at my parent's prone bodies, I saw the faint outline of a symbol carved into their skin. I wanted to inspect further, something about it was familiar, but the memory went dark as I closed my eyes and fell to my knees next to them.

"Who would do something like that?" I asked, my voice barely above a whisper.

"His name is Aiden Patridge. The same man who keeps sending people to kill you," Aunt Beth answered. Her voice held a cold, dark edge to it I'd never heard before.

"But couldn't you see what was going to happen and warn them?"

Aunt Beth closed her eyes and her bottom lip quivered. "I did know. I had always known they would die before seeing you grow into a beautiful young woman, but I was never able to pinpoint when. Your mother knew her fate, though. I didn't keep it from her. But she didn't want to live in fear, so she asked me not to look ahead for her anymore."

"But you were there that day, before the police showed up. How did you know something had happened?"

She placed her hand on mine. "I knew because, for the first time in my life, I had a vision of what had happened without having to use touch as a medium. It hit me with such force, I rushed right over." She looked down at her hands.

"Is it unusual for someone... like you to see something without the use of touch?" I asked.

"Yes," she said, taking her hand off mine and placing it in her lap. "You need touch to make the connection, but sometimes visions reach out to you and if you're strong enough, you can see their message."

We sat, looking over the water for a quiet moment. Bright streaks of orange and red flew across the sky with the slowly setting sun. I thought about the past as I sifted through my new memories, remembering all the little slips my parents had in front of me. I felt like I knew them better now.

"Aunt Beth?"

"Hmm?"

"How come you never told me any of this after they died?"

"It was their wish that if anything ever happened to them

that you would remain in the dark about Magic. They just wanted you to have a normal life."

"So much for that," I chuckled, shaking my head at the irony.

"I knew we could never keep you from the Magical world forever. It's your destiny. It's been your destiny for hundreds of years."

We stood up and the swing rocked back and forth.

As we walked side-by-side back to the house I asked, "So I never had a choice then?"

"Of course you do. You can choose to walk away from all of this," my aunt clarified as we reached the French doors.

"But I won't, will I?"

"No, you won't." She smiled.

Before we went back inside, where Robert and his family were undoubtedly waiting for us, I wanted to ask her one more thing.

"Aunt Beth?"

"Yes, sweetie?"

"Thank you for everything." I hugged her tight.

"You're very welcome," she said, kissing the top of my head.

"I need you to promise me something though." I released her.

"What is it?" Her brow furrowed with concern.

"Promise me you'll never take my memories from me again."

"I promise." She patted my hand and nodded reassuringly.

CHAPTER THIRTEEN

My Aunt left shortly after our talk, but promised me she would be in touch to teach me how to control my visions. Robert had been by my side since the moment my aunt and I came back in the house. I could tell he was anxious to hear about what she had told me, but he had enough common sense not to ask me in front of his entire family.

I wanted to go home, crawl into bed and enjoy my new memories, but Robert's mother, Aniela, had insisted we stay for dinner. I couldn't begrudge her a meal with the son she never got to see, and I knew Robert wasn't going to let me go home without him. And honestly, after last night, I'd rather not spend the night alone in my house.

I didn't say much over the next couple of hours. No one paid much attention to me anyway, which I was grateful for. As the evening went on, my mood rapidly decreased. I was emotionally drained and just wanted some time to myself to process everything my aunt had told me.

"Violet?" Aniela called as Robert said goodbye to his brother.

"Yes, Mrs. Maxwell?"

"Please call me Aniela," she said with a warm smile.

"Okay, Aniela. Thank you again for a wonderful dinner." I smiled, but my heart wasn't in it.

"Of course, anytime, dear." She waved her hand dismissively. "I want you to know that if you ever need anything, anything at all, you always have people to come to." She glanced in the direction of her family.

"Thank you."

"I mean it." She spoke to me with a motherly tone of voice, authoritative and loving.

"I appreciate it, thank you very much."

She looked over her shoulder again and then back at me. "And be good to my son. He cares about you a great deal."

I opened my mouth to say something, but she raised her hand in protest.

"No need to make excuses," she said with finality.

Aniela smiled and walked over to her husband, wrapping her arm around him. She was such a regal woman. It was nice to know she had a compassionate side too.

Annabel kept glancing in my direction, and every time she took a step toward me, Jake would pull her a little tighter to his side. I felt bad that I wasn't being a very social guest, but my mind was fried and I didn't have it in me to play the nice house guest.

After another round of goodbyes, Robert and I headed off toward the garage. He didn't say anything as we walked through the house. I knew he was still dying to know what had transpired between Aunt Beth and me, but being with his family had eased his curiosity some and lightened his mood. We reached the car and he opened my door for me. His gentlemanly ways never ceased to surprise me.

"You okay?" he asked, sliding into the driver's seat.

"Yeah, just out of it." I sighed and stared out the window.

"Do you want to talk about it?"

"Not right now." I let out a grunting exhalation. I knew I was going to have to face him sooner or later, but I just wasn't ready yet.

"I'm here for you when you're ready."

"Thank you."

We spent the rest of the ride in silence. When we got back to my place, I went straight to my room, changed into sweats and a cotton t-shirt and went to brush my teeth. I'd been so preoccupied with everything I had learned about my parents that I hadn't given much thought to what Aunt Beth had said about mine and Robert's souls. Could he really be a part of me? I rinsed my mouth and couldn't help going back into the living room.

Robert flapped a clean sheet in the air, making up his bed on the couch with his back to me, and didn't notice me enter the room. I watched him unfold the blankets and fluff his pillow. Not only had he saved my life, but he had become my friend. Granted, it was a tense friendship most of the time, but I felt like the pieces inside of me were finally falling into place.

"I'm gonna head to bed now. Do you need anything?"

"I can fend for myself," he said and smiled. "Get some sleep. It's been a long day."

"Alright, night."

"Goodnight," he said softly.

I checked the front door out of habit and dragged myself to bed.

I spent the next couple hours tossing and turning. The memory of my parents' lifeless bodies covered in blood played in my mind every time I closed my eyes. *My aunt was right to alter this memory when I was a child*, I thought. If it was too much for me as an adult, there was no way I could have dealt with it when I was young. I'd always considered myself a strong person that could handle anything life threw at me, but lately life had been trying to bury me. Every time I broke through the surface, another wave of information crashed on top of me, threatening to drown me entirely.

Sitting up, I switched on the bedside lamp. I wanted to go to the kitchen and make some tea, but I didn't want to wake Robert if he was sleeping. Sitting on the edge of the bed, I picked at my cuticles, wrestling with myself to get up or try to go back to sleep. Chewing off half of my nails, I decided to get up and go to the kitchen.

As I walked down the hall, I noticed it wasn't as dark as I expected. *One of the lamps in the living room must still be on.* Which meant Robert was probably still awake. I breathed a sigh of relief. If he was still awake, then maybe he could help take my mind off things. I turned the corner and saw Robert lying on the couch with a book propped open.

"You're still awake," I said, a little breathless. He wasn't wearing a shirt, and the sight of his bare chest completely took me off guard. The dim light grazed his skin, softening the hard lines of his body and showing a gentler, more vulnerable side to him.

"And so are you, I see. Is everything alright?" he asked, sitting up and putting the book on the coffee table.

"Yeah, I umm… couldn't sleep," I said, tripping over my tongue. "I was going to make some tea, do you want some?"

I did my best to ignore the primal hunger rumbling inside me. Though my hands shook with the desire to feel his body close to mine, this wasn't the time or place to be having a clandestine affair. Becky's voice popped into my head, *"Hello, there couldn't be a better time for a frisky midnight romp!"*

"Sure, let me help you." Robert stood up and threw on a cotton t-shirt. I pushed Becky out of my head and forced my feet to take me to the kitchen.

I searched through the darkness and pulled out the tea kettle Harriet had given me as a housewarming gift and filled it with enough water for two.

"Can I help you with anything?" Robert asked as I placed the kettle on the stove and lit the burner.

"I'm good. Making tea isn't exactly rocket science," I teased and turned to face him.

Robert leaned against the sink opposite from me, his hands on the counter for support. His shirt clung to him and did very little to hide his well-muscled body. I looked up at the window above his head and focused my attention on the half-crescent moon shining brightly in the sky. Unconsciously, I reached for the pendant around my neck and traced the curve of one of the moons. Soon there would be a new moon and night would fall into a quiet darkness.

"Violet, are you alright?" Robert finally said, breaking the silence.

"I'm fine." I tried to make the words sound convincing.

"You're not fine, you've barely said a word after talking to Bethany, and now you can't sleep." A hard edge marred his voice and his eyes narrowed in apprehension.

"You weren't sleeping either," I pointed out. "Does that mean there's something bothering you?"

"Don't try to turn this around on me." His voice turned pleading, but his jaw maintained its hard edge. He wasn't used to people not answering him.

"It's just…" I paused and turned my back on him to remove two mugs from the cabinet behind me.

"Violet," Robert said and put his hands on my shoulders. "Let me help you." He turned me around to face him. The proximity of his body to mine made my head spin.

Resting my head against his chest, I tried to regain control. "You can't help me."

"Won't you at least let me try?" He placed his hand under my chin and pulled my head up to look at him.

I searched his eyes. I could feel every emotion I'd ever felt in my life boil to the surface. Any other time when I felt overwhelmed, I always had Becky to talk to. She was the one person I could trust, the one person who knew all the deep dark corners of my heart. I trusted Robert with my life, but letting him into my heart was something I wasn't sure I was ready for. I didn't even know if I could let *anyone* in anymore. I'd spent my whole life building walls to protect myself, but lately, my walls had been taking a lot of hit's and they looked more like Swiss cheese than a fortress.

"I don't know, Robert," I sighed and removed his hand from my face. "I just, I don't know who I am anymore." I kept my voice low, not wanting to say the words aloud. I swallowed the lump in my throat and took a deep breath.

He didn't say anything but patiently waited for me to continue.

"Everything I've learned since I was attacked…it's just too much," I said. "Nothing is what I thought it was; nothing in my life has been real."

The kettle rattled on the stove.

"How am I supposed to deal with any of this?" My voice rose in utter frustration as I pushed away from Robert's intoxicating touch.

Steam slowly rose from the kettle.

"I never asked for any of this!" I started pacing. "I don't want to know any more, I just want things to go back to how they were!"

The kettle screamed and shook.

I stomped over to the stove and turned off the burner. Slowly the screaming turned to a whisper and the jet of hot steam settled to a calm haze.

"I'm so sorry, Violet," Robert said, his eyes on the floor.

"It's not your fault," I exhaled heavily, feeling guilty for letting my emotions boil over. It wasn't true that I wanted everything to go back to the way it was.

"Still, I'm very sorry. All of this is a lot to put on a person."

I pulled two tea bags from the pantry along with a small bottle of whiskey and plucked a lemon from the refrigerator.

"It's not that, it's just…" I sighed, not knowing how to explain everything I was feeling. "I feel like I'm learning about someone else's life." I put the tea bags in the cups and poured the water over them. "And it's not just because you came into my life with Magic. Even before I knew you, everything I thought was real, every memory, I just found out it was all a lie. I don't know who I am anymore." Pulling a knife from the block by the stove, I began to cut a wedge out of the lemon.

"You are who you are because of everything you've been through. That hasn't changed."

"Yes, it has. Everything I thought I went through, everything I thought I dealt with, it wasn't real, it didn't happen."

"What do you mean?" Robert crossed his arms and propped himself against the stove.

I sighed and poured a dollop of whiskey into my glass and squeezed the lemon wedge into the steaming liquid. "Warm your cup?" I asked, holding up the bottle.

"Violet…" Robert gave me a disapproving frown.

"Don't judge me. Do you want some or not?"

"Can't let you drink alone, now can I?"

Pouring a healthy amount into his cup, I handed the mug to him.

"Thank you," he said and took a sip. "Now, what do you mean none of it really happened?"

"My aunt. She told me… well, she showed me my memories. Memories of things I have no recollection of. I sipped my tea as well, tasting its warm bitterness. I felt the liquid making its way to my stomach, warming my chest and sending a wave of calmness through my body.

"You mean someone altered your memories?"

"Yeah, you know about that?" I raised my eyebrow, only half surprised.

"Of course I do. But it takes very powerful magic to alter someone's mind."

"She said the same thing." I turned and walked into the living room.

I heard Robert's footsteps on the carpet behind me, but he didn't say anything. Taking another sip of my tea, I grabbed the blanket hanging off the back of the loveseat and made my way to the couch. Robert made his way around me and moved his makeshift bed out of the way for me to sit. Curling my legs underneath me, I threw the blanket over my feet and rested my cup on my knee. I'd spent many nights curled up like this, a nightcap warming my fingers.

"What did she show you?" Sitting beside me, he left almost a whole cushion between us. A small piece of me didn't like the distance, but I ignored it.

"A few of the memories were of my parents using Magic in front of me. My mother didn't want me to be exposed to Magic. She thought that if she kept me from the Magical world, I'd be spared." I laughed without humor. *So much for that.*

"It was wishful thinking at best. Prophecies aren't made lightly," Robert sounded apologetic, but I knew he understood how futile my parents' efforts had been.

"What else did she show you?" he asked when I didn't say anything.

Looking at him, I wished he could see what was in my head so I wouldn't have to say it out loud. I took a large sip of tea, letting the whiskey give me courage. The warmth coated my throat and moved swiftly down my torso. My head spun as the whiskey burned in my chest.

I took a deep breath and exhaled. "She showed me how my parents really died." I pulled the blanket more fully over my legs.

"I'm so sorry," he said and reached out to squeeze my foot.

"I understand why she altered the memory. It was the right thing to do."

"It's never the right thing to do." His voice was stern and the little wrinkle between his eyebrows appeared as he furrowed his brow.

If only he could see in my head, he would understand what my Aunt did for me.

"Do you know the truth about how they died?"

"No, I only know they died when you were young. No one's ever elaborated more on the topic."

"They were murdered." I paused as tears stung my eyes and threatened to spill over. "Because of me." A single tear escaped and rolled down my cheek. I quickly wiped it away.

Robert didn't say anything. He grabbed my hand and held it in his.

"I was the one who found them," I continued, "when I got home from school."

"Violet, you don't have to do this. You don't have to tell me," Robert said and moved closer.

"Yes, I do." Another tear fell from my eye. Robert gently wiped the tear away and let his hand rest on my shoulder. "I could still feel the Magic when I found them. The air was thick with it. The killer wanted to send a message. There was blood everywhere."

Pausing, I took another sip of my tea as I summoned the last bit of my courage.

"I spent the night at a friend's house the night before," I explained. "That's when it happened. My aunt said she stopped looking ahead for my parents because they didn't want to know when they would die, but I wonder if they knew. I wonder if that's why they sent me to my friend's house for the night, to protect me."

I pulled the blanket tighter around me, suddenly feeling cold despite the tea. "I was in shock. I walked over to their bodies and sat in their blood, not knowing what to do. I never cried, I just sat with them until my aunt showed up and called the police. She tried to get me to talk for days, but I wouldn't say anything. So finally she altered my memory and I grew up thinking I'd lost my parents in a car accident. I even thought I gave a speech at their funeral, but it was all a lie. They were murdered and it was all my fault."

Unable to fight it anymore, I let myself cry.

"Listen to me. None of this is your fault. Look at me," Robert insisted, taking my face in his hand and pulling it up so I'd lock with his eyes. "Your parents' death is not your fault."

"But they died because I was their daughter," I sniffled and wiped my nose with the back of my hand.

"Your parents, whether they wanted to admit it or not, knew who you'd become. They died protecting you so that you could fulfill your destiny. The only person who can accept fault for their death is the person who killed them."

"But if I'd never been born-"

"You were meant to be born to them. Your soul chose them. When they found out who you were, they could have given you up to be protected and hidden away, but they didn't. They chose to keep you and care for you themselves. They knew the consequences of their actions, but you were worth it. You can't blame yourself, do you understand me?"

"But-"

"Do you understand me?" he asked with fierce determination.

I looked at him for a long moment, letting myself get lost in the haze of the whiskey. How could I make him understand that maybe if I had died instead of my parents, everyone would be better off?

Tears streamed down my face as the pain of their death gripped me. Robert took the teacup from my hand and set it on the table next to his. He pulled me to his chest and let the grief consume me.

I don't know how long we stayed like that, but as my tears

started to fade, exhaustion swept over me. Letting everything out did make me feel a little better. I'd been holding so much in lately that my heart was a tangled mess. I still felt guilty for my parents' death, and I was still overwhelmed by the Magical world. But after today, I was finally ready to accept that all of this is real. I guess that means *I'm not in Kansas anymore*, I thought with a wry smile.

I pulled away from Robert and sighed heavily. "I think I'm ready to sleep now," I said.

"I'll say. You smell like a distillery," he teased.

"Not nice." I stood up and nearly lost my balance.

Robert grabbed hold of my waist to steady me. "Come on, let's get you to bed."

I thought about protesting his help, but my head was starting to spin a little. "Let's," I said as we walked toward my bedroom.

Robert helped me into bed and threw the covers over me. The sheets were cold and I shivered a little. I closed my eyes as Robert started to shut the door and my parents' faces flashed across my vision.

"Robert?" I chirped against my better judgment. This was a horrible idea, but I couldn't stand being alone all night.

"Yeah?" he said, poking his head back in.

"Will you…will you stay with me tonight?"

He hesitated in the doorway. "Violet, I…"

"I just don't want to be alone. I can't stop the memories," I said under my breath.

He sighed and closed the door.

"Do you have an extra blanket?"

"Yeah, in the chest." I pointed toward the foot of the bed.

He pulled a quilt out of the chest and laid down on top of the duvet next to me, then threw the quilt over himself.

"I'm right here if you need me," he said and settled into bed.

"Thank you."

Darkness concealed all but the faintest outline of his face. I smiled knowing I was safe with him here next to me and with that little surety in my mind, my anxiety faded a little.

I laid down on my side with my back to him. His steady breathing was like the tide moving in and out. With each breath he took, my eyes grew heavy. I tried to keep them open so I could enjoy the calmness of the moment, but I couldn't fight it any longer. My eyelids felt like barbells and I gave way to exhaustion. This time I saw my parents just as I'd remembered them: loving and alive.

CHAPTER FOURTEEN

Somewhere between reality and dreams, I heard what sounded like a blunt object banging against wood. I stirred and lifted the covers to my chin as I tried to chase the wispy edges of my fading dream.

"Violet," a warm voice whispered, "someone's at the door."

My eyes shot open and I lifted my head up to find Robert looking down at me, a smile on his face. I must have rolled over at some point in the night because I was now lying on top of him. My arm lay across his chest and his arm was wrapped around my lower back. Blood rushed to my cheeks as I sat up and pushed away from him.

"Sorry," I said, clearing my throat as I shuffled to the other side of the bed. The sheets felt cold from the lack of body heat and I fought the urge to roll back into his warm arms.

The same voice from my dreams yelled again and the doorbell buzzed, dashing away any hope of five more minutes of sleep.

"Alright, alright, I'm up," I grumbled. I pulled myself out of bed and went to open the door.

"Where the hell have you been?" Becky asked and stormed right in.

"What're you talking about?" I rubbed my eyes, still half asleep.

"I've left you a million messages. I thought something happened to you."

"Messages… shit, my phone!" I walked over to my purse on the table and started digging. "I'm sorry, Beck, I've just been really busy with this project." I pulled my phone out. It was dead.

"I'll say," Becky replied. The tone of her voice caught me off-guard and I turned to find her staring at Robert, who had clearly just rolled out of bed, my bed.

"I can explain." I hated how cliché I sounded.

"Uh huh," Becky mumbled, raising an eyebrow in my direction.

"I'm going to make some coffee," Robert said, excusing himself.

"You better dish," Becky said as soon as Robert was out of earshot.

I sighed and motioned her to the living room. How was I going to explain to her what was going on when I couldn't tell her the truth? I wanted to tell her about my parents, about what really happened to them. I didn't want to lie to her again - I just couldn't do that to her. Maybe if I stayed away from anything Magical, I could tell her just enough without having to lie.

"It's kind of a long story," I began as we sat on the couch.

"I've got time" Becky's eye lit up.

"It's not what it looks like."

"You said that."

"I'm serious. He was just comforting me."

"Oh, is that what you call it now?"

"Knock it off, I'm being serious."

"Okay, what was he *comforting* you about?" Her eyes went up and down as she searched me suspiciously.

"My parents."

"Your parents?" She balked.

"Yeah, turns out they didn't die in a car accident." The initial shock had worn off and even though I was still upset about what had happened, I was better equipped to deal with it after my breakdown last night.

"What do you mean? What happened to them?"

I was dabbling in dangerous waters. How much could I tell her without giving anything else away? I had to keep the Magical parts secret, but I wanted to stick as close to the truth as possible.

"They were murdered," I said, my eyes closed as I took a solemn breath.

"What!" Becky gaped at me.

"It was a robbery at our house." It wasn't exactly the truth. Their murderer did break in and kill them, but not with the intention of robbing the house.

"Oh my God, Violet. I'm so sorry," she said, wrapping her arms around me. "Are you okay? I mean, of course, you're not okay, but how are you dealing?" She pulled away from me, and her loving expression nearly made me lose it all over again.

Robert walked into the room with two cups of coffee. He handed one to me and offered the other to Becky.

"Thank you," I said, feeling the warmth of the dark liquid radiate through the ceramic mug.

"No thanks, I've already had enough caffeine this morning." Becky waved him off.

Robert kept the second cup for himself and sat down on the loveseat to the right of us.

"I'm dealing the best I can. I mean, it doesn't change the fact that they're gone."

"Do you know who killed them?" Becky asked.

My eye flickered to Robert for half a second. I did know, but how was I supposed to explain that to her. "There are a few leads," I sighed and admitted.

"And how do you fit into all this?" Becky asked, looking over at Robert.

"My family stumbled upon Violet and the truth about her parents," he explained. *That was mostly true,* I thought, taking a sip of my coffee. They did stumble upon me. He was much better at telling careful truths than I was. "When I told her, well, you can imagine her reaction, so I offered to stay with her if she didn't want to be alone."

"You should have called me," Becky lamented as she turned back to me. She didn't like being out of the loop. "Although, I can see why you didn't," she added under her breath as she tilted her head toward Robert.

Leave it to Becky to lighten the mood with sex. Looking at Robert over the top of my coffee cup, a small smile spread across his face as he took a sip.

"I know I should have called you. I've just been so preoccupied with my parents and with this rush project I've been working on the past few days. I'm sorry."

"Don't be. I'd forget about me too in your… err… situation."

"Still, I didn't mean to make you worry."

Becky waved off my apology and added, "I've been trying to get a hold of you because I wanted to make sure you didn't forget about the Yosemite trip this weekend."

Every year Becky, myself and a couple of our girlfriends took a trip to Yosemite before the summer was over. It was nice to get away from the city, even if only for a couple of days.

"Damn, that's right." *When it rains it pours,* I thought. I had so much going on right now with the winery shoot and the sudden emergence of the Magical world that the Yosemite trip never even entered my mind.

"Thanks, I did forget about it," I said, glancing at Robert.

"Well, you can't bail. Christy will kill you if she has to hear from me about your *preoccupations.*"

"I'm not bailing, I just need to get some things done faster than I had planned." I knew that now was probably not the time for a trip, but a part of me relished the thought of getting away from everything.

I sighed, if not for editing pictures yesterday morning before my life had blown up, I'd be way behind schedule.

"Alright, well now that I know you're still alive, I'll let you get back to whatever it was you were doing," Becky said and stood up.

"Sleeping," I noted with a roll of my eyes and a shake of my head, "and I think that ship has sailed." I yawned.

"Why don't you come by later? We can talk more and maybe catch a movie. I know Aaron would love to see you again," Becky suggested. She glanced at Robert. "You're welcome to come along too."

"Thank you," he said. It wasn't a yes or a no.

"Yeah, sure. I'll call you later." Becky and I exchanged a quick kiss on the cheek and she headed out the door.

With the door once more locked, I plopped back down on the couch and let my head fall back.

"She's something else," Robert remarked.

"Yeah, she's a little high strung," I added, taking a sip of my coffee.

Everything was still a little awkward between Robert and me, and neither one of us knew what to say to each other. I wondered how long I had laid on top of him and how long he'd been aware of it. My heart started to pick up in tempo and I fought a smile as I remembered how warm and relaxing it had been sleeping next to him.

"So what are your plans for today?" he asked, interrupting my thoughts.

"Well, we're leaving for Yosemite on Friday night so I have

today and all day tomorrow to get everything printed for Caltome." The opening wasn't for another week and a half, but with how unpredictable my life has been lately, I wanted to finish that project sooner rather than later.

"About Yosemite."

"You think I shouldn't go," I said, not really surprised. Robert liked having me on house arrest. I was surprised when he didn't insist on coming with me for the Caltome shoot, but apparently, I'd been with people he knew and trusted.

"No, you should go. I just want to coordinate with you."

"Oh, okay. So you're going too?" I already knew the answer and honestly, I wasn't opposed to him always being around anymore.

"Of course I'm going, but I think Brett or Annabel should accompany you since you have no way of protecting yourself against Magic and I won't be able to stay close to you."

"Oh, okay," I said, unsure of how I felt about Brett or Annabel babysitting me. Having Robert around was one thing, but I didn't know his sister or Annabel.

"That won't be a problem, will it?" He cocked to the side as he studied the confused expression on my face.

"No, not at all. I'll let Becky know we have one more person coming." My voice sounded stiff, even to my own ears.

"Great." His smile was all business and lacked the warmth I'd grown accustomed to.

"Now if we could just figure out what your vision is all about…" he trailed off.

"About that," I said, realizing I hadn't told him about the rest of my conversation with my Aunt.

He raised his eyebrow at me.

"I guess I didn't tell you because I was so distracted about my parents. My aunt talked to me about the visions and about…" I hesitated, pausing to take a breath. "About my Magic."

Robert cocked his head to the side and a small smile caught

the corners of his mouth. Admitting I had magic was a big win for him. I could tell he was jumping for joy inside, but he was doing a really good job of keeping his composure.

"And?" he asked, wanting more details.

"It's kinda convoluted. Let me shower and get ready and then we can talk about everything," I offered.

"Alright." He smiled and I saw the relief wash off of him.

I bounced back to my room with hurried steps and jumped into the shower. In a rush to get to work and get everything done, I didn't spend as much time under the hot water as I would have liked. While getting dressed, I realized I also hadn't said anything to Robert about our souls. I wondered if he already knew and if he knew the story about King Arthur? I was sure he did, but why hadn't he ever mentioned it before? I brushed my teeth as quickly as I could and threw on some foundation before heading back toward the living room forty-five minutes later.

Robert had also showered and changed into a dark blue button-up shirt and jeans. He sat at the kitchen table writing in his journal again. His hair was still a little damp and he'd shaved. He looked up as I walked over, and we both appraised each other for a moment. *Damn, he was good looking.* A small smile played at the corner of my mouth as our eyes met.

"You don't mind if I come along with you to the studio, do you?" he asked, standing up. "I know you want to get to work, but I'd like to hear what Bethany told you."

"I don't mind if you want to tag along, but I do need to get things done so you can't be too much of a distraction."

His lips spread into a mischievous smile. "I'll try my best to behave," he promised, though didn't hide his playful grin.

"Right." I exhaled. "Let's go then." I felt a little taken back by Robert's good mood. He was always so serious. I wasn't used to him being playful.

We walked outside and saw clouds dotting the sky. The

temperature had dropped at least ten degrees in the past few days. Sliding into the driver's seat, I turned the key over and the engine roared to life.

"About the visions, what did Bethany tell you?" Robert asked as I turned the first corner. He wasn't wasting any time.

"Well, you were right. The visions are happening because I'm the same as her."

"A Soothsayer?"

"Yeah," I mumbled this admission. Just because I was coming around and starting to accept everything didn't mean I was able to call myself a Soothsayer just yet.

"What did she say exactly?"

"She said I could learn to control my visions."

"What else did she say? Did she tell you how you were able to come into your magic?"

"She did, actually." I paused, taking a slow, nervous breath. I didn't know how to tell him that when he saved me a piece of his soul infused with mine. What if that was the only reason for the attraction between us?

"Care to share?" he asked, sounding impatient.

"Robert, I don't know if I want to tell you."

"You can tell me anything, you know that." He tried his best to make his voice sound soothing.

"I know but…"

"It can't be that bad."

He placed his hand on my leg. The electricity that had been crackling between us since we woke up this morning coursed through me. What I felt, the way Robert looked at me, it couldn't just be because our souls were connected. There had to be more going on between us than some Magical bond, right?

His touch broke down my walls and I caved. "It happened because of you," I explained, "because you saved me." I pulled up to a red light and looked at him.

"What do you mean, because I saved you?"

"You know how you said you were either born with a Magical soul or you weren't?"

"Yes."

"Well, because I wasn't born with a Magical soul, I had to be given Magic by other means. When you saved me, a piece of your soul bonded with mine and vice versa."

"Arthur," Robert whispered and removed his hand from my leg.

"You know the story about Arthur and Merlin?"

"Of course." He shook his head, still lost in his own thoughts.

"So it's real then?"

"Yes, it's real. This is incredible. Healers have tried countless times to duplicate what happened with Arthur and Merlin, but very few have ever been able to."

"What do you mean healers have tried to duplicate what happened?"

"Some healers aren't as ethical as others. They experiment with humans by trying to pass on their magic to them, but I've only heard of a handful of cases where it actually worked."

"Why would healers want to pass on their magic?"

"There are two reasons. The most noble, but by no means accepted one is when a child is born to a Magical family with no magic."

"And the other reason?" I asked, hesitant. If it wasn't acceptable to try to give a child magic, I wasn't sure I wanted to know what the other reason might be.

"To create your own army of Magical people."

"Why would someone want to do that?"

"Control, power. The usual reasons people do inhumane things." He shrugged his shoulders matter-of-factly.

I shivered at the thought of someone experimenting with human life so callously.

"My aunt said I was always meant to get my magic from

you," I said, bringing the topic back to us as I parked in front of the studio.

"I suppose she's right." He exited the car in one swift motion.

I unlocked the front door to the studio and flipped on the lights as I walked in. I was a little surprised with myself, at how calmly I was talking about all of this. I put my purse on my desk and turned on my computer. Robert had followed me in and sat down in the chair across from me. I looked him over while his eyes wandered the studio.

Robert had changed my life so much and had become someone I really trusted. I felt safe with him. It had been a long time since I'd really felt safe with someone. My heart swelled and I realized I had fallen for him. I'd been so preoccupied fighting against the Magical world that I couldn't see him slowly sneaking his way up and over my walls.

I felt ridiculous, but I had to ask. I had to know if what I was feeling was just because of our soul connection or if it was something more.

"Robert?"

"Yes?" he asked, turning his gaze to me.

"Does the connection between us... I mean, is our souls being connected why I feel..." I paused. I sounded like a bumbling idiot. I felt incredibly self-conscious, more than I'd ever felt in my entire life.

His expression softened in understanding. "No, we're not drawn to each other because of our souls being connected. It's just a way to pass on Magic to someone who doesn't have a Magical soul."

So it wasn't just me then. He felt drawn to me too. I smiled. "That's it, then? It's just a way magic is transferred between two people?"

"Well, no," he said, hesitating as he tapped his finger in thought. "That's not it."

"What else is there?"

"Now don't quote me on this. I don't have a lot of information to go on. But it's been said that Arthur and Merlin were able to wield very powerful magic when the two of them worked together."

"Have you felt a difference at all?"

"No, at least I don't think so. Let me make a few calls and see if I can get some more information."

"Sure, I need to get to work too."

We didn't talk much the rest of the day. Robert left me to my task and he made phone call after phone call, taking notes in his journal after every one. I kept glancing over at him, wondering what he was writing about. If he had found something new, I wanted to know. After all, this connection affected me too.

Around lunchtime, he went and got us sandwiches from the deli a couple doors down and told me what little more he knew about Arthur and Merlin.

So much of what happened back then had been lost or turned into fictitious stories. The only hope was to find a family journal, like Robert's, that had been passed down through the generations. That was a long shot.

Jessie showed up a couple hours later in her P.E. clothes and chatted with Robert about school. She clearly had a crush on him, and it was cute how she shamelessly flirted with him.

After finishing a little more than half of the pictures, I went through the messages I'd pushed aside earlier. The elementary school had called me back with a date next month for picture day. I called them back to confirm the date and moved on to the next message. It was from Matthew. He had called yesterday afternoon.

I dialed the number Jessie had jotted down and Matthew picked up on the second ring.

"Hello?"

"Hey, it's Violet. You called yesterday, but I wasn't in," I said.

"Off playing hooky, huh?"

I laughed. "No, just working from home. Did you need something?"

"Yeah, I'm going to be in the area tomorrow and Meredith wanted me to check with you and see if you had anything done I could bring back with me."

"I have a little more than half the pictures printed. I should be able to get everything else finished by tomorrow."

"Alright, perfect. I'll give you a call tomorrow."

"Sounds good. Talk to you later, Matty," I said. I couldn't help myself.

"Just when I was starting to like you," he laughed.

We both hung up and I went through the rest of the messages. I had a few from Becky that made me feel guilty I'd completely forgotten about her the past few days. I dialed her cell to see if she still wanted to do something later tonight.

"Hey, what's up?" she answered after a few rings.

"Not much. I'm finishing up here at the studio and wanted to check in with you about dinner and a movie tonight."

"Yeah, I'm still going to be a couple hours and I won't have time to make food but Aaron's at the house."

"No worries. I have a few things I want to do at home first." I eyed Robert. He was still talking with Jessie, but looking in my direction. "I'll pick up some takeout on my way over."

"Alright, see you in a bit."

"See ya," I said and hung up.

"Ready when you are," I told Robert as I walked over to him and Jessie.

He nodded and said, "It was good talking to you again, Jessie."

"You too." She smiled ear to ear.

"Why don't you get out of here," I suggested to Jessie.

"Are you sure? Day's not over yet."

"Yeah, but the clouds cleared up and it's still pretty nice out. Take the rest of the day on me."

"Alright, thanks so much, Violet!" Jessie pulled her phone from her bag and started texting away the moment she was out the door.

"That was nice of you," Robert said.

"She's young. She should be out enjoying life, not being around what I'm going through."

"So we're heading back to your place?"

"Yep, there's something I want to try if you're up for it." I was determined to learn a little more about my Magic.

Robert gave me a skeptical look, but then a small smile played at his lips. "I'm up for anything."

CHAPTER FIFTEEN

We left the studio and got back to my place in a matter of minutes. Robert didn't ask what it was I wanted to do, and I was grateful. I needed the drive home to think about what I would ask him and wanted to be sure I was ready. If I went through with this, there was no going back.

I parked the car down the street and we walked up to my complex. The sun hadn't begun setting, but the cool ocean air made it clear that night was fast approaching.

"So, are you going to tell me what we'll be doing?" His eyebrows rose innocently.

"Yes," I replied and looked him up and down.

"Anytime soon?" His lips curled into a smile that would have any girl at his mercy.

"Yes," I said, a little breathless. I swung the gate open and headed down the path, trying to stay in control of the emotions bubbling inside me.

He placed his hand on my lower back as we walked down the shaded path. I could feel the warmth of his hand through my thin, cotton t-shirt and my skin tingled at his touch.

"Violet, tell me," he whispered. His breath on the back of my neck sent chills all over my body. I felt like I was overheating despite the cool air. He was good at this, but so was I.

I turned to face him and placed my hand on his chest. Following my movement, his fingers now rested on my hip. Surprise flickered in his eyes and his grip tightened around me.

"Can we just get inside first?" I held his gaze as my fingers fiddled with one of the buttons on his shirt.

He hesitated a moment, giving himself away. In that brief moment, I could see just how much of an effect I had on him. I smiled, glad it wasn't just me, and turned away from him, needing to put a little distance between us.

Unlocking the front door, I walked inside and Robert followed a good distance behind me. Tossing my purse on the kitchen table, I took a deep breath and turned to face him as he closed the door.

"I want you to teach me how to use Magic," I blurted out.

His eyes still held a hint of desire from our playful banter, but the look on his face was pure shock. I waited for him to say something, but he just stared at me.

Uncomfortable with the silence, I took a step toward him and said, "You said yourself I'm not able to protect myself against Magic."

"Well yes, but-"

I cut him off. "No more buts or excuses from either of us. If I'm going to do this, if I'm really going to accept this part of myself, then I have to be all in."

"Are you sure you're ready, though?" he asked, frowning with concern. He looked worried, and rightfully so. Only a few days ago, I'd been fighting him tooth and nail about all of this.

"Yes, I'm sure. Robert, my life's been turned upside down and I need to regain control." I felt like a child asking permission to go to the school dance. It made me uncomfortable, and I crossed my arms to keep the agitation from showing on my face.

"I don't want you to move too fast. You need to really believe first."

"I do believe. I want…" I faltered. "I need this."

"Why the sudden need for control?"

"Because I'm sick of other people telling me who I am or who I'm supposed to be. I need to know for myself. I need to experience it for myself."

He looked at me for a long moment and then smiled. "Alright, close your eyes."

I took a deep breath and did as he instructed.

"Clear your mind," he continued with a soft voice. "Feel the beat of your heart and follow it inward."

I let out a heavy breath and tried to do as he said.

"There's an energy inside you that wasn't there before. Clear your mind and try to focus. It'll be very subtle at first."

I wasn't sure what exactly I was supposed to focus on, so I listened to my heartbeat from within and focused on my lungs expanding with each breath. In and out. *Thump-thump, thump-thump.* In and out. *Thump-thump, thump-thump.*

Robert wrapped his hands around my wrists like gentle manacles and lifted them from my sides.

"Let me guide you." He caressed the insides of my palms.

I let out a ragged breath and gave myself over to his influence. A tingling sensation started in the tips of my fingers. It slowly moved up my arms and throughout my entire body. The hunger that had been growing just under my ribcage the last few weeks relished in the sensation and expanded to fill me from head to toe. Bit by bit, the energy left my extremities and rushed to my core. It coursed through my veins, ready to be freed from the shell of my body.

"Now try thinking about a blanket of protection. Let it wrap around you and feel its defense," Robert instructed. "Use the energy inside you to make that blanket into a barrier between us."

The room had grown so quiet that his voice startled me. I took a breath in cadence with the hum inside me and tried to picture an impenetrable blanket wrapped around me.

"Open your eyes."

I hesitated for a moment. *This is it. No turning back now.* I still had some reservations about Magic, but I'd honestly come to terms with it. Now it was time to let go and release the Magic within me.

Cautiously, I opened my eyes and glanced at my extended hands. Robert was no longer holding onto me. Looking up, I couldn't believe what I saw. A beautiful, golden shimmer hung between Robert and me. The barrier rippled like the ocean and was transparent enough that I could see Robert standing on the other side of it. I looked up again and the golden barrier disappeared.

"What happened?" I asked. The smile faded from my face.

Robert chuckled. "It takes a lot of concentration to keep up a shield."

"So I did it then?"

"Yes. Now that you've seen how your shield manifests itself, it should be easier to bring it up again."

"Manifests itself?"

"Everyone's shield is different. When you tap into your Magic, you're tapping into the essence of who you are. Even though I can teach you everything I know, healing aside, your Magic will manifest different than it does for me."

"What does your shield look like?"

Before I could blink, a burning red shield flew up between us. It was the most remarkable thing I'd ever seen. It rippled as different shades of crimson wove in and out of each other, flowing to an unheard beat. The shield hung between us like a piece of transparent fabric. I reached out and let my fingers graze the shield in front of me, the way I used to run my fingers across the water when I was a kid. I could feel his energy and tried to push my fingers through the sea of red but couldn't penetrate the barrier. I looked up at Robert, amazed as a smile spread across his face.

"This is unbelievable," I said under my breath.

"It's all real. The world is at your fingertips." He grabbed my hand and pulled me through the red curtain. I felt his energy as I passed through the shield, the same warmth I felt the night he healed me.

"How'd you-"

"It's my shield," he explained before I could finish my question. "I'm in control of what comes through it." One of his arms found its way around my waist.

I reached out to touch the crimson waves and the shield disappeared, leaving a current in the air that was almost palpable. Robert watched me carefully, curiosity written in all the lines of his face. He still had his arm wrapped around me and it brought all my emotions bubbling to the surface.

"What?" I asked, trying not to blush.

"I'm just surprised. You're handling this much better than I thought you would."

I sighed and picked a piece of lint off his shirt. "It's important for me to accept this side of my life."

"Violet." He lifted my chin, so I had to look at him. "It won't matter that it's important if you don't truly embrace this side of you."

"I'm getting there." I smiled and leaned in a little closer to him. My heart had gained some speed with his arm around me and I desperately wanted to break the tension between us.

"Shall we try again?" he asked, releasing me and taking a deep breath.

"Sure." I stepped away and closed my eyes.

This time I found the energy inside me without Robert's help. Now that I knew what I was looking for and how it felt, it was easier to stay focused. It took much longer to summon up the same force Robert had on my own, but slowly the electric hum built up inside me. I saw the beautiful golden shield in my head and tried to focus on seeing it in front of me. Robert stood quietly in the room somewhere, watching and waiting. I felt the electricity ease some and opened my eyes. A golden shimmer hung in the air and quickly fizzled into nothing.

"That was really good," Robert said with a proud smile.

"Really good? Nothing happened. It didn't look anything like it did the first time."

"It's not easy. For doing it on your own, that was perfect. It didn't take you nearly as long as I thought it would for you to summon the Magic."

"How long did it take you before you were able to do it instantly?"

"Just try again," he said, avoiding my question.

I closed my eyes again and found the flicker of electricity inside me once more. It took even longer this time to build up the same sort of intensity, and I felt like I was going to break a sweat as I wrinkled up my face in focus. Once I thought I was strong enough, I imagined my shield. I pictured the golden shimmer wrapping around me like a cocoon. I felt the electricity bubble over and let it flow out of me with ease.

The cloth-like shield glowed all around me. Not at all as vibrant as when Robert helped me, but it was there. I smiled. I was really doing this. This was real. I looked at Robert, my smile still in place as the shimmering light faded around me.

I tried twice more to produce the shield, but both times nothing happened. Feeling like the wind had been knocked out of me, I sat down next to Robert on the couch.

"Why can't I do it anymore?" I asked, near panting as I caught my breath.

"It takes a lot of energy to use your Magic. It'll get easier with time. You'll build up your strength, but for now you did amazing," he beaming.

Robert's eyes held mine and I let myself fall into their warm, russet depths. He had accomplished the impossible; he had helped me believe in the Magical world, and he couldn't be happier. I let the moment linger on a little longer and then tore myself away from his warmth and happiness.

Despite being absolutely spent, I sighed with wonderful relief. I felt like a huge weight had been lifted from me, the anxiety and torment that had been living inside me was gone. I wondered if that was what my aunt meant when she said it went against our nature to abstain from Magic. Had the unused Magic inside me caused my anxiety? I let my head fall back and gave myself over to my senses. The raw, ancient hunger that had been gnawing at me flickered with satisfaction deep at my core.

"Huh," I said.

"What are you thinking?"

I sat up and pulled a pillow into my lap. "Have you ever gone a long stretch without using Magic?"

"No, why?"

"It's just something my aunt said."

"Care to enlighten me?"

"She said that it goes against our nature not to use Magic."

"That's true. Using Magic is like breathing for us. It just happens naturally, sometimes without thinking."

"Well, I was wondering, if our souls became a part of each other the night you saved me, then I've gone quite a long time without using Magic."

"And what exactly were you wondering?"

"I was wondering..." I rolled my head his direction. "If that's why I've been so anxious lately because the Magic was building up inside me."

"It's possible, but you've been having visions since that night, right?"

"Yes," I said, furrowing my brow, unsure where this train of thought would take him.

"When you had the visions, were you emotional in any way?" he asked, picking up on my mood.

I thought back to all the times I'd had visions of the future, the past. I guessed my emotions were heightened somewhat in those moments. Whenever I thought about the night, I was attacked I seemed to get sucked back into that moment. And then there were the couple times Robert's touch had sent my heart into overdrive, which resulted in my seeing that kiss I so desperately wanted.

"Yeah, I guess you could say that," I finally replied.

"Well, that's probably why you had the visions. Your Magic had been building up inside you, and when you were in an emotional state, the Magic bubbled over and resulted in your visions," Robert explained.

"Hmm, I guess this isn't an exact science is it?" I laughed.

"No, it's not."

"Thank you, by the way."

"And what might you be thanking me for?" he asked, sounding surprised.

"Everything. You've been so patient and understanding."

"You're worth it." Robert winked and nudged me with his elbow.

I smiled and didn't try to hide the blush rushing to my cheeks. "We should probably head over to Becky's soon."

"You don't mind me tagging along?"

"No. Besides, who's going to save me from Becky's twenty questions if you're not there," I said with a laugh.

Robert gave me a hesitant look. "I don't want to impose."

"It'll be good for both of us to do something fun and easy," I said and stood from the couch.

"Alright, I'm in."

I did a quick freshening up and we were off. Dusk had finally arrived and a damp chill clung to the air as the marine layer moved in. I placed an order with this little hole-in-the-wall Chinese place Becky and I both loved and swung by the store to pick up a few bottles of wine. Robert and I discussed the link between my emotions and my visions as we drove to Becky's but we didn't come up with anything more enlightening.

We pulled up to Becky's house about an hour after leaving my place and headed inside. Becky wasn't home yet, but Aaron let us in. We popped open a bottle of wine as soon as the introductions were through and sat in the living room to wait for Becky. Robert had a way with people, and he and Aaron chatted like they'd known each other their whole lives. I'd normally have been much more a part of the conversation, but I was exhausted and they started talking about the stock market, which was something I knew nothing about.

I got up to pour myself another glass when Becky came through the front door.

"Hey," I said, heading to the kitchen.

"Hey, hope I didn't keep you guys waiting too long." She plopped her stuff down on the floor and followed me into the kitchen.

"Not at all."

"I see you brought Robert with you." Becky gave me a meaningful look.

"I believe it was you who invited him," I noted as I filled my glass.

Becky smiled and pulled a glass from the cabinet for herself. "It was the polite thing to do." She went about making herself a cocktail, pouring vodka and a whole collection of colorful bottles together to make something she claimed tasted just like a cherry Jolly Rancher.

"Uh huh," I said, appraising her bartending abilities.

"Hey, you could have gotten out of it if you wanted."

"True," I said into my wine glass.

"How are you dealing with everything?" Becky finished pouring her cocktail and clinked her glass against mine.

"I'm okay."

"Any more news about your parents?" She threw the takeout containers in the microwave.

"No, nothing new."

"I still can't believe it. All these years you thought it was a car accident."

"I know, but my aunt did what they thought was right. They were gone no matter what. It was better for me to grow up thinking it was an accident."

"You really think so?" Becky asked, frowning as she sipped her drink.

I knew so. The image of my parents flashed through my head. I had been furious at my aunt for altering my memories, but the more time I spent with the truth, the more I realized it was the right thing to do.

"Yeah," I concluded. "I don't think I'd have been able to handle this as a kid."

The guys laughed in the other room and drew our attention.

"They seem to be getting along," Becky noted. She was always the best at changing the subject.

"They haven't come up for air once," I joked and took a healthy sip of wine.

I pulled some plates down for dinner and Becky took the food out of the microwave, setting it on the counter.

"Hey, chatty Kathies, let's eat!" Becky yelled to the guys.

Both men stood up without acknowledging Becky and came into the kitchen to help with dinner.

Robert and Aaron poured themselves another glass of wine, and Aaron grabbed a few of the cartons off the counter. I started grabbing the stack of plates when Robert stopped me.

"Allow me."

"Thanks," I replied as I grabbed the remaining containers.

"You okay? You look a little pale," he said under his breath.

"Just tired." I fought a yawn as I took my seat at the table.

Everyone passed the cartons back and forth, dumping mounds of food onto our plates. I hadn't realized how famished I was until the smell of spicy eggplant and orange chicken wafted up from my plate. Words escaped me as I deftly twirled Chow Mein onto my chopsticks and shoveled chicken into my mouth. Thankfully, Robert took the conversational reins and regaled Becky with stories about Europe. She clung to his every word. If there was anything Becky loved more than her computer, it was traveling.

After dinner, Becky and Aaron refused to let us help clean, so Robert and I went to the living room and sat on the couch to nurse our full stomachs.

"How you doing?" Robert asked as he gave me a thoughtful smile. We sat close together. The smell of his cologne hung in the air. I was already a little lightheaded from the wine, and the smell of Robert so near made my head spin.

"I'm fine, why do you keep asking?" I cocked my head to the side.

"I'm just making sure." He leaned even closer so he could keep his voice low. "You used a lot of Magic today. That's not something your body's used to yet."

"I'm much better now that I have food in me."

"Good." Robert smiled and brushed my hair behind my ear.

I returned his smile and held his gaze for a moment. His eyes were soft and tender. I looked down, trying to hide the blush that had rushed to my cheeks, but Robert lifted my chin back up to look at him. The tenderness remained, but I saw a fire that wasn't there a moment ago. I leaned a little closer to him and he moved his hand from my chin to my hair. I could feel the hesitation in his shoulders as our lips grazed and he pulled me against him.

A loud crash came from the kitchen and the magic of the

moment disappeared. His hand fell from my neck and I backed away from him.

"Everything alright?" Robert called out, clearing his throat.

"Yeah!" Becky yelled from the kitchen, followed shortly by angry mumbling between her and her brother.

Becky and Aaron joined us a minute later, and Aaron selected a movie on Netflix. Becky sat on the couch next to me in a way that made it impossible for me not to be pushed against Robert and Aaron sprawled out on the loveseat to the left of us. The movie was a thriller, and while I normally loved them, I found myself not in the mood to see people get hunted down and killed. I thought Robert could sense I wasn't enjoying the film because he put his arm around me and gave me a slight squeeze. It was a reassuring gesture, and I was grateful to have someone who knew the ins and outs of what was going on with me. I did feel a little guilty that Becky wasn't this person. She had always been my rock to lean on in the past, but there was no way she could comfort me now. I picked up my glass to take another sip of wine but discovered it was empty.

"Let me," Robert said, taking my glass.

Aaron stood, needing a refill as well. "Another one, Beck?"

"Yes, please," she said with a smile. Becky paused the movie and the guys went to the kitchen to refill our drinks.

"You seem different with him."

"I feel different," I bit my lip trying to keep my feelings from gushing out of me. After all, the guys were just in the other room.

"You guys balance each other out." Becky's smile stretched from ear to ear as she lightly bounced up and down next to me. "He seems good for you."

"Don't get ahead of yourself," I said, needing to hear the words myself.

"You can't honestly tell me nothing's happened between you guys." Becky leaned closer, anticipating some juicy gossip.

"Not a thing." Resentment laced my reply. Had Becky and Aaron not caused such a ruckus in the kitchen then maybe something more would have happened, but c'est la vie.

"Well why not?" she asked, near whining with disappointment. She eyed me and I could tell that she assumed I was the one holding things up.

I shrugged. I really didn't have a good answer for her, and it frustrated me as much as it did her.

"So you do want something more to happen." Becky'd always had a knack for picking up on my emotions.

"It's complicated."

"What's holding you back?"

"Honestly, nothing on my part. He's the one who's hesitant." I let out another sigh. I did want something to happen between us and knew it would, eventually. I flushed, thinking about the kiss from my vision. It was filled with so much passion, so much need. My skin tingled at the thought of his touch. I really did hope this was a vision and not just a fantasy.

"Bullshit, I've had my eyes on him since I got home. He watches you when you're not looking, and he dotes on you like you walk on water," Becky challenged.

"He's just worried about me," I mumbled. Of course, he looked at me like I was royalty. The Magical world had been waiting for me for generations.

Robert and Aaron came back in the room and Becky let the topic drop. Robert handed me my glass and sat back down beside me. We finished watching the movie and I had to turn my head from the screen for the last half. I couldn't stomach watching people be brutally murdered, even if the blood was just red-dyed corn syrup and the victims were just actors. Robert put his arm around me and I rested my head against his chest. As I listened to the even beating of his heart, exhaustion took hold of me and I fell asleep in his arms.

CHAPTER SIXTEEN

I awoke the next morning still feeling a little worn out. A low hum resonated deep within my bones. My magic wasn't the monster of anxiety it had been before, but it had definitely grown in strength while I slept. I stretched my arms and legs and rolled over to look at the clock on the nightstand. Seven thirty-two. I had a good half hour before I actually needed to start getting ready for the day, so I grabbed the journal Robert had given me from off the nightstand.

Propping myself up with a couple pillows, I got comfortable. The journal felt like a ton of bricks in my hand as I ran my fingers over the soft leather cover and gently flipped it open. The binding crackled like kindling as I slowly turned each page. I stopped a couple of entries in and began to read.

14 December, 1789

Belinda's words fill my thoughts. My bones will be dust in the earth by the time her prophecy comes to pass, but I cannot help wondering about the future. It must be such a curse to know all that has passed and what is to come, to not be able to live in the present moment. I admit to seeing the benefit of getting a glimpse of the future now and again, but what would I do with that sort of information?

Would I stop trying in the now and simply wait for the future to come? Would my inaction lead to an alternative future? It is silly of me to ponder such things. Soothsayers aren't like the rest of us. The blood in their veins gives them the strength to harness their ability. Still, I can't help but wonder if it must be hard for them to always know.

"Aren't like the rest of us?" I re-read the line. What could the writer possibly mean by that? I rose from bed and walked to the living room in search of Robert. As I turned the corner, I re-read the paragraph again.

I looked up from the journal as I reached the back of the couch to see Robert still fast asleep. One arm lay across his chest while the other lay on the pillow above his head. He wore a grey t-shirt and a quilt over the bottom half of his body. His hair was messy and his face wore the stubble of a long night. My heart tugged at the sight of him, and I smiled at how peaceful he looked. I wanted to go to his side and run my fingers through his unkempt hair, but instead, I settled for the loveseat adjacent to him. Turning my attention back to the journal, I flipped forward a couple pages while I waited for Robert to wake up.

9 April, 1790

My love's betrothed has been sent on an errand that will take him away for a week at the very least. We've made plans today to meet behind her father's barn, where we can steal away for the afternoon. My heart swells with the thought of our meeting, and the reality of the present situation is suspended momentarily. If only I could get a glimpse of our future, to be certain that we will find a way to be together for all of time.

I smiled and traced the words on the page with my index finger. I could feel the magic growing at my core, so I closed my eyes and let it take me.

When I opened my eyes, I found myself standing in front of a modest two-story house. The stones making up the exterior looked smooth and worn by countless storms. Several steps led up to a large front door. Curtains hung closed in all the windows, and if not for the smoke rising from the chimney, I would have thought the house was empty.

A crisp, cool breeze wafted through the grey sky. Dust rose around me as someone rode past on horseback. I looked around, but there wasn't much to see, nothing but tree-lined, open fields beside the house. I could just barely make out another house down the block and through the trees.

A young man came out of the house just then, taking the stone steps two at a time. He wore a white linen shirt, a dark-colored jacket, and matching pants. He was very handsome and walked with a regal posture. His brass-buttoned clothing indicated I was definitely somewhere in the past, but I still wasn't sure what I was seeing. He looked up and down the path as if to make sure the coast was clear. Satisfied no one was in sight, he tore off down the street. I followed him, curious where this vision would take me.

A long, wooden fence held up by stone columns stretched as far as I could see in each direction. Once the house the gentleman had come from was out of sight, he jumped over the fence. I followed close behind him. He looked over his shoulder as I landed in the tall grass and my heart leapt into my throat. He couldn't see me, could he? I looked over my shoulder but saw nothing behind me. Cautiously I turned back toward the gentleman and to my relief found him already walking away from me.

His frantic, urgent demeanor seemed to transform into something more peaceful the longer we walked up the low, grassy hill. I followed him through the tall grass at an easy pace until we reached the top of a hill where he paused. I stopped beside him. At that moment, I knew exactly where I was and where we were going. A small barn sat at the bottom of the hill. Further out, I could see a few more houses and a small town off to the left. The barn just below us must have been where the lovers were meeting. I couldn't help but smile as I watched William run down the hill toward the barn. When he was about fifty yards away, Constance appeared out of the shadows to meet him. She *flung herself into his arms and they kissed with a longing that pulled at my heart.*

I could feel reality pulling me back, but I watched the lovers for as long as I could. Robert had told me they would end up together, and I wished I could tell William he would get to be with the woman he loved so much.

The vision gave way to my living room, and I smiled at the love I had just witnessed. "Welcome back," Robert smiled up at me from his makeshift bed on the couch.

"How'd you-"

"I could see in your eyes that you were somewhere else."

"I saw William and Constance." I let out a small chuckle of delight and looked at the journal in my hand. Something about putting a face to the man whose journal I read was kind of thrilling.

"Really?" Robert sat up.

I nodded. "They were meeting each other behind her father's barn."

"I'm glad you're reading through the journal." Robert tossed the quilt off of him and sat up.

"Yeah, I haven't really looked at it much since you gave it to me, but I was curious what else was in here besides the prophecy."

"It's a diary just as much as it's a way of passing information on to the next generation."

"I gathered that." I smiled again, thinking about William and Constance.

"So, is there a reason you're reading in my bedroom instead of yours?" Robert gestured around the living room.

"Actually, yes. I came across something I wanted to ask you about, but you were still sleeping."

"Alright, but coffee first. Some of us aren't morning people," Robert noted as he pushed to his feet and stretched his arms above his head.

I followed him to the kitchen and flipped the journal open to the entry I had read first that morning.

"Soothsayers aren't like the rest of us. The blood in their veins gives them the strength to harness their ability," I read out loud. "What does he mean, Soothsayers aren't like the rest of us?"

"Bethany didn't tell you?" Robert asked, pouring grounds and water into the coffee machine.

"Tell me what?"

"The only way a person can be a Soothsayer is if they're a direct descendant of Merlin. That's what William means by the blood in your veins."

"Okay, but what does that have to do with Soothsayers being different?" I asked with only a little difficulty. The fact that I was a descendant of Merlin was a hard pill to swallow, but I had decided to accept all of this and stamped out the screaming doubt in my mind.

"Your Magic is directly connected to the most powerful person the Magical world has ever known," Robert continued.

"I still don't know what that has to do with anything."

"Magic comes from your soul. Where does your soul come from?" He asked as his eyebrows rose on his forehead.

"I don't know," I replied, a little shocked at the turn of the conversation.

"Ever heard someone say that a trait in a person must have skipped a generation?"

"Yeah."

"It's because each generation before you is a part of your soul. Your soul happens to be connected to Merlin and that's what gives you the ability to be a Soothsayer."

"What do you mean each generation is a part of my soul?" I shook my head, trying to decipher what he meant.

Robert took a breath and explained, "When you were born,

your ancestors were already a part of you. Their essence, their souls played a part in creating you. It takes more than just DNA to create a person, Magical or not. Your families' Magic has had an influence on you since the day you were born." The coffeemaker groaned and spat the last remnants of the dark liquid into the pot below. Robert reached for it enthusiastically to pour himself a cup.

I set the journal on the counter as he handed me the mug of steaming hot coffee and proceeded to pour himself one.

"Then why wasn't I born with a Magical soul? It doesn't make sense." I emptied a sugar packet into the steaming drink and stirring in a splash of French vanilla creamer.

"Your soul is still unique to you, they just influence you a little. It's the same way genes work. No other combination could have made you exactly as you are. You were born the way you were meant to be born, without Magic."

"So anyone in my family has the potential to be a Soothsayer?"

"No. I can assume since your Aunt is a Soothsayer and she is your mother's sister that the bloodline is on your mother's side. No one on your father's side of the family could ever be a Soothsayer. But if you or your Aunt were to have children, they would have the possibility of being a Soothsayer." He poured a little creamer into his own coffee and took a sip.

"I wasn't expecting a lesson in genetics this morning." I rubbed my forehead, mildly dazed.

"I know it can be a little convoluted, but that's why you're different from the rest of the Magical world."

"What does he mean though, that Soothsayers have the strength to harness their ability?" I asked, reading from the journal again.

"You've seen things already in the past and future, correct?"

"Yeah, and?"

"And what did you do with what you saw?"

"Nothing." I shrugged. What was I supposed to do with what I saw?

"Exactly," he said, taking a sip of coffee and leaning against the counter. "Your gift comes with the ability to know but not let that knowledge rule you. Any other person, Magical or not, would either try to prevent it or drive themselves crazy waiting for the vision to come to pass."

I thought about all the things I'd seen so far, including the electric kiss between Robert and myself. I started to blush. Robert, consumed by his coffee, didn't notice and I quickly pushed my thoughts in a different direction. Would William have been able to handle knowing his future? Could he have been able to know he would end up with Constance but still be able to wait? I yearned for that kiss, but knowing it was somewhere in my future comforted me instead of making me anxious.

"What are you thinking?" Robert asked, letting his fingers trace the cover of the journal.

"Nothing." I took a sip of my coffee and propped myself against the counter next to him.

"Still feel the need to keep secrets from me?" There was a playfulness to Robert's voice that made me smile.

"No, it's just... I was thinking about some of the things I've seen," I said, staring down at the toffee colored liquid in my cup.

"What about them?" Robert asked, sipping his coffee.

"I was just thinking about how it makes me feel, knowing the future."

"And how does it make you feel?"

"Calm," I said with certainty.

"Really?" His eyes opened wide and he pursed his lips together.

"Yeah, it's weird. It's like I don't have to worry about that particular event because it's out there somewhere in time, waiting to happen."

"That doesn't drive you crazy though, waiting for something you know is going to happen?"

I blushed again, and this time I couldn't hide it from him.

"What is it?"

"I do get a little anxious sometimes," I said and took a sip of coffee in an attempt to hide my embarrassment.

"About anything in particular?"

"No," I blurted out too quickly.

I saw Robert smile out of the corner of my eye and hoped he wouldn't push to learn more.

"What's it feel like for you, when you see something?" he asked, thankfully changing the subject as he cradled his steaming cup.

"Depends on what I'm seeing. Like when I saw William and Constance just now, I felt comforted. It was warm and loving there," I explained. I looked up and smiled, remembering the feel of the tall grass and the smell of the crisp, cool air in my vision.

"And other times?"

I grimaced. "Well, when I go back to the night I was stabbed, there is some comfort because I know how it all turns out, but I can also feel everything I was feeling that night. It's suffocating." I set my coffee down and wrapped my arms around my shoulders.

"Do you see that night often?"

"Not so much anymore. I used to dream about it. Well, I thought they were dreams. And then that day when we were on the pier, your touch took me back to that night, but nothing since then."

"I'm sorry you were hurt."

"Robert, don't. It all turned out fine." I waved off his concern.

He looked up at me and our eyes caught for just a second. Warmth spread through me like wildfire, and I let my hair fall across my face to hide my uncontrollable emotions. It frustrated me that just one look from him made me feel like a schoolgirl with a crush. I wished I could get my feelings in check, but somehow he always managed to get my guard down.

"I should probably get ready," I said, taking one last sip of my coffee before placing the cup in the sink.

"Do you mind if I tag along with you again today?"

"Do I have a choice?" I gave him a playful grin.

"Not really." Robert smiled with all his charm and pushed himself off the counter. "But it's polite to ask," he whispered into my ear as he leaned around me to put his cup in the sink.

My hand started reaching up to cradle his cheek, but I made myself take a step around him and head out of the kitchen.

"Be ready to go in an hour," I said without looking back. I took a deep breath as I closed my bedroom door behind me and proceeded to get ready for the day.

An hour later we were out the door and I had pushed any lingering attraction between us to the back of my mind. On the way to the studio, I stopped by the framing shop I frequented to pick up what I needed for the Caltome project.

"Your phone went off while you were inside," Robert said as I got back in the car.

I dug through my purse and pulled out my cell. Becky had sent me a text. *6pm call time. See you tonight!*

"Everything okay?" Robert asked as I threw my phone back in my purse.

"Yeah, it was just Becky letting me know they're going to pick me up around six tonight."

"Do you think you can get everything done in time?" Something sounded off about Robert's voice just then. I looked over at him and he seemed to be perfectly fine, so I shrugged off the odd feeling.

"Of course. Plus I have someone to help me just in case it comes down to the wire." I nudged him with my elbow.

"I'm better at supervising." He grinned and shrugged his shoulders.

I rolled my eyes at him. "Of course you are."

Pulling up to the studio, I parked right in front. Robert grabbed the box of frames from the backseat while I unlocked the front door, flipping on the lights and holding the door open for him.

"Where would you like me to put this?"

"Umm... there's a table in the back you can set it on," I pointed toward the back door as I walked over to my desk.

Turning on my computer, I followed Robert into the back room to warm up the printing equipment. I still needed to print all the larger portraits, and each one took a good amount of time. As I flipped each machine on, they groaned to life and cycled through their components to prepare for printing. It always reminded me of someone getting out of bed, yawning, stretching and cracking in various places. I pulled the smaller-sized pictures I'd printed yesterday from the filing cabinet and put them on the table next to the box of frames. Turning to walk back into the main office, I saw Robert leaning against the wall, watching me.

"You don't have to watch over me like I'm a prisoner," I said, walking back to my desk.

"Maybe if my prisoner wasn't so easy on the eyes, I wouldn't," he replied. I could hear the smile in his voice and refused to look at him, not wanting to be distracted for even a moment.

I sat down in front of my computer and double-clicked on the printing software. Robert had followed me back to my desk and I looked up at him while I waited for the program to open.

"What's going on with you?" I asked. "You seem tense this morning."

"I'm fine, just didn't get a lot of sleep last night."

"Is everything alright?"

"Of course," Robert said, leaning against the side of my desk so I could no longer see his face.

I pushed my chair back so I could at least see his profile. "Would you tell me if everything wasn't okay?" I asked, unable to hide a suspicious frown.

The set of his shoulders tightened ever so slightly. He was definitely keeping something from me, but what?

"Violet, just trust me." He turned his head to look at me. A sad smile touched his lips.

"Alright," I said, pushing my chair closer to my desk.

"I need to make a few phone calls. I'll be outside if you need me." Robert abruptly pushed himself off my desk.

I didn't say anything as I watched him walk out the front door. Turning back to my computer, I pushed Robert out of my mind. I didn't have time to sit here and wonder what could be bothering him.

I spent the next couple of hours printing the larger photos and fitting the portraits into the frames while Robert went in and out of the store taking and making calls. His mood hadn't improved much since leaving the house that morning, and it started putting me on edge. If he wasn't on the phone outside talking to someone, he was inside frantically typing away on a text message. Something was definitely going on, and he was trying to keep it from me.

Toward the middle of the day, food arrived in the form of a pizza I'd ordered. I took a slice and ate without really tasting it. I was in deadline mode and nothing else really mattered until I had everything done. Jessie showed up at three-thirty like always, and I put her straight to work. With Jessie putting together the rest of the frames and Robert outside again, pacing back and forth in front of the store, I decided to call Matthew and let him know I'd have everything ready in about an hour.

"Hello?" Matthew's voice came through after just one ring.

"Hey, it's Violet," I said, startled. I hadn't expected him to answer so fast.

"Is everything okay?" His voice sounded off, tense. I shot a glance at Robert. He was still outside on the phone.

"Yeah, why wouldn't it be?"

"Just checking. What's up?" Matthew asked, his voice suddenly light and carefree.

"I just wanted to let you know you can come by in about an hour and pick everything up." I debated whether I should ask him what was going on, but kept my mouth shut.

"Sounds good, see you in a bit." The line went dead before I could utter a response.

I removed the phone from my ear and stared at it for a second, surprised that Matthew had been so abrupt. I got up from my chair and went outside to confront Robert, who still chatted away on his phone.

"What the hell is going on?" I demanded, bursting through the front door.

"I'm going to have to call you back," Robert said into his cell, eyeballing me. He ended the call and put the phone in his pocket. "Now, what's the problem?" He glanced at me as if I hadn't just burst through the door yelling at the top of my lungs.

"I want to know what's going on and don't you dare tell me everything's fine," I demanded. I could feel my frustration crackle just under the surface. One wrong word from him and I'd lose it.

Robert frowned. "Why do you think there's something wrong?"

"Well for starters, you've been distant all day and your phone hasn't left your hand the whole time. Also, I called Matthew." Robert's shoulders tightened at the mention of Matthew's name.

"And the first thing he wanted to know was if I was okay. Why wouldn't I be okay, Robert?"

He sighed. "Fine, but inside." He wrapped his hand around the crook of my arm and led me back into the studio.

"There's been a lead on the man who attacked you." Robert released my arm once the door closed behind us.

"What kind of lead?" I asked as my heart plunged into my stomach.

"We think we may have tracked him down here in Pismo."

"So what does this mean?" I asked under my breath. My frustration teetered on becoming full-blown panic.

"Violet?" Jessie called, poking her head around the door to the back room.

Robert and I backed away from each other at the intrusion, and I took a deep breath. "Yeah, Jessie?"

"Sorry," she said, blushing after interrupting what was clearly a charged conversation.

"It's alright, what's up?" I smiled, trying my best to keep my voice light.

"One of the larger photos jammed."

I let out a heavy sigh. "Okay, just give me a minute and I'll be right there."

Jessie nodded and disappeared behind the door.

"Robert, what are-"

"We're gonna get this guy, Violet." He cut me off.

"And what about the next guy and the next guy? This isn't just going to stop with him."

"I know, but you have to trust me," he said, reaching up and placing his hand against my cheek.

"I do trust you." I covered his hand with mine and removed it from my face. "But you can't keep me out of the loop. I'm not a child, Robert," I said, trying to stay in control of the wide range of emotions battling inside of me. I knew he thought he was protecting me by not telling me what was happening, but keeping me in the dark wouldn't help either of us.

"I know you're not, but it's more important that I find out what's going on than it is to fill you in on every little detail." He frowned, irritation seeping into his voice.

Like a spark to gasoline, the anger ignited inside me. Some part of me knew the fear I'd been keeping at bay since the night I was attacked was driving my anger toward Robert. It was much easier to be mad at him than have to think about the fact that my life was in danger.

"You don't get to decide what's more important when it's my life on the line," I said through gritted teeth.

"Violet, you have to-"

"No," I cut him off, "you need to stop pretending you know what's best for me. I let you follow me around and keep me out of harm's way, but don't think I won't kick you out of my studio if you can't be honest with me." I turned and walked away before he could add anything else to the conversation. I opened the door to the backroom and slipped inside without so much as a glance back in Robert's direction.

Taking a deep breath to steady myself, I stepped over to the machine that needed un-jamming. Once I pulled out the ruined portrait and hit the reprint button, I set to work with Jessie on the rest of the frames. Working helped abate my anger and just as we were finishing the last few frames, Matthew came into the backroom.

He was normally all smiles, and I could tell he was trying to keep up appearances. But he couldn't seem to look me in the eye. I found it impossible to be mad at him, though. It wasn't his place to update me on the latest Magical news. Not wanting to keep him waiting any longer than necessary, I quickly showed him all the portrait's and put them back in the box the frames had come in. He thanked me on behalf of the Deardons and gave me a check as payment.

"Take care of yourself, Violet," Matthew said as he kicked the front door open. His eyes met mine for just a second. There was a sadness to them I hadn't seen before.

"You too."

I found Robert sitting in the front of the studio in the small waiting area. I glanced over at him before heading back to my desk. He didn't move to follow me, which was all the best since I really didn't know what to say to him. I sat down in front of my computer and stared at the screen. We finally had more information on the guy who attacked me, but the news offered no comfort. I felt more afraid now than ever. Knowing I might have to face him again made me sick to my stomach. If he got to me before we got to him, would I survive a second time? I tried to focus on the hum inside me, to force myself to see the future. Nothing happened.

The thought of William suddenly came to mind and how he wished he could get a glimpse of the future. I had the ability but not the know-how to make my visions work. I closed my eyes, feeling completely helpless. Maybe Robert was right, maybe it would take too much time to explain everything to me. I didn't know anything about the Magical world. I couldn't even use my own Magic when I wanted to.

My cell phone vibrated across the desk, jolting me back to reality. I took a deep breath and answered. "Hey, Becky. What's up?"

"I just wanted to check in and make sure you'd be ready to go in about an hour?"

I looked at the time on my computer. It was already five o'clock. How long had I been lost in my thoughts?

"Yeah, I'll be ready and waiting," I said, trying to sound excited.

"Perfect. Can you grab a few extra blankets? It's always freezing at night, and Aaron is using all my spare stuff right now."

"Sure, no problem."

"Alright, see you in a bit."

"See ya."

I saved all the changes on my computer and closed out the programs. When I went into the backroom, I found Jessie cleaning up and shutting down. I let her know I was heading out and that she should probably head home too.

I turned the lights out as Jessie and I walked back into the front office and I locked the door behind me. Walking over to my desk, I switched off the computer monitor and grabbed my purse. After everything was locked, powered down and put away, I took a deep, reluctant breath and walked to the front of the studio where Jessie and Robert were chatting. I was the last one out the door and turned the lights off before securing the deadbolt.

I looked at my darkened studio through the glass window for a moment. Everything was still, and the late afternoon sun made the room glow orange. I felt a small pang of sadness as I turned away from the building and toward my car. A piece of me knew this might be the last time I ever locked up after a long day.

Robert and I stayed quiet on the quick car ride home. As we walked up to the gate, I finally decided to break the silence.

"Maybe I shouldn't go to Yosemite." I kept my eyes on my keys as I turned them in the lock and swung the gate open.

"No, you should go. If your attacker really is here in Pismo, it'd be best if you were nowhere in sight while we take care of him."

I unlocked the front door and walked inside, but didn't hear Robert's footsteps behind me. I turned around and saw him standing in the doorway.

"Aren't you going to come in?"

"No."

"Why not?" I furrowed my brow and took a few steps back toward him.

"I have to go by the house and tie up a few loose ends before I follow you." He laced his fingers around my wrist and pulled me close.

"You're leaving me alone? Now? With everything that's going on?" I placed my other hand on his chest, needing to feel his solid presence.

"You won't be alone. Harriet is just next door and she can protect you until I get back."

"But Harriet-"

"Is perfectly capable of watching over you for an hour," Robert insisted, putting his finger to my lips and cutting me off.

"Robert." His name came in a whisper on my lips. My anger toward him had completely faded. I was terrified of being alone, especially knowing we were so close to finding the man who attacked me.

"It'll be okay." He pulled me against his chest and wrapped his arms around me. I pressed the side of my face against his warm, solid body.

"It'll be okay," I said, repeating his words under my breath.

I started to pull away from him, but he didn't completely release me. Looking up at him, our eyes locked. I felt stupid for being so angry with him earlier. He'd done nothing but try to keep me safe, and I'd acted like an undeserving brat every chance I got. I didn't realize how much I'd grown accustomed to having him around. Having to say goodbye to him, even for just an hour, felt like tearing away some essential part of me.

I started unwrapping myself from the circle of his arms but never broke our gaze. I couldn't even if I wanted to. I saw something flash across his eyes as his arms slid away from me. He wrapped his arms tighter around my waist and pulled me back to him. He slid one of his hands into my hair and around the back of my neck. I felt his warmth spreading through me. I didn't know if it was anxiety at the thought of our parting or the tension that had been building between us since the day we met, but something had finally snapped.

The warmth at the closeness of our bodies burned through every part of me. It was the same undeniable warmth I had felt when he saved me. It coursed through my body, bringing my blood to a boil. I thought I was going to melt into a puddle when he slowly leaned toward me. His warm breath sent a wave of pleasure through me. He hesitated for just a second before he gently placed his lips against mine. Wrapping my arms around his neck, I closed what little distance was left between us. Our bodies pressed together, forming against one another and closing the circuit of warmth. Every nerve in my body burst at his touch. I squeezed my arms tighter around his neck, needing to be closer to him. Nothing had ever felt so right in my life, the comfortable feel of his lips on mine, the way our bodies fit perfectly together.

Slowly, he pulled away and looked down at me. His eyes blazed with the same fire I felt inside of me. He kissed me gently once more and then reluctantly pulled away.

"I won't be long," he said. He let his hand stroke my cheek, then turned and walked away without another word.

CHAPTER SEVENTEEN

I located the duffel bag in my closet and started packing for Yosemite, still in a haze from the kiss. I strained to focus on the task at hand, but it was a lost cause. Robert had completely taken me off guard. I'd known a kiss was in our future, but that wasn't the one I'd seen. My heart sped up at the memory of his lips on mine and I packed on autopilot, completely lost in my thoughts.

Annabel appeared in my living room with a duffle bag just a few minutes before Becky and the girls arrived. I knew Robert would be close behind, but not having him in sight made me jumpy. I'd never been more thankful than I was in this moment that Christy liked to hear herself talk. Too many thoughts bounced around in my head for me to be able to participate in a normal conversation, but that didn't seem to keep Christy from chatting away. Becky kept eying me in the rearview mirror, though. She knew there was something up with me but wouldn't dare broach the subject in front of the other girls, who were clueless to my mood.

I watched the landscape change colors with the sunset and finally plunge into darkness. I kept looking behind us, hoping

I'd get a glimpse of Robert's car. Since I didn't know what he would be driving, I soon realized how futile this was. A feeling of dread settled in the pit of my stomach every time I turned to look for him and came up empty. What if he wasn't following us? What if something held him up? I tried to keep the trepidation building with each passing minute at bay. *This isn't the time or place to have a panic attack, Violet*, I told myself.

"He's right behind us," Annabel whispered and gave my arm a gentle squeeze.

I gave her a small smile and took a deep breath. I guess I wasn't doing a very good job at hiding my feelings.

Despite trying to stay at the moment, my mind kept wandering back to Robert and that kiss. My stomach tightened at the memory of his body pressed against mine. Each time it did, I had to fight for control of my emotions. Something was developing between us, but I wasn't sure what that might be.

We stopped for fast food on our way to Yosemite, and Becky cornered me while the rest of our group visited the restroom.

"Is everything okay with you?" Becky asked.

"Fine, why?" I replied, trying to blow off her concern.

"I'm your best friend, I know when you're lying so spit it out already."

I debated for a moment over what I could safely tell her. Nothing Magical of course. I could tell her about Robert, but I had to be careful what I did and didn't say.

I sighed. "I'm just trying to sort some things out. He keeps giving me mixed signals."

"Are we talking about Robert?" Becky smiled.

"It's just, there's so much more to him, to all of this, that I'm not sure about starting a relationship." I trailed off, frustrated. "It's just complicated I guess." I did my best to be vague about the situation. I didn't want to drag Becky into the Magical world.

"It shouldn't be. Look, Violet, I've seen you guys together and there's something really right about the two of you."

"I don't know, maybe," I admitted, thinking about the kiss. I could feel myself blush and a small smile started forming on my lips.

"There's something you're not telling me." Becky studied my face with a wry grin.

"Something may have happened just before you picked me up tonight." I pinched my lips together, hesitating. Part of me wanted to keep it secret and safe from the rest of the world.

"I knew it! Tell me everything," she said, excitement oozing out of her.

"You guys ready to get back on the road?" Christy asked as she, Rachel and Annabel exited the bathroom, ending any further conversation between Becky and me. Christy and Rachel didn't even know Robert was in my life, and if we opened that can of worms now, we'd never get out of here.

"Yep, let's go," I replied, standing up from the table and giving Becky a meaningful look.

She nodded in acknowledgment, but I knew I'd have to answer to her later. Becky was relentless when she was after something, and right now she was like a hawk circling her prey.

The further we got from Pismo, the more I felt like me again, the old me. I slowly started falling back into a rhythm with the girls as the night went on. That being said, I still wasn't one hundred percent in the moment. My thoughts kept finding their way back to Robert and in the back of my mind, I was acutely aware that my attacker was still out there. But being with the girls was like breathing fresh air. For the first time in a long while, I felt myself start to relax. By the time we pulled up to the cabin in Yosemite, I was joking and laughing right along with them.

I made a beeline to one of the bedrooms when we arrived, in desperate need to freshen up. Moonlight spilled across the floor and filled the room with an otherworldly glow. I placed my bag on the bed, tore off my sweater, grabbed my toiletries bag and headed to the adjoining bathroom. I closed the door and went to flip the light on when someone grabbed me by the wrist and threw their other hand over my mouth.

My body tensed and I bit into the hand over my mouth. My heart slammed against my ribcage. *This is it, he's going to kill me*, I thought.

"Violet, it's me, it's Robert," he said, trying to shake off my bite. He slowly released my hand and took a step away from me.

I swung my bag at him, clipping the side of his head, and shoved him into the wood-paneled wall.

"What was that for?" He flinched. I could barely make out his shape in the dark, but his voice held a humorous edge to it. I contemplated swinging at him again, but thought better of it.

"You scared the shit out of me!" I said, grinding my teeth to keep from yelling. My heart still pounded and my body was tensed for a fight.

"Keep your voice down. We don't need an audience." Robert flipped on the light and locked the door.

The bathroom was small and made of the same dark wood as the rest of the cabin. It had a small porcelain sink that matched the toilet and shower-tub. A shelf above the toilet held folded red towels, and little mountain trinkets placed around the room added a rustic ambiance.

I turned the water on and let it run, then spun around to face Robert while it warmed up.

"What are you doing in here?" I whispered.

"I just wanted to check in with you." He leaned against the door.

"But how did you get in here?" I tested the water with the tips of my fingers, still freezing. I wiped the icy water off of my hand with a towel hanging to the right of the sink.

"Do I really need to answer that?" He pushed himself off the door and placed his hand over the faucet. "That should do," he said as steam rose from the sink.

I ran my fingers under the water again and this time found the temperature perfectly warm.

"Right, Magic," I said under my breath. I pulled my hair into a messy bun and splashed some water on my face. "So did you get all your loose ends tied up?"

"Most of them, but there's something I need your permission to do."

"And what might that be?" I asked, grabbing my face wash and rubbing it into my skin.

Robert hesitated and said, "I need to cast a spell on you." I could feel him holding his breath as he waited for my response.

"What kind of spell?" I grimaced but continued thoroughly rubbing the face wash into my skin. It was a waste of time being surprised by anything anymore.

"It's a connection spell. It allows me to feel your emotions. That way I'll know if you're in trouble. I can't keep close enough to you with the girls around."

"Isn't that why Annabel's here?"

"Yes, but if something happens, I won't know about it until it's too late."

"I see, and what exactly will you be able to feel?" I asked, bending over the sink to rinse the soap off.

"Everything. Every emotion that passes through you, I'll feel inside me." He handed me a towel as I turned the faucet off.

"Why haven't you asked me to let you do this before?" The towel muffling my voice as I dried off.

"It's a complete invasion of your privacy, plus putting a spell on someone isn't something one just does whenever the mood strikes." He pulled the towel away from my face to look me in the eye.

"Would I be able to feel you too?" I was curious at the thought of finally getting under his tough exterior.

Robert smiled. "No, I would make the spell only go one way. You don't need the added distraction."

"But it can go both ways?" I raised an eyebrow, scrutinizing him.

"Yes."

"And you'll undo it when we're back home?" As I studied the lines of his face, his mouth twitched to the side and I could tell he was uncomfortable asking me to do this.

"Of course."

"Alright, go ahead." I threw the towel in the sink and took a deep breath.

"You're sure?"

"Yes," I lied, but nodded. I was getting used to the idea that Magic was a real part of my life, but it still unnerved me.

Robert stepped toward me and took my hands in his. He gave me a small smile and closed his eyes. *"Tiegan mín sáwol eac hie sáwol,"* he chanted. His hands began to glow as he continued and the bright light made its way up our arms and over our bodies. *"Alætan mec áfindan eall breóstwylm fléding geond hie."* He looked up at me and we were both wrapped in the soft silvery light. It was the most beautiful and amazing thing I'd ever seen. Tendrils of light crawled over my skin like ivy. As each coil danced up my arms, another vine would branch off until my shoulders were completely covered in the silvery light. Looking down, the ivy light curled down my chest and settled over my heart. Every emotion I was feeling bubbled to the surface: awe, excitement, fear. It was overwhelming and my eyes began to fill with tears from the raw sensation. Just as quickly as they had come, the vines began to recede back over my chest, down my arms, and up Robert's arms until all the light moved from me to him. He dropped his hands and inhaled deeply as the last tendril vanished over his chest.

"Did it work?" I asked, my voice barely a whisper.

"Yes, but just to be sure..." Robert said, trailing off as he closed the gap between us. He tucked a loose strand of hair behind my ear and let his hand linger on my cheek. I tried to swallow, but my throat dried up, clenching shut. My heart accelerated and the butterflies in my stomach alighted in full flutter. Our bodies were less than an inch apart as he leaned toward me. My hand found its way around his neck and I closed my eyes.

Someone knocked at the door. "Violet, are you okay in there?" Annabel asked. Her voice sounded muffled through the heavy wood door.

Robert and I both jumped at the noise. I could feel his breath on my lips and desperately wanted to curse Annabel for the intrusion.

Robert smiled. "That was interesting," he said under his breath as he pulled away from me.

"Violet?" Annabel called again.

"Yeah," I said and cleared my throat. "I'll be right out." I did my best to keep my voice even as I whispered, "You've got to get out of here."

"Don't worry, they won't see me leave." He leaned against the door again and crossed his arms.

I put my face wash back in my bag and fiddled with the zipper. "I should get back to the girls."

"You should," Robert agreed but didn't move away from the door.

I took a step toward him and put my hand on the door handle. He shifted his body, so we were face to face and his shoulder leaned against the door. I looked up at him and saw the uneasiness in his eyes.

"I'll be fine… and if anything happens you'll feel it," I said and turned off the light, placing my hand flat on his chest. I could barely make him out, but I still felt the warmth radiating off of him.

"Just be careful," he said, taking my hand from his chest and kissing the back of my palm.

"I will," I promised with a hushed voice. My heart gave a gentle squeeze as I undid the lock and turned the handle.

Robert leaned away from the door so I could step through.

"Goodnight, Violet," he whispered.

"Night," I whispered back and closed the door behind me.

I leaned back against the smooth wooden door and let out a shaky sigh. *This is going to be a long weekend,* I thought as I made my way back to the girls in the living room.

The next morning we got up early and made a quick breakfast. Yosemite could get crowded this time of year, so it was best to hit the trails just after sunrise. I finished putting my pack together and checked again to make sure I had remembered my zoom lens. Becky tried several times to get me alone so we could finish our conversation from last night, but thank goodness we found little privacy in a cabin with five people. I couldn't avoid Becky forever, but I hoped I could delay this conversation at least until we got home.

Rachel took charge of picking which trails we hiked. She loved the outdoors and always came prepared with a new and exciting trail. She promised this hike would give me an excellent view of Half Dome once we got to the top. Every year I tried to get a shot of the mountain, but the weather had never been on my side. The straight smooth surface juxtaposed with the half circle dome was not only one of the main tourist attractions but also one of the most beautiful sights in the whole park.

Supplied with plenty of water and lunch, we headed out the door a little after eight o'clock. The trailhead was only about a ten-minute walk from our cabin. Once we arrived, we started up into the wilderness. Rachel took the lead of course and I picked up the rear with Annabel. I wanted to be able to stop and get the shots I wanted without holding up the rest of the group.

Yosemite was photography heaven for me. The trees sprung out of the ground and stood with stoic beauty, creating a world of lush green leaves and pockets of blue sky above. The contrast between the hard granite rocks blanketing Yosemite and the softness of the pine trees made a beautiful photographic composition.

"You sure are quiet back there, Violet," Rachel said about forty-five minutes up the marked path. "Are you struggling that much? I didn't think this trail would be that bad."

"Not that bad!" Christy gasped, struggling for air. "I feel like I'm gonna keel over!"

"Stop your complaining, Christy, exercise is good for you," Becky laughed.

"Exercise, yes… having a heart attack on the side of a mountain, not so much." Christy planted her hands on her knees and panted.

"Here you go." Annabel handed a water bottle to Christy and helped her sit down.

"Why don't we take a short water break?" I suggested, trying to keep the peace.

"Yes, water break!" Christy said taking another sip from the bottle Annabel had given her.

"So what gives, Violet? You're never this quiet," Rachel noted as she sat on the rock next to me.

"She's just a little… preoccupied, shall we say," Becky said in a teasing voice as she wiggled her eyebrows at me.

If looks could kill, Becky would have burst into flames with the glare I was giving her. Putting me on the spot like this was her way of guaranteeing she would get her questions answered. There was no way I could get away with short, noncommittal answers with all of them ganging up on me. Everyone's eyes turned to me then, and I squirmed under their scrutiny. There was no escape.

"Preoccupied?" Christy looked at me with raised eyebrows and a smile.

"That's right," Becky squeaked with excitement.

"About what, exactly?" Rachel asked.

"Oh, isn't it obvious," Becky said. "There's a new man in Violet's life."

Annabel and I shared a glance. This was going to be mortifying.

"Who?" Christy asked with more excitement than necessary.

"Thanks a lot," I said, shaking my head at Becky. "Yes, there is someone, but it's not what you think. We're just friends."

A short laugh escaped Becky's throat.

"Violet, seriously, who is he?" Christy asked as she leaned on the edge of her rock.

"It's Robert Maxwell!" Becky blurted out.

"Do you wanna tell them, then?" I seethed at Becky.

"No, sorry. I'll be quiet now." She mimed locking her mouth and threw away the key.

"Robert Maxwell, like *the* Robert Maxwell? Steamy, rich, mysterious Robert Maxwell?" Christy asked with a gaping mouth.

Annabel laughed out loud and I covered my eyes with my hand.

"He doesn't usually put an article before his name, but that would be him." My cheeks flushed as I pinched the bridge of my nose.

"Well good for you! You need yourself a good man," Rachel announced.

"I have to say, I do approve," Annabel chimed in.

"Start at the beginning and tell us everything!" Christy clapped her hands together.

I sighed. "We met at the bookstore a week before your

wedding," I said, looking at Annabel. "I was searching for a few books when he walked up to me."

"So he came on to you, that's a good sign," Rachel noted, smiling enthusiastically.

"He came over and suggested a book. I could hardly string a sentence together, I was so taken off guard," I continued, laughing at the memory. So much had happened since that day it was almost humorous remembering how tongue-tied I'd been the first time we met. "I didn't know who he was at the time. It wasn't until I met with Annabel later that day, that I put two and two together." Everyone looked between Annabel and me.

"I ran into him again, at the wedding, in one of the bedrooms," I continued.

"One of the bedrooms?" Christy said, raising her eyebrows with barely contained excitement.

"I didn't know that." Annabel's voice was accusatory.

I shook my head, embarrassed by what I was about to say, "Yeah, he was naked." I paused. "Well, half naked." A grin formed on my lips as they each stared at me with rapt expressions. If I was going to be forced to tell them about Robert, then I might as well enjoy it.

"What I wouldn't give." Rachel sighed and shook her head.

"That's what I said," Becky laughed.

"You better give us every little detail," Christy added.

God, I hope Robert can't interpret the meaning behind my emotions right now, I thought.

"He came walking out of the bathroom with a towel around his waist the same time I walked into the room from the balcony where I was taking pictures," I explained. "I was so embarrassed at having intruded on someone that it took me a minute to realize I recognized him. As handsome as he already is, he gets even better with his clothes off." I had to pause then to catch my breath.

"Okay, that's my brother-in-law, you're talking about." Annabel threw her hands up.

The rest of the girls stared at me, picturing Robert half-naked and dripping wet. I couldn't help but laugh. Christy and Rachel's faces were glazed over with forbidden fantasies of the man they thought I was involved with.

"So are you guys together now?" Christy asked.

"It's complicated," I answered and looked up at Annabel. We were getting into a sticky topic.

"Oh stop being shy. I saw him come out of your bedroom the other day," Becky chimed in.

"Oh my God, I could just imagine," Christy fawned.

Annabel cleared her throat to stifle a laugh. Robert and I were never going to hear the end of this from her.

"We aren't sleeping together. I told you, all we did was... well, sleep," I explained, leveling my gaze at Becky. She rolled her eyes. Clearly, she still thought I was lying about what happened on that particular occasion.

"Really? So nothing's happened between you guys?" Rachel asked.

"Well, not nothing." I bit my lip, trying to hide a smile as I remembered his lips and body pressed against every inch of me.

"So, details?" Becky asked with anticipation. Rachel and Christy kept their eyes glued to me. I had them completely hooked.

"We kissed, just before you guys picked me up yesterday," I admitted.

"Finally," Annabel exclaimed.

Becky looked at Annabel out of the corner of her eye, sizing her up.

"What?" She said, noticing Becky's glance, "They've been dancing around each other for far too long."

Becky nodded in agreement and the tension eased a bit. Becky could get a little territorial sometimes and I didn't think she liked that I invited Annabel along, who seemed to know more about Robert and I than she did.

"So that's it?" Christy asked, frowning with disappointment.

"I definitely think she's holding out on us," Rachel said, taking a bite of a granola bar.

"I'm not holding out. Honestly, that's all that's happened between us."

"I've seen the way he looks at you. Whether you want to admit it or not, he's got it bad for you," Becky said.

I looked away, unable to meet her glare.

"What do you mean?" Christy asked, saving me from having to come up with something to say.

"It's just this look," Becky started. Christy, Rachel, and Annabel turned their attention toward Becky. Sadly, I did too. I couldn't help but wonder what she saw when Robert looked at me. "It's like Violet's the whole world to him. When they were over for dinner the other night, he never took his eyes off her, even when we were watching the movie. He kept staring at her like she was going to vanish at any moment." Becky kept her focus on me.

Little did Becky know Robert looked at me like that because he believed I was The Waker, not because he was in love with me. Although, that kiss we shared had nothing to do with being The Waker. I frowned, unsure about how wrong Becky was.

"I think you're seeing what you want to see," I said and sighed.

"Maybe, but he did kiss you," Becky pointed out.

"What was it like?" Christy asked, smiling at me.

I laughed, "You know that feeling you get when you're at the top of a roller coaster?" I looked up at the trees above us.

"Excited," Rachel said with a wicked grin.

"Terrified," Christy said.

"Thrilled," Becky added.

"It was all those things and more," I explained. I could almost feel his lips on mine once more.

"It's been way too long since I've had a kiss like that," Rachel sighed.

"I don't know," I said as I played with the end of my ponytail.

"What don't you know?" Christy asked.

"It's just so hard to stay in control when I'm with him. After everything that happened with Nick, it just scares me, falling for someone again." I tossed my ponytail back over my shoulder.

"Nick?" Annabel asked.

"My ex."

"He was a walking nightmare," Becky added. "He was into this voodoo, spiritual crap."

"Voodoo?" Annabel looked at me with a hidden question in her eyes.

I shook my head. "He was just mixed up in some kind of spiritual cult."

"I see." Annabel nodded her head once in understanding.

"I know Nick was nuts, but it might not be such a bad thing to lose a little control." Rachel gave me an endearing smile.

"Maybe, but I don't know if that's a risk I'm willing to take though."

"You're going to have to sooner or later," Becky noted and eyed me matter-of-factly.

"Is that all you're worried about? That you don't want to be vulnerable to him?" Christy asked, hopeful. To her, not wanting to be vulnerable was an easily solved problem.

"No, that's not all I'm worried about," I admitted and stood. Being vulnerable to Robert was really the least of my worries at the moment. What scared me the most was knowing someone out there wanted me dead. I might not be alive long enough to worry about being vulnerable to anyone, but I couldn't tell them that. "We should get moving again."

"But we're not done talking," Christy protested. She loved

coming on these trips, but she always hated the hikes and would do just about anything to delay anymore exploration.

"Yes, we are," I said and took the lead.

No one said anything for a long time. I made my way briskly up the trail, taking pictures along the way. It really was one of the park's easier trails, and I used the adrenalin pumping through my body from our conversation to propel me up the steeper paths. It wasn't just fear running through me; it was also the electricity arcing through my senses when I thought of Robert. He didn't have to be close to me lately to have an effect on my heart rate. Just thinking about him made my vitals go into overdrive.

"Violet?" I heard Becky's voice behind me. "Can you wait up?"

Annabel and I stopped and turned around. Becky was the only person standing there; the other girls were nowhere in sight. "Christy needed to stop again, so I said I'd catch up with you," Becky said as she looked over her shoulder toward the rest of our group.

"Oh, okay. How far back did they stop?" I asked, taking a step back down the trail.

"They're just around the bend, but I wanted to talk to you real quick."

"Say no more," Annabel said, bouncing back toward the other girls.

Once she was out of earshot, Becky said, "I wanted to say sorry. I didn't mean to out you like that."

"Yes, you did." I smiled. It was Becky's nature to get in everyone's business. I learned a long time ago not to hold a grudge.

The tension in her shoulders eased as her guilt quickly abated. "I just don't want you to feel like you can't talk to us. I know you have your reasons for being guarded, but we're your friends."

"I know you guys are, but you know how private I am. And

this thing with Robert is complicated. Now you've got 'Miss Happily Ever After' down there all excited about something that might never happen," I said, motioning back in Christy's direction.

"I know, I know. It's just, he seems like a nice guy and you should be excited about him. It may be complicated but good God, Violet, have you taken a good look at the man who happens to be completely engrossed with you?"

I couldn't help but laugh. It was true, Robert really was an attractive man and that kiss proved I was more than just The Waker to him. In a perfect world, I should be able to enjoy being with him and get excited about where this might lead. But one simple fact remained: he was only in my life because someone wanted me dead.

"Why don't we go grab the girls? We're almost to the end of the trail and I'm itching to get to the top," I suggested, changing the subject. I put my arm around Becky's shoulder and pulled her back down the trail toward our companions.

CHAPTER EIGHTEEN

I got up the next morning and put on a pot of coffee for everyone. I didn't need caffeine to get me moving with the rest of the waking world, but the girls did. Over dinner last night, Becky said she wanted to head over to the waterfall and have a nice picnic lunch. As much as I loved the outdoors, I just wanted to relax and do nothing for one day. My life had been so chaotic lately that a day of lounging around seemed like heaven. I knew getting rid of the girls wouldn't be easy, but I formulated a plan while they slept.

In the back of my mind, I knew I should probably stay with them and not make myself vulnerable. But Annabel would stay with me, and Robert was close by if anything happened. I thought about calling Robert and having him join us since the girls would be nowhere in sight, but I had to admit it was nice not having him around watching my every move.

Once everyone was awake and getting ready, I told them I wasn't going to join them today because I wanted to get lost in the woods and take pictures. Annabel dutifully volunteered to assist me against the other girl's protest. I was ninety-eight percent sure this would get them to leave me alone. No one ever liked coming with me to take pictures. I tended to be very focused when I was trying to get the perfect shot and spent a lot of time in one place, sometimes just making small adjustments. It wasn't much fun for anyone tagging along.

"You sure you guys don't want to come with us?" Becky asked again as they got ready to leave. She wasn't too keen on leaving us behind, but the thought of spending the day with me in the woods taking pictures of things she wouldn't find interesting in a million years kept her from offering to stay with us.

"Yeah, we'll be fine," I replied. "There are a few shots that didn't come out the way I wanted them to last year, so I'm going to try to get the pictures right this time around."

Becky laughed. "Alright, we'll only be a couple hours though so don't disappear into the woods for too long." She was anxious to get out of the house.

"We won't. Besides, I don't think the weather is going to hold out much longer," Annabel noted.

Looking out the window, I grimaced at the dark clouds descending on the cabin.

"Christy, come on already!" Becky yelled.

"Coming, coming, geez," Christy said, shuffling to the front door while juggling her jacket, a Power Bar and a cup of coffee.

"Have fun." I waved to them from the porch.

"You too," Becky called over her shoulder.

With the girls out of sight, I went into the bedroom and pulled Robert's family journal out from my bag. I made myself comfortable on the couch with a small blanket and sifted through the pages.

"What's that?" Annabel asked, grabbing her own blanket and curling up on the leather chair adjacent to me.

"Family journal that Robert gave to me," I said, flipping the pages back and forth.

"Any juicy family gossip?" She wiggled her eyebrows suggestively.

I laughed, "So far, nothing too scandalous."

"So you and Robert, huh?"

I groaned. "I'm sorry about yesterday. That was humiliating."

"Naw, don't worry about it." She waved off my apology. "It was nice, pretending to be normal for a change. We get so caught up with Magic sometimes that we forget the little things."

"I've noticed. It's been a bit of a rollercoaster." I bit the inside of my cheek.

"With Robert or with Magic?" Cocking her head to the side, she watched me with an amused expression.

"Both." I laughed as I tucked my hair behind my ear.

"They can both be a handful at first. But you were made for this." For the first time, Annabel looked at me with the same sort of reverence that Robert did.

"Right, because I'm The Waker." I shifted on the couch to avoid her gaze.

"No." She shook her head and sat up, adjusting the blanket on her lap. "Because you're you. Robert can be a stick in the mud sometimes, but you bring him to life. And Magic, sure it's a lot to take in," she shrugged, "but you didn't run for the hills when you found out it was real." She paused, letting her words sink in. "You were meant for this life."

I looked at the journal in my hands and let my fingers graze the front cover. Maybe she was right. Destiny aside, I did choose to stay. "I guess. I've never been one to run from a challenge." I shrugged and a small smile played on my lips.

It was so nice talking to someone I didn't have to lie to. Magic had changed my life so much already and it was hard having only Robert to talk to. Relaxing into the couch, the tension I always held in my shoulders melted away.

"So how old were you when you found out about Magic?" I asked.

"I was four when I realized I was different. But my ability-"

"The vanishing thing?" I interrupted her.

"Orbing," she corrected me. "I didn't find out about that until I was about twelve. Sometimes it takes longer for an ability to manifest itself," she said casually, as if we were talking about shoe size.

Annabel's phone rang in her lap before I could ask her anything else.

"It's Jake." She smiled from ear to ear, "I'll be right back." She hopped off the couch and bounced into one of the bedrooms.

I smiled to myself. Annabel was intoxicating and you couldn't help but feel lighter when she was around.

Turning my attention back to the journal in my lap, I flipped to one of William's entries. I felt like I knew him somehow. Every time I read the words he'd written, it felt like I was visiting an old friend. Robert reminded me a little of William. They used some of the same phrases and both held a secret passion.

I skipped forward a few pages and came across a whole section of writing that looked like spells. The words weren't in any language I recognized, but they still drew me in. Under each spell, I found a description detailing their different uses. I idly wondered if the spell Robert put on me was in this journal, but I didn't see anything that looked familiar.

Seeing the spells made me want to explore my magic. I really couldn't do anything except bring up a shield and have visions, neither of which I had very much control over. I wished I knew how to do more so I could practice and get stronger. I thought about asking Annabel to teach me some Magic, but the girls would be back soon enough and I didn't want to risk getting caught. I decided I would ask Robert to teach me everything he knew after this trip ended. I had accepted the Magical world. Now it was time to start being a part of it.

Annabel was still locked up in one of the bedrooms and needing a break from reading, I made my way to the kitchen.

My stomach growled as I looked through the contents of the refrigerator, but nothing looked appetizing. The lodge food court was only a five, ten-minute walk from the cabin, but I wasn't sure I wanted to venture outside. The clouds had wiped away any trace of blue sky while I'd read the journal, and I doubted the weather would hold out much longer. I stood in front of the kitchen sink, looking out the window at the clouds and weighing my options. After a moment's pause, I decided a little rain never hurt anyone.

"Annabel," I yelled as I walked back into the living room.

"Yeah, everything okay?" I almost crashed into her as she orbed in front of me.

"Everything's fine. Want to grab some lunch with me?" I asked, throwing on a sweater.

"Sure thing, boss."

A chill in the air gave off a heavy smell of rain as we walked toward the lodge. I took a deep breath and enjoyed the clean mountain breeze. I'd always loved the atmosphere just before a big storm: the thick, humid wind, the electricity coursing through you and warning you to take cover. With each step, the fresh air cleansed me from the inside out. I finally began to relax and gave over to the Magic building and growing stronger inside me. I let it fill every nook and cranny and acquainted myself with the physical presence of my Magic. I felt strong and more secure than I had in a long time. I may not have known how to use my Magic, but it was a comfort knowing it would always be with me.

The smell of baked goods and meat being cooked on a grill assaulted my senses as we walked inside the food court. The aroma floating through the food court was intoxicating, and the sweet smell reminded me of my aunt's cooking. My stomach growled and my mouth salivated, pushing all thoughts of Magic from my brain.

"Everything sounds good," Annabel said, looking up at menus hanging from the ceiling.

I nodded my head in agreement. "I'll have the chili," I said to the cashier.

"Would you like that in a sourdough bread bowl?"

"Umm, yeah that sounds good. Can I also get a large drink?"

"One chili bread bowl and a large drink, is that all?"

I eyed the dessert menu but decided against it. "That's it."

Annabel put in her order while I filled my cup with Coke.

Before we could find a place to sit, the kitchen called out our order, I picked up my chili bowl and Annabel grabbed her burger and garlic fries.

"I'm going to have to steal some of those fries from you," I said as we made our way to an empty table near the windows.

She laughed, "You're going to have to fight me for them."

Sitting down, I immediately dug my spoon into the bread bowl with ravenous enthusiasm. Steam rose from my spoon and my stomach grumbled in anticipation. I took a small bite and the chili melted in my mouth. It tasted spicy, which I liked, but there was also a sweetness to it that made it one of the best chili's I'd ever tasted. I tore off a piece of the bowl and dipped it in the chili to take another bite. I was in food heaven.

As we ate, a few raindrops appeared on the window and we quickly finished our meal in an attempt to make it back before the rain started coming down in sheets.

The thickness of the air had been cut in half as the clouds opened up. We walked quickly but were no match for Mother Nature. Within minutes the dark, angry clouds unleashed a torrential downpour.

"Shit, I left my wallet back at the food court," Annabel yelled over the din.

"Go grab it real quick and I'll meet you back at the house."

She nodded and doubled back.

Making a run for it, I tried to avoid the small puddles already forming along the path. I could see the cabin off in the distance and pushed my legs a little harder. I was already completely soaked through and the cold started seeping into my bones.

I unlocked the door and rushed inside, shaking off the rain. Throwing the keys down on the coffee table, I moved toward the bedroom to change my clothes when I saw something move out of the corner of my eye. I took a step back toward the living room, searching for anything that might be out of place. My shoes squeaked on the wooden floor as I made my way through the cabin.

The menacing clouds hovering outside gave everything a dark hue as the rain thundered against the roof. My heart pounded in my chest and my breath grew slightly ragged.

Moving to the wall adjacent to the couch, I pressed my back against it, feeling the cool wood through my soaked shirt. I peered around the couch but saw nothing. I took a deep breath to steady myself and then swiftly walked into the living room, flipping on the light switch as I passed it.

Nothing. Everything looked just as I'd left it. I let out a sigh of relief as I took in the empty living room. The doorbell rang and I nearly jumped out of my skin. *That couldn't be Annabel already, could it?*

"Ian?" My eyes almost popped out of my head. "What are you doing here?" I asked as I swung open the door.

"I saw you leaving the food court. I called your name, but you didn't hear me."

"Oh, well, come in, come in," I said, ushering him inside. "Let me get you a towel."

I quickly shed my wet sweater, grabbed a towel for Ian and headed back to the living room.

"So what are you doing in Yosemite?" I asked, handing him the towel.

"We're shooting a few scenes for a movie. The storm got

everyone the day off. How about you, what're you doing up here?"

"Oh, I come up every year with a few girlfriends."

"And where are your friends?" Ian asked, stepping toward me and looking around.

A small warning bell went off in the back of my head. "They went to the waterfall this morning, but they should be on their way back now," I explained, taking a step back and looking out the window.

I had no reason to be afraid of Ian, but something about him felt off. We stood there in the living room, not saying anything. My skin crawled as I felt him looking at me.

"Would you like some tea?" I tried to break the tension.

"No," he said with a stern voice as his eyes studied me.

"Coffee?" My voice cracked. Something was wrong. My every instinct told me to run. I hoped Robert was already on his way. All I had to do was stall Ian for a few more minutes.

"No coffee," Ian said and took a step toward me, leaving only a small gap between us.

I put my hand against his chest to keep a little distance between us. Just the feel of him sent a jolt of nervous energy through me. *Where the hell was Annabel?*

I tried to focus and open myself up to my Magic so I could see something, anything, from him, but I got nothing.

"Tisk, tisk. You really think I wouldn't be prepared for your little tricks?" Ian said, tapping his forehead.

"What tricks?" My voice squeaked and my stomach hollowed out. I stepped back toward the kitchen. Without missing a beat, Ian stepped forward and followed me as if we were a pair of dancers. He couldn't possibly know what I was capable of. The last time I saw him, *I* didn't even know what I was capable of.

"Don't play dumb with me. It really doesn't suit you." He followed me as I kept trying to put some distance between us.

"Really, I don't know what you're talking about," I said as my nerves crept into my voice, making it sound like I'd swallowed a butterfly. I took another few steps away from him, placing the kitchen island between us. I could see the back door from where I stood and tried to think of a way to reach it before he reached me.

"Please," Ian sneered and circled the island. I made a dash for the sliding door at the back of the house, but he was on me in an instant. He grabbed me by the arm and turned me around to face him before shoving me against the cold, hard glass of the sliding door.

"You think I don't know who you really are, Violet?" Ian whispered, his nose brushing against my cheek and his breath hot on my neck. I suppressed a shudder, determined not to let him see how terrified I really was. The smell of his cologne and body odor was so thick it choked me and left me fighting for clean air.

"What do you want from me?" I asked. The words barely escaped my lips as I tried to push myself closer to the glass and away from his invading body.

My right hand slowly made its way to the lock on the handle. Chills ran all over my body, along with a sick feeling in the pit of my stomach. He'd somehow blocked my ability to see, but I wasn't completely blind. I could still feel the tenor of his future, and it was surrounded by darkness and death. It wasn't something I wanted to be a part of.

"Well, I want you, my dear," he said, pulling back to look at me. He caught my wrist just as I flicked the latch to the unlock position.

"Don't bother," The latch clicked back down into place without him touching it.

"You… you're," I tried to say, the words caught in my throat. He was Magical. Panic consumed me and left me frozen against the glass door.

"Yes, that's right," he interrupted. "Now you see why there's no reason to bullshit me. I know all about you and the *Prophecy*." He emphasized the last word with disgust. "I told you you're different." He smiled, reminding me of our blind date.

"What do you want with me?" I asked, trying to sound calm and in control, but my voice barely came out as a whisper. My pulse raced and the sting of tears forming blurred my vision.

"Let's not rush things. It'll all be over soon and it'd be such a shame to fight the whole time." He pushed himself against me, his hand still tight on my wrist and a disgusting smile across his face. "We had such a wonderful evening when I was in town. I think it's time we move forward in our relationship, don't you?" He pushed his lips hard against mine.

Rage and disgust replaced the panic, and I hit him across the face as hard as I could with my free hand. His lips pulled back and his grip loosened on my wrist for a split second. I took the opportunity to knee him in the stomach and make a run for it. I got halfway to the door when Ian's hands wrapped around my waist and he tackled me to the floor, pinning my arms down and pushing his body hard against mine. I couldn't move.

"Don't fight me, love. You're on the losing end," he promised as he pushed his hips harder into mine. "Now where were we?" His revolting lips landed on my neck and slowly made their way down the v-cut of my shirt. I squirmed under him, trying to free myself, but it was no use. He pinned me down with too strong a hold.

"Why are you doing this?" I begged, trying to free my arms as tears streamed down the side of my face. I just needed to keep him talking until Robert or Annabel showed up. There was no way Robert couldn't be on his way with all the emotions running through me right now.

"Don't you think we should finish up where we left off?" Ian asked, flicking his tongue against my ear.

"Where we left off? We never started anything," I managed to yell as I tried to push him off of me with my hips. This couldn't be happening; I had to get away from him!

"Didn't we, though? After the wedding?" he whispered into my ear.

Fear and darkness surrounded me. For a split second, Ian's mental guard slipped and everything around me changed. The world grew dark and foggy. I heard music playing in the distance. My eyes focused and I saw myself walking across the street to my car. I gasped, recognizing the scenery. I was seeing the night I was attacked! A man came out from behind a car and headed toward me. But it wasn't just any man: it was Ian. Ian was my attacker! The scene shifted and I saw myself on the ground with him on top of me, my voice begging him to stop. I moved up close to make sure of what I saw, only to see the enjoyment and satisfaction on Ian's face as he slid the knife into my helpless body. Blue light crashed into Ian and tossed him off of me.

I closed my eyes and when I opened them again, I was back in the living room with Ian on top of me.

"That... that was you?" I squeaked, terrified. The man who attacked me and left me living in fear that he might return was... was Ian. My body rejected what my brain was telling it, and I went numb. Everything came rushing back to me, the emptiness in his eyes at the Cantina, the detailed questions about my life. He'd been planning his next move all along. "But why didn't... why didn't you..."

"Why didn't I finish you off then?" Ian finished the words caught in my throat. "I wanted to, but that filthy healer attacked me before I could finish the job." He brushed the hair tenderly off my face.

The blue light, I thought. It was Robert attacking Ian with Magic.

My body finally caught back up with my brain and started thrashing against his, violently trying to get away. My elbow caught on the wooden floors and gave me a little leverage. Before

I could push myself up though, Ian regained his hold on my arms and pressed me back against the floor. Our hip bones crushed together and it took all the strength I had not to cry out in pain.

"Why didn't you just kill me when you drove me home after dinner?"

"I wanted to so badly," he whispered, his breath hot on my face. "But once I reported that you didn't have Magic, things changed." He bit down on my bottom lip, drawing blood as I tried to pull free. The warm, copper taste turned my stomach upside down and brought bile to the back of my throat. I fought to keep myself from throwing up and swallowed a mouthful of blood. "By the time I returned to finish what I started, Robert was all over you, protecting his little pet." He seethed and scowled at me.

I pulled one hand free from his grasp and pushed on his shoulder, trying to force him off of me. Without skipping a beat, he grabbed my arm right as I swung to hit him, slamming it back to the floor. He slapped me across the face with his other hand. My eyes watered and I felt the blood from my lips trickle down my chin.

"He'll never let you get away with this," I vowed, turning my head back to look at him.

"I'm counting on that, love." He gathered both of my hands above my head, crushing my wrists together.

A burst of red light hit Ian and he flew off of me. Scrambling to my feet, I made a run toward the front door where Annabel stood.

"Get down," Annabel yelled and I threw myself to the floor as something flew over my head and crashed into the wall next to her.

Plaster exploded around the room as an orange globe formed in Annabel's hand. She threw it at Ian and he jumped out of the way just in time.

"Come on, let's get you out of here." Annabel motioned for me to come to her.

As I stood, green tendrils of electricity shot past me and hit Annabel directly in the chest.

I watched horror stuck as she fell to the ground like a sack of potatoes. "You're not going anywhere." Ian seethed from behind me.

"What did you do to her?" I dropped to my knees and crawled over to her writhing body. *Where the hell was Robert?*

Ian leapt across the room and grabbed my arm. "You should have stuck with the Healer as your body guard."

He kicked Annabel out of the way, her body still convulsing, and dragged me toward the front door. His grip on my arm wasn't as strong now that I had the rest of my body free. I kicked and squirmed until I slid from his grasp. I made a run for it but hit an invisible wall. Ian lunged on me in an instant and we rolled over each other on the floor. I ended up on top of him and pressed my forearm against his throat, cutting off his air supply.

He squirmed under me and then without warning a un-seeable force sent me flying across the room. I tumbled over the couch and slammed into the bookshelf. Several books fell on top of me as I scrambled to my feet. Before I could feel the pain from any of it, I jumped up and ran to the back door, sliding it open and stepping onto the balcony. I placed my hand on the ledge to jump over the veranda when Ian caught my arm and ripped me back inside, throwing me over the coffee table and onto the couch. I twisted off the couch, kicking the cushions to the floor as I hopped over the back and ran for the front door. I swung the door open but before I could take a step, the door slammed shut in front of me with some invisible force of Magic.

"I told you. You're on the losing side. It was a nice try, though," Ian said as he stood up and adjusted his clothes.

I turned to face him, wracking my brain for a way out of

this. Nothing presented itself. He was too strong to physically fight, and his Magic was far more advanced than mine.

"You don't have to do this." I shrank back against the wall.

"Oh, yes I do." He closed the gap between us.

I threw up my hands, focusing on creating a shield. I'd never needed it to work more than I did at that moment. He reached out to grab me when a transparent, golden veil appeared in front of me and blocked his hand. The colorful barrier was beautiful and kept Ian from getting any closer. I sighed in relief and kept my focus on the shield.

"Very cute," he said. Ian waved his palm in front of me and my shield disintegrated. "And now we're going to do this without any more interference from you." He grabbed me by the neck and cut off my air supply.

I clawed at his hand and tried to kick myself free, but to no avail. The corners of my eyes blurred and my body started tingling. I kept kicking and pulling at his hands, but the darkness soon closed in on me and my body went limp.

CHAPTER NINETEEN

$\mathcal{A}$ low ringing pierced the darkness around me and my body jostled back and forth. Every inch of me felt bruised and tender as I bumped around on a cold, hard surface. My eyes refused to focus and my mouth tasted like salt and copper from the blood that had pooled on my tongue.

"Why didn't you take the connection spell off her?" A woman's voice screeched.

I strained to focus my eyes but couldn't see anything. My vision was blurry and when I tried to lift my head, and I felt like I might throw up.

"Because I want him to feel her die." A menacing grin spread across Ian's face.

My body bounced up and down as we hit a pothole. My head hit the floor and stars shot across my vision as I desperately tried to hold on to consciousness.

"You're brilliant, you know," the woman said. I could hear the admiration in her voice and it made me sick.

I tried to sit up again, only to fumble and slam into several boxes that fell over with a loud crash.

"I thought you said she was out?"

"She was. I'll handle it, just keep driving," Ian ordered.

Ian grabbed me by my waist and I kicked him in the stomach. As I wiggled away from him, I slipped and my head crashed into the side of the van. Darkness bled into my vision as I fought to stay conscious.

"Bitch!" he exclaimed and grabbed me again. He flipped me over and pressed his full weight against me so I could barely move.

"Get off me!" I yelled and struggled to squirm free.

Ian slapped me hard across the face, stunning me into submission. My left eye watered and my cheek stung where his hand had caught me. He grabbed me by the neck and I clawed at his hands. Terror burst through me as I struggled to breathe.

"*Cyspan*." My arms and legs went rigid.

He smashed my head against the van's bare metal floor and my vision went black. He got off of me and kicked me in the ribs, sending me over on my side stiff as a board.

"Some Waker," the woman huffed from the driver's seat. Her low, cruel laugh was the last thing I heard before I blacked out.

I woke up again with a splitting headache. Blinking my eyes open, I realized I was sitting up with my back against something wooden. The ground felt soft beneath me. Water lapped at my legs, and the even rhythm of the tide soothed me into a false sense of ease. My arms had been wrapped around a wooden pillar that dug into my skin where it had splintered. Turning my head, I took a cautious look around. My vision was still a little blurry, but I could make out the scenery by squinting. I was under a pier and facing the ocean. The rain had calmed to a light drizzle, but the wind had picked up, bringing the dark, ominous clouds on the horizon closer with every gust.

Ian and the woman were nowhere in sight, but I could hear muffled voices coming from somewhere behind me. I tried to pull my hands-free but found it impossible. Whatever bound me to the pillar refused to budge. A million thoughts ran through my head as I tried not to panic. Robert should have reached me by now. I cursed myself for not asking him to spend the day with me. Peace and quiet seemed like the last thing in the world I wanted now. I searched my surroundings for a sharp rock or stick that I might be able to turn into a weapon, but saw nothing but sand. How ironic that I might die on the beach when it had always been such a place of peace for me.

I pulled my legs in close in an attempt to keep them out of the cold water, but the tide started coming in and I knew the water would reach me soon.

"Finally awake, I see," the woman said as she came into view and stood in front of me.

"Lila." Horror gripped me.

"So Robert told you about me then." She knelt down in front of me. "I'm sure he didn't tell you everything." Venom coated her voice.

"What are you going to do to me?"

"Kill you, of course." She chuckled as if the answer was humorously obvious. "You see, you're a burden to the Magical world and my father wants to stop you before it's too late." The corner of her mouth pulled up.

I shivered at her words. "Why doesn't the coward do it himself?"

"How dare you!" she yelled and backhanded me across the face. The cut on my lip split open and started bleeding again.

I stared right back and spat a mouthful of blood and saliva at her.

Ian grabbed me by the hair and yanked me to the side so my face lay in the sand. "Stop fighting the inevitable."

I didn't say anything. His grip on my hair made me want to scream out in pain, but I refused to give him the satisfaction.

"Alright then." Ian released me and stepped back and tended to Lila.

"We should start the ritual. It'll be sunset soon," Lila ordered. She stood up and pushed Ian away from her. Ian nodded and walked around the pillar behind me.

"What ritual?" I asked, afraid that Robert was nowhere in sight and I'd have to face my fate alone.

"That's none of your concern," Lila spat.

I felt the Magic start to rise in me but couldn't do anything with it. I was helpless and going to die. I wanted to cry, but my pride wouldn't allow me to show them any more weakness. I pulled and pushed against my restraints, but still, they wouldn't budge. My heart pounded so hard I could feel it in my temples, in my teeth and deep in my bones. My pulse beat with the ferocity of a caged lion. Each moment that passed, the magic inside me grew stronger and burned to be released. Fire coursed through my veins and like a volcanic eruption, the Magic took over and exploded in a blistering fury.

Suddenly I was standing on the porch of the cabin. A car pulled up and skidded to a halt in the mud. Robert jumped out and ran up the porch to Annabel, who was still lying on the floor, but no longer convulsing.

He checked her pulse and let out a sigh of relief. "Violet? Violet, are you here, please tell me you're here?" He ran from room to room searching for me.

"She's gone, they took her," Annabel croaked.

"Are you alright?" He said helping her to her feet.

"I'll be fine," she grimaced. "Just get Violet. I'll orb home and get the others."

"Alright, and contact Bethany, maybe she knows where they're taking her."

Annabel nodded, holding her side, and vanished into thin air.

The rush of energy faded and I was back on the beach. Ian had just finished placing five stones around me. He recited some sort of spell and they all started glowing an eerie, soft green. I steeled myself and shook off both the fear and cold seeping into my soul. Help was on the way. I just had to stall them a little longer.

Lila approached me then with a small knife. She pressed my head against the pillar and began to carve something into my forehead. The wound stung as blood began to streak down my face and drip into the sand.

"Couldn't you do this back in Yosemite?" I winced.

"No, the ritual draws power from the elements and the salt in the ocean acts as a binding agent. Once the spell is complete, all we have to do is wait for you to die." She looked over her shoulder at the water rolling in, "The tide should take care of that bit." She smirked.

I looked down at the water. It had completely submerged my legs and now lapped at my waist.

"I'm ready for you, Ian," she announced.

Ian bounded over to her and she handed him a green crude looking stone.

No, this can't be happening. Where are they? I pleaded.

They cupped the stones in their hands and the green light shone upon their faces as they began to chant, "*Ætniman hie sáwol.*"

I kicked my legs and splashed water all over the three of us, but they didn't notice. The salt water stung the cut on my face, but I could barely feel it. Adrenaline coursed through me in a desperate attempt to stop them.

"*Áfeorsian hie æt gást léoht,*" they continued.

Something stirred in me, something unnatural. I tried to squirm free from my bindings, but the harder I fought, the tighter they seemed to get.

"Insegel hie sáwol innan déaðbærlic. Llandcofa næfre æt géan-hworfennes," Ian and Lila chanted.

A guttural scream escaped my throat as they finished reciting the spell. My insides were in knots and I felt sick to my stomach. Whatever they were doing to me, it was working.

They repeated the spell and the light from the stones grew brighter. I turned away from Ian and Lila and saw the water rising around me, reaching up to my chest now. If Robert and the others didn't get here soon, it would be too late. I tried again to pull free from the pillar, twisting and kicking, but it was no use. Whatever spell they used to tie me to the wood was too strong for me to break with sheer force. I needed to use Magic to fight Magic, but I didn't know how. I cursed myself for not getting on board with all of this sooner. Maybe Robert could have taught me how to defend myself if only I'd listened to him from the beginning.

A loud explosion pulled me from my reverie and I looked up to find Lila and Ian in the water ten feet away. I tried to look behind me but couldn't see anyone. Maybe the spell had backfired?

"You're too late," Lila said, standing up in the surf. "You can't save her."

"Watch me." I recognized the voice: it was Brett. She came into view on my left side along with Annabel, Jake and a few other people I didn't recognize. I searched their faces again, but Robert wasn't among them. The sick feeling in my stomach started spreading through me and made me dizzy.

Ian yelled something at the top of his lungs and five or six people appeared next to him out of thin air. No one moved at first, each side sizing up the other.

In the blink of an eye, all hell broke loose. I wasn't sure who struck first, Lila or Brett, but everyone joined in, the moment the first blow was cast.

Brett kept a shield around her as she raised her hands to the sky. Dark clouds formed above her and the wind and rain picked up. Lighting struck her, and a deafening crack of thunder exploded around us. Brett's entire form crackled with electricity as she lowered her hands toward the enemy. Hot white electricity shot across the beach toward Ian and his cohorts. At the very last second, Ian threw up a shield and the lightning deflected away from him in a shower of blue sparks. Angry red light shot across the beach toward Brett and Annabel. Jake leapt in front of them and threw up his shield just in time.

I was so caught up in what was going on around me that I had forgotten about the ocean closing in until it slapped me in the face and I inhaled saltwater.

Coughing and spitting, I heard Robert yell over the din, "Annabel, get her out of here!" He came running down the beach and our eyes caught for a brief moment before he turned to face our adversaries.

Annabel ran toward me, disappearing and reappearing at intervals while dodging fireballs and explosions as the sandy shore turned into a vicious battlefield.

"Don't worry, I'll get you out of here," Annabel said as she reappeared next to me. She placed her hand on my shoulder. While standing the water only reached her thighs. But for me, it was starting to get dangerous. I tried to push myself up with my legs, but I was too weak. The spell was taking its toll on me and I didn't have much time left. Annabel wrapped both arms around me and her whole body moved in and out of focus, but I stayed tied to the pillar.

"Annabel!" Robert yelled.

"I can't!" she yelled back, "she's been anchored to this plane."

"Do something, we can't lose her!" Robert blocked a giant wall of fire with his shield, covering himself and Brett. Brett, for her part, made the ocean rise into a giant wave and directed it at the swirling fire hammering down on them.

"Violet, I'll be right back. Just hold on a little longer,"

Annabel yelled over the roar of the battle and then vanished into thin air.

"Stop her!" someone yelled as a wave crashed on top of me. This time it covered me completely and then quickly receded.

I turned my gaze back to the fight and saw Annabel on the ground writhing in pain. Lila stood a few feet in front of her, a sick green light coming from her hands and keeping Annabel pressed to the ground.

"Someone…" I started to yell when another wave slammed into me. The sting of the cold water burned my face and I couldn't focus on anything. My thoughts jumbled together and my vision blurred as the water receded once more. Colorful flashes burst into my sight, but I couldn't discern who it came from. What sounded like a freight train hitting a wall boomed all around me and rattled my bones as another roaring wave almost knocked the breath right out of me.

My head resurfaced, only to be pelted with furious rain and wind. I didn't know if the weather was getting worse because of Magic or if the storm had finally hit the beach. Trying to open my eyes and get a glimpse of what was happening, the saltwater stung and blurred my vision.

I tried to yell for help but couldn't muster enough energy to scream. I wanted to cry. I wanted to fight my way out of this, but I was helpless and scared. Most of all, I didn't want to die. I couldn't die. I was The Waker!

Another wave assaulted me and filled my mouth with salt water. I struggled to hold on to the little air I had left in my lungs until I resurfaced. It felt like my chest was going to explode and I gasped for air. I fought against the weight of the water to hold on just a little longer. Little stars appeared behind my eyelids and I felt my limbs start to go numb. The water still hadn't receded and the stale air burned my lungs. I exhaled my last breath and my reflexes took over. I inhaled a large gulp of seawater just as my head resurfaced. My face hit the cold air and

I tried to take a breath, but there was too much water in the way. My body convulsed and salty vomit came back up my throat and out of my body. I coughed so hard my body shook and I gasped for air. My throat felt raw from both swallowing and throwing up saltwater. I coughed again, gagging myself and spewing another mouthful of water. My entire body was being stretched to its limit as I drew in another ragged breath.

My vision cleared a little and I looked back toward the fight. Annabel was struggling to get to her feet while Brett stood in front of her and absorbed the green light coming from Lila.

"Help Violet!" Brett yelled back to Annabel.

Brett almost glowed as Annabel scrambled toward me. I glanced at Lila, who looked to be focusing all her energy toward Brett. Brett stood motionless, staring at Lila as the light entered her body and coursed through her.

I looked back at the water just in time to take a breath before another wave pummeled me down. The water was growing too high, the sets of waves getting closer together. I didn't have much more time. If the water completely consumed me I'd die and what if Robert couldn't get to me in time?

Annabel appeared by my side again, along with someone else I didn't recognize. They stood on either side of me and tried to undo the magic binding me to the pillar. I heard Jake yell Annabel's name just as another set of waves came toward me and I felt the pillar vibrate against my body. I held my breath and kept my eyes closed tight. The water didn't recede in between waves, and I fought with everything I had to hold on. I could feel someone's hands on my shoulders and then their lips on my mouth. They held my nose and blew air into my mouth as another wave crested above me.

The wooden pillar vibrated again as my head resurfaced and yellow sparks danced all around me. I kept my head tilted back in order to keep it out of the water and coughed again. Remnants of saltwater and bile spewed from my mouth. I blinked a few times to get the water off my lashes. I could just make out the fight to the left of me through my blurry, squinting vision. The next set of waves came toward me, and I knew I wouldn't resurface this time.

This was it. I took a deep breath as the first wave approached. I knew that there wasn't anything I could do. An eerie calm settled over me as the water swirled around me. The sounds of the battle disappeared and darkness overwhelmed every other sensation. The rumble of the next wave passed over me as I held onto life as long as I could. A third wave passed over me and I exhaled the last bit of air I would ever taste. The *whoosh* of the water and the sound of my heart faltering were the last things I heard as death gripped me.

~

Every muscle in my body ached. I felt frozen to my core. Darkness surrounded me and I felt like I was floating, permanently suspended in this cold, lightless place. Every so often a blurry face would break the darkness, but I could never quite make out who the face belonged to. I had no concept of time, but somewhere in the back of my mind, I knew time was passing me by.

Slowly, my body stopped aching and the bone-cold chill subsided. The darkness began to lighten and I began to feel restless, trapped in my own body. I heard the muffled sounds of voices and wondered if I'd finally found my place in the afterlife. I hoped; I didn't think I could stand an eternity of darkness.

"Violet, are you awake?" an angelic voice called to me. It was like her voice alone cleared away the cold emptiness engulfing me.

I felt my eyelids flutter open. Deep blue eyes looked down at me with intense focus.

"There you are," Brett said and smiled.

"Where am I?" I squeaked. My voice cracked through a hoarse and dry throat.

"You're home."

"Home? What… I mean, I'm dead. Why am I here and what are you doing here?"

"You're not dead," she said emphatically.

"But how? The ritual?" I tried to clear my throat, but swallowing was hard.

"We stopped them before they were able to recite the spell three times. We saved you."

"I'm alive?"

"Yes." She didn't offer any more comfort and a small part of me didn't believe her. She knew something, I could see it in her eyes, there was something important she wasn't telling me.

"How long have I been out?"

She moved her eyes up and down and watched me carefully. After a lengthy hesitation, she said, "A little over a week."

"What! What about my friends… Yosemite! They must be worried sick. Becky's going to kill me," I groaned.

"We handled them," Brett said rather shortly.

"What do you mean… handled?" I eyed her.

"You're not going to like this."

"Like what? What did you do to them?" I tried to sit up so I wasn't looking up at her helplessly, but my strength hadn't returned. Instead, I adjusted myself onto my side.

"They're fine, I promise. We just had to… alter their minds a bit." Brett frowned.

"Brett, how could you?"

"Well, if you must know, it was your Aunt who did it. She did it to protect you, I might add."

"You mean protect the Magical world, not me."

"You and the Magical world are one and the same." Brett gave my shoulder a light touch and I looked up at her. I saw a sadness in the set of her shoulders that made me uncomfortable.

I looked away from her and asked the first thing that came to mind: "What did you alter?"

"You and Annabel still went to Yosemite with them. We couldn't change everything. But you had to leave early for a project you booked. They think you guys drove separately and then left while they were out hiking."

Anger filled me and gave me enough energy to sit up. How could they lie so easily?

"You guys think of everything, don't you?" I seethed.

"That's right," Brett said and smiled, completely ignoring the anger radiating off of me.

A glass of water had been left on the nightstand and I reached for it. I needed a moment to try to cool down. The glass felt much heavier than it should have, and I held onto it with both hands. I looked around the room. It was the same room Robert had stayed in at the Maxwell's' during the wedding. Everything looked the same as it did that day, and I took a small comfort in that.

"Where is everyone?" I asked, taking a sip of water.

"They're downstairs. I came up to check on you. Bethany said you'd wake up today," Brett replied.

"Is she here?"

"No, I'm sorry. But she sends her best."

"Oh, right… yeah," I mumbled, disappointed. "Can I see Robert?" I put down the glass of water. I was surprised that he wasn't the one to come check up on me.

Brett looked away from me and dread crept over my skin.

"He's gone." She wouldn't look at me, but I could see that her eyes were glassy. I felt the sting of my own tears and fought to keep them at bay.

Closing my eyes, I willed myself to remember what had happened on the beach, but no memories appeared. My heart ached for Robert, for some image of him alive and well that day.

"What do you mean gone?" I asked as a single tear spilled down my cheek.

"I mean gone," Brett said and grabbed my hand. She looked me in the eyes. "That day on the beach… there was so much chaos. Annabel was trying to save you and… before we knew it…" She took a deep breath to steady herself. "Before we knew it, they all disappeared, including Robert."

"What do you mean disappeared?"

"One second he was fighting on the beach in front of me and the next they were all gone."

I felt like I'd been hit with a stun gun. Nothing made sense. How could he just disappear?

"We all ran straight to you," Brett continued, "but Robert wasn't with us. He never came."

"But what does that mean?"

"Nothing good." Brett sighed and let go of my hand. "Either he's been taken prisoner or he's a traitor."

"Can't Aunt Beth see anything?"

"No, she tried. They're blocking her out."

"May I?" I asked, reaching out to her.

"If Bethany can't see where he is, what makes you think you can?" Brett gave me a sideways look.

"I'm not going to try to look forward. I want to see what happened on the beach."

Brett thought about this a moment, then nodded in consent.

"I'm still really weak, so I'll need your help," I said. "Try to focus on that day at the beach, just before he disappeared."

"Okay," Brett replied. She closed her eyes and let out a sigh.

I put my hand on top of hers and let the Magic build inside me. Then I released it.

The room swirled around me and we dropped onto the beach. Brett was with me this time; that was new.

The beach was in complete chaos. A wall of fire surged toward

Robert and Brett, but he blocked it. I looked beneath the pier and saw myself struggling to survive. Lightning erupted from Brett's outstretched arms, and Annabel ran across the sand toward me. Lila and Ian focused their energy on Robert. Green and yellow light assaulted his shield with such force it knocked him unconscious to the ground.

"We have to get him out of here," Lila yelled.

A few of Ian's henchmen shimmered and disappeared.

Brett swung her arms open then brought them together as forcefully as she could, sending Ian and Lila flying with hurricane-force winds.

"Are you okay?" she asked and knelt next to Robert.

"I'm fine, get Violet," Robert ordered.

Brett nodded and ran toward everyone else who had gathered under the pier.

I looked back at Robert. He stood up and dusted sand off of himself.

Lila and Ian approached him, and they stared each other down.

"Lila," Robert said through gritted teeth.

"It's nice to see you again, Robert," Lila replied, a wicked smile spread across her face. She reached out to him and before he could make a move, they vanished into thin air, just like the rest of Ian's men.

The beach blurred and Brett and I were back at the Maxwell's estate.

"Like I said, Violet, he's either a traitor or a prisoner. Either way, we have to let him go," Brett replied.

"We can't!" I refused to believe what I'd just seen. "He can't be, he wouldn't leave me like that. Brett, you can't believe he's with them."

"Then why did it take him so long to reach you when you were taken?" She raised her eyebrows at me.

My mouth opened to defend him, but I had wondered the same thing that day. Robert could feel everything I did. He must have known something was terribly wrong when Ian got to the house, so why didn't he come for me?

"Did he or did he not put a binding spell on you?" Brett asked.

I nodded and whispered back, "He did."

"He played us. He led them right to you." Brett shook her head.

"Brett, there has to be some sort of explanation. You can't believe Robert would do that."

"You saw him with your own eyes. He left with them without a fight," she snapped.

"I'm not giving up on him." I flipped the comforter back and got out of bed with a newfound strength. I wouldn't believe he was a traitor. I knew Robert; he was a part of me and my heartfelt certain there was no way he would sell me out to the enemy. There had to be another explanation for what happened.

I had to find him and get the truth, no matter what the cost.

THANK YOU!

I hope you enjoyed *Soothsayer*. I have been with these characters for many years now and it's such a privilege to share them with you. I'm sure you're wondering what happened to Robert and whether or not he's turned on us.

Well, you're in luck! On the next page you can read the first chapter of Avalon, or you can go ahead and buy the next book at your favorite retailer or directly from me on my website, allisonsipe.com

I love to hear from my readers, so please feel free to email me any questions or just drop me a line and say hello on my website, allisonsipe.com And again, thank you for taking this journey with Violet and Robert!

Until next time, Embrace Your Magic!

INTRODUCING AVALON!

The second installment in the series is here!
Enjoy a free sample on the next page and pick up your copy today!

My tires squealed against the pavement as I made a sharp right turn, racing toward the coast. I could feel Violet's heart starting to race as I floored the accelerator against the carpeted Tesla floor mat.

"Hold on, Violet. I'm coming," I said through gritted teeth.

My phone rang through the car speakers and I answered it on the first ring, effortlessly pressing the Bluetooth button on the steering wheel with my thumb. "Did you find her?" I asked, my words rushed and clipped.

"Yes. Bethany said she's being held on the beach at *Pacifica Pier*. Annabel is orbing us now," Brett, my ever-serious sister, said. Normally I'd find her militaristic no-nonsense attitude irritating, but things were different now that Violet's life was on the line.

"Okay, see you shortly." I took another corner faster than I should've.

"Robert, take a deep breath. We'll get her out of this." Brett did her best to sound reassuring.

"I'll breathe easy once Violet's safe." I pressed the end button on the screen and quickly typed Pacifica Pier into the navigation. I was fifteen minutes away. I could only hope I wouldn't be too late.

A searing pain shot through me from the bond. My vision blurred and I had to fight the throbbing radiating from my head. Gripping the steering wheel so tightly I thought it might snap, I took a deep breath, gathered my senses and accelerated forward.

I needed to get to Violet. Now.

Throwing the gearshift into park the second I arrived, I shoved the door open and sprinted toward the beach. With a quick jump over the railing, I landed on the rocks below and scanned the shoreline.

"Annabel, get her out of here!" I yelled over the din as my eyes caught Violet's for a brief moment. With the connection spell still active, I could feel her fear ripping through her like a jagged blade. The urge to run to her and shield her from any more pain propelled me forward.

Quickly I maneuvered across the beach, dodging Cinder orbs and fireballs. Someone released a Galvin spell and green tendrils of electricity crackled across the shore like tentacles, electrocuting anything they came in contact with and causing uncontrollable muscle spasms.

Annabel ran toward Violet, disappearing and reappearing at intervals, dodging both people and explosions as I took advantage of the fact that most of Aiden's people had their backs turned to me. Running up behind one of them, I quickly snapped his neck before taking my place next to Brett.

Another wave of Violet's emotions surged through me. I tried to push what she was feeling aside, but she was beginning to panic and the shock of it choked me and left me gasping for air. We needed to get her out of here before it was too late.

"Annabel!" I yelled again. She was the only one who could get Violet out of here quick enough to survive the firestorm of Magic around us.

"I can't!" she yelled back, "she's been anchored to this plane."

"Do something, we can't lose her!" I turned my head just in time to see a massive wall of fire barreling down on Brett and I. My shield materialized on instinct and stopped the flames from engulfing us. Brett dropped to her knees, dug her hands into the wet sand and summoned the ocean water, making it rise high above us and douse the blazing inferno battering against my shield.

"Stop her!" someone yelled. Searching the beach, I saw green sparks flying toward Annabel while she was mid-orb. Her body blinked for a moment, shimmering as she struggled to stay grounded and then reappeared as she fell to the sand, convulsing and screaming. I looked in the direction where the sparks were coming from and recognized Lila's sharp features and long blonde hair. A part of me hoped she wouldn't be here. Our history made things complicated, and even though I'd moved on, it would still pain me to kill her.

Running toward Annabel, I watched her writhe in the sand as the Galvin spell kept her pressed against the ground, when suddenly I found myself gasping for air. No matter how much oxygen I sucked into my lungs, I couldn't breathe. Looking toward the pier, searching for Violet, I realized she was under water. She was suffocating and I could feel the agony of her last breath burning in my own chest and throat. Looking back toward Annabel, I saw her take off toward Violet while Jake was busy fighting off Lila.

My feet tossed sand into the air as I ran toward Violet. The connection spell was getting stronger the more she struggled to survive. My vision blurred and my throat burned as I made my way across the shore.

A stout, portly man and a woman who was more limbs than body appeared in front of me out of thin air, blocking my path to Violet. I looked behind me to see if anyone else could get to her, but everyone was busy with their own fight. Brett stood in front of Lila and absorbed the woman's Galvin spell into her body. She was the only person I'd ever known who could withstand the effects of the spell. In fact, it seemed to make her stronger. Jake fought against two guys and Annabel rolled on the ground in a brawling struggle with a red-headed woman.

"Go help Violet!" Brett ordered at Annabel again.

My anger and Violet's terror surged through me with a force I'd never felt before. Every nerve in my body pulsed with an energy that begged to be released. The gangly woman ran at me as the man raised his hands above the sand, making each tiny pebble rise from the ground into a twister. I didn't have time for this. Each one of my muscles tensed and the rage pumping through my blood pulsed off of me in a circular formation, sending the two assailants flying backward. The sand twister crumbled, throwing grains of rock and seashells flying in all directions. Taking a fraction of a second to assess myself, I patted my torso. I'd never felt so much Magic course through me before.

My two opponents rebounded quickly and before I could take more than two steps, the woman stood blocking my way again while the stout man circled around me.

"You know what to do, Jo," the heavy man growled and the lanky woman smirked and nodded.

I looked between Jo and the pier to gauge the distance. Annabel had just orbed next to Violet with Taylor Deardon and they worked together to untie Violet from the pillar.

Another wave of energy burst out of me but this time they blocked the blow and threw two Cinder orbs my direction. I raised my shield just as the first one hit. It bounced off of me into one of their other men. He froze mid-run, then disintegrated into a pile of ash.

Jo's unnaturally long fingers held her cheeks as she screamed like a wolf in pain. Arms flailing, she made a run for me again. Her partner vanished into thin air, and I knew I needed to keep my guard up. She jumped into a spin-kick formation and I ducked out of the way just in time. Landing gracefully back on her feet, I caught her by the waist and tackled her to the ground. A ball of Arcane Magic formed on my palm, ready to take her out when I fell forward with someone on my back. Jo disappeared from underneath me and the Arcane orb in my hand reabsorbed into my palm. Snarling at my missed opportunity, I grabbed the guy on my back and threw him over my shoulder. He landed in the shallows with an audible *thud.*

Violet's emotions gripped me again and I doubled over in pain. The air in my lungs burned in concert with Violet's agony. A thousand tiny knives pricked over my skin, forcing another uncontrollable pulse of energy to erupt out of me. The dark-haired man I'd thrown over my shoulder flew backward as the pulse of Magic hit his body.

"Annabel," Jake's voice tore across the shore with an edge of urgency.

Looking in Annabel's direction, a stream of Devil's Flame licked across the beach, aiming directly for her. Blinding yellow light moved unnaturally, changing directions on a whim and hitting the pillar Violet was strapped to. Annabel and Taylor quickly jumped out of the way, diving into the ocean and out of sight.

Enough was enough, I put up my shield and made a beeline for Violet. Nothing would stop me from reaching her this time. The cold water stung my legs as I rushed into the surf. The pain in my chest grew the closer I got to her and I had to fight against the overwhelming surge of terror, panic, and anguish coursing through me from the binding spell.

About fifty yards away, I dove into the waste-deep water and began to swim. When I reached the pillar, I took a deep breath and submerged myself. My hands fell on Violet's shoulders and I quickly found her mouth. Pinching her nose, I placed my mouth on hers. She tensed for a moment and then seemed to understand what I was trying to do. Relaxing against my lips, she let me blow air into her mouth.

Another wave roared above us, and I knew that she would die if we didn't get her out of the water soon.

The pillar Violet was tied to vibrated as the battle for her life waged on above us. I squeezed her shoulder for reassurance and then resurfaced.

"Robert, give her this," Annabel said. She threw an oxygen tank and mouthpiece to me. I grabbed it, gave her a quick nod of thanks, and took another deep breath before dunking back below the water line.

I felt around for Violet's shoulders again and found her body limp under my hands as I placed the mouthpiece between her lips. I put my hand on her chest and gently pushed, telling her to breathe, but she didn't move.

Resurfacing, I yelled at Taylor and Annabel, "Get her out of here, she's dying."

"We're trying!" Annabel snapped back. "We just need one more minute."

"Get back to the fight, they need you," Taylor yelled over the rumble of the ocean as he worked on the ropes tying Violet to this plane.

As I pushed through the water, I made a run toward Lila and her companion.

With his back turned toward me, I knew I had a clean shot. Summoning a stunning orb, I aimed it at the center of his spine. The orange orb flew across the beach as I ran toward them, but he turned just in time to deflect the spell. His maneuver, however, allowed me to close the gap and land a clean punch to his jaw. His face swept to the side and then he was back on me in the blink of an eye. A black orb appeared in his hand and I threw up my shield. Instead of throwing the sphere as I expected, he held the ball of Magic against my shield and stared at me with eyes like death.

My defense crackled under the pressure and darkness spread out from the orb like tentacles where it touched my shield. I couldn't hold the Cinder spell at bay much longer, so I took a gamble. Retracting my Magic, I let my only defense shimmer away, as I ducked down and swung my leg out to throw him off balance.

He fell to the ground and the Cinder orb disappeared.

I gathered my fist to take another swing at him, but he jumped up and stepped back toward Lila.

It was then that I realized a bright light was glowing just behind me. Looking over my shoulder at the source of the light, I saw Brett glowing like the sun, brilliant and terrifying. Lightning erupted from her outstretched arms and crackled down her entire body.

Lila and the man I'd just been fighting turned their attention toward Brett. *That's not good,* I thought. I ran in front of my sister and summoned my shield just as Lila's spell flew at us.

The force of it knocked the wind out of me and I fell to the ground.

"We need to make sure Robert comes with us!" Lila yelled over the roar of the battle.

A few of Lila's henchmen shimmered and disappeared. They were retreating.

Brett swung her arms open and then brought them together as forcefully as she could, sending our attackers flying as a stream of raw electricity arced into each of them.

"Are you okay?" Brett asked as she knelt next to me.

"I'm fine, get Violet." I winced as I got to my feet.

Brett nodded and ran toward the pier where everyone was gathering to help Violet. As she did, Lila approached me with arms raised in surrender while I dusted the sand off of my jeans.

"Lila," I said through gritted teeth.

"It's nice to see you again, Robert." A wicked smile spread across her face.

In one quick motion, she reached out to me, bound my wrist and said a spell under her breath. The ground disappeared beneath me as the world swirled around me in an array of colors.

A moment later, my legs hit something solid and gave out beneath me. I lay still for a moment to catch my breath before opening my eyes. We weren't on the beach anymore, that much I knew. I could feel it in the air.

Rolling onto my side, I pushed myself up and healed all of my wounds. Then I scanned the area, looking for any sign of a threat, but it was just the three of us.

We had landed on an unnaturally green lawn that had been manicured to perfection. A large stone estate loomed to the right of us, just out of reach of the tree line. Seagulls squawked overhead as dark, ominous clouds pressed down on us, promising rain.

We must be close to the sea, I thought as I watched a few of the seagulls land on the grass nearby. That was a start. At least there might be boats nearby I could use to escape. Still, I couldn't shake the feeling that we had come a very long way from the California coast. There was something familiar about the cold, humid air, but I couldn't quite put my finger on what it was.

"Let's go. He'll be waiting for us," Lila said, starting toward the estate.

I took a hesitant step forward. I could make a run for it, but where would I go? I had no idea where I was or where I could find help.

"Ian," Lila snapped at him, "Will you please." She smiled and motioned toward me.

Ian shoved me by the shoulder and I resigned myself to getting more information before trying to escape.

As we approached the estate, an older gentleman emerged, meeting us at the front of the property.

"We have a present for you," Lila announced, her deep voice purring with affection.

Ian walked alongside me, looking utterly dejected. I wondered idly what could've made him so distraught. Violet was struggling for her life on the beach and they had me prisoner. What more could he want?

"Is The Waker dead?" the older gentleman asked. He folded his arms across his chest as we came to a stop in front of him. His slender build did nothing to detract from the unspoken authority emanating off of his presence as his eyes narrowed in an appraising gaze.

"Of course. We performed the ritual like you said and stole their Healer just to be safe." Lila's voice cracked when she used my moniker instead of my name.

Ian shoved me down on my knees as realization began to set in as to who this man was. A small tremor of fear settled in the pit of my stomach and I prayed I was wrong.

"Very nice." He eyed me up and down. "But what am I supposed to do with him?" He looked at Lila in disgust. Out of the corner of my eye, I saw Ian smile as he shifted back and forth from one foot to the other in a nervous little dance.

"I thought you'd be happy, Father," Lila said. Her voice still held an edge of pride, but she wrung her hands together with a child-like worry.

My instincts were correct. The old man was the infamous Aiden Partridge. I looked him over more carefully and measured him against every horror story I'd ever heard. He wasn't what I pictured, but he was cold and stiff as if his heart had truly frozen over.

"You're sure she's dead?" Aiden asked, addressing Ian this time.

"I wouldn't be here if I thought she was alive," he said with pride. I wanted to punch my fist through someone's skull. How could they speak so casually about someone's death? The hope that Brett and the others had found a way to save her was the only thing keeping me from lunging at Aiden in a suicidal rage. I tried to reach out through the Connection spell but felt nothing. Ice froze my heart and I rationalized that I must be too far away from her to feel anything. But deep down, I knew the spell wasn't hindered by distance.

I glared at Aiden with utter disdain and spat at his feet. "Such a big man you are, having your daughter do your dirty work," I said through gritted teeth.

"How dare you speak to-" Ian erupted, but Aiden cut him off with a simple, silencing raise of his hand.

Aiden knelt down in front of me, grabbed my face between his thumb and finger and forced me to look him full in the eye, "It must be difficult to know that you failed not only Violet, but your destiny," he chided with a wry grin.

I tried to pull my head free, but he tightened his grip and leaned in closer. "Robert must find her before it's too late," he whispered and let go of my face.

Those were Belinda's words to William. I was the one who was meant to find Violet. I was the one who was meant to protect her. But how could he possibly know that? William was the only one Belinda told that night. Only another Soothsayer would know what Belinda shared with William, but how could any Soothsayer betray their gift and work with Aiden?

Aiden rose to his feet and looked me over once more. "Throw him in one of the cells for now. I'm sure we can find some use for him." He turned on his heel and walked back the way he'd come.

Lila followed after her father and they disappeared inside.

"Get up." Ian kicked me with his thick, leather boot.

We trudged across the lawn to the back of the house. There we came across a set of double doors in the ground, like a tornado shelter or an old root cellar. Ian pulled one of the doors open and pushed me down the stairs. We passed a few empty cells as we made our way down the concrete path. One cell, second to last on my left, held an older woman who had honestly seen better days. A plastic tray holding a sandwich and a bottle of water sat on the floor of her cell, untouched. Her eyes tracked me as we passed and her mouth parted slightly as if she wanted to say something but thought better of it.

We arrived at the furthest cell from the entrance. Ian slid the bars open and shoved me inside. Following me into the cell, he slammed the bars closed behind him and waved his hand over the lock. An electric blue force field shimmered across the metal, and suddenly I felt empty.

"Healers, always thinking you're so much better than the rest of us." Ian fumed and punched me square in the stomach.

I coughed and doubled over. With my hands still bound, I couldn't defend myself. Looking inward, I tried to summon my shield but found nothing. My Magic was gone. But how?

Ian chuckled and said, "Did you really think we wouldn't take precautions?" He tapped the bars with his knuckles and the force field rippled across my prison.

"What purpose can you possibly have for keeping me here?" I asked as I righted myself.

"I was wondering the same thing." Ian's voice held an edge of jealousy as he took a step toward me. He didn't want me here, that much was clear, and the way he looked at Lila when she wasn't watching made me wonder.

"You're upset Lila brought me here at all, aren't you?" I guessed.

"Don't you dare speak to me about Lila." Ian shot toward me and grabbed my shirt in his fist.

I laughed. "Do you really think you have a chance with her?"

"I'm warning you." He clenched his jaw and balled his other hand into a fist.

I looked him up and down and said, "You're not really her type, trust me," I paused and looked him straight in the eye, "I would know."

Ian swung at me, his fist landing right on the bridge of my nose. A loud crack and an explosion of pain radiated from the center of my face. Blood sprayed from my nose and dripped at a steady pace. Ian reached back to punch me again, but I threw my weight against him and caught him off-guard. Dodging to the right and then left, I quickly got behind him and threw my bound arms over his head. Getting his thick neck in the crook of my arm, I pulled tight, cutting off his airway. His elbow shot backward into my torso and knocked the wind out of me. My grip loosened and he reached around, grabbing the back of my shirt and throwing me over his shoulder. Landing on the cold, hard cement, I struggled to breathe. Before I could right myself, Ian was on top of me. His fists came at me with a one-two punch as I rolled him off of me in one quick motion.

A dark chuckle escaped my throat as I rose to my feet and said, "She doesn't even notice you, does she?" I spat a mouthful of blood to the floor. I knew I shouldn't goad him, but I needed a way to release everything I was feeling. Anger, fear, anxiety, they all clawed at me and propelled me forward.

Ian lunged at me again, but I quickly dodged out of the way.

"After everything you've done for her, she still doesn't even take a second glance at you," I cackled.

"That's enough!" he yelled and closed the gap between us in two strides.

"It must be so hard knowing that some of us don't even have to try to get her attention." I shrugged and pain shot down my left side.

He punched me across the jaw and grabbed me by the shirt again. His face was only a couple inches from mine, his breath warm on my face as dark amusement glistened in his eyes. The *click* of a switchblade being opened caught my attention and I shook my head in disapproval.

"You can't kill me. Aiden wants me alive," I said through bloody teeth. My mouth tasted like salty pennies as blood dribbled down the back of my throat.

"For now. But I will be the one to kill you when the time comes." His fist connected with my stomach again and I sunk to the floor. My body throbbed in cadence with Ian's footsteps as he stepped away from me.

"Pathetic," Ian scoffed as he unlocked my cell.

"Give Lila my best." I struggled to get the words out as I stood up.

"Don't push me, *Healer.*" His head twitched to the side as the bars slid closed in front of me.

"You think I'm afraid of you?" A short, dark laugh escaped my throat. "I have nothing left to lose." I held his eyes. It was true. If Violet really was dead, then my entire life had been a waste.

"You always have something to lose." A wry smile spread across his face as he waved his hand again and my wrists fell free from their shackles.

Without another word, that sick smile still plastered on his face, Ian left.

He really was unhinged. I realized it was only a matter of time before Aiden lost his hold over him, and I sure as hell didn't want to be around when he did.

"You should be careful what you tinker with. The puzzle pieces don't quite fit together if you know what I mean," the old woman said and nodded in the direction Ian had just exited.

"I'll keep that in mind," I replied and smiled as kindly as I could manage given the circumstances.

Pulling my shirt over my head and using it as a rag, I wiped as much of the blood off of my face as I could. I tried to tap into my Magic again to heal myself, but nothing happened. I felt empty and naked without my Magic. It felt wrong to feel so normal. And for the first time, I finally understood how Violet must have felt when she first got her Magic. Being normal now, I realized how different having Magic felt.

"Oh Violet," I said under my breath. I needed to find a way out so I could get back to her. I wouldn't believe she was dead. Our souls were connected, after all. Wouldn't I be able to feel it if she was really gone? There had to be some way for me to reach out to her and make sure she was alright. I sat down on the edge of the two-inch thick mattress and closed my eyes. I focused my energy inward, hoping I could feel something or get a sense of what she was feeling.

"If you keep concentrating that hard you might lay an egg," the old woman said, breaking my concentration.

I sighed. As much as I wanted to believe I could still feel Violet through our connection, I knew it wasn't possible if I couldn't use Magic.

"I just wish I knew for sure that she was alright," I admitted without looking up.

"Of course she is, dear. It's going to take a lot more than a little spell to kill The Waker," the old woman said with a light chuckle.

I raised my head then. "You mean you can see her? Violet, she's alive?" Hope sprung up inside me as I pictured Violet unharmed and safe. I crossed the small space to the metal bars in three strides and searched for the old woman's face hidden in the shadows.

"She's alive," the woman said with a warm smile.

I breathed a sigh of relief. "You're a Soothsayer then?"

"Once I went by that title, but *he's* made a disgrace out of my gift. It's nothing but a curse now." She looked up at the ceiling, toward the house above us.

So that's how Aiden was able to quote Belinda's words, I thought as I looked her over carefully.

"Why serve him at all?" My broken nose made my voice sound stuffy and I cringed at the thought of having to pop it back into place.

"I don't have a choice." She shook her head as a shadow crept into her eyes.

"How long have you been down here?" I reached my arms through the bars and let them rest on the cool metal.

"Too many sunsets to count." She sighed and looked up at the small window above her head.

"I didn't catch your name. I'm Robert."

"Clara." The old Soothsayer placed her hand against her chest and inclined her head. "And I know who you are, Mr. Maxwell. I've had many visions of you."

I looked away, suddenly self-conscious. It was always an odd experience interacting with a Soothsayer. They seemed to know more about you than you knew about yourself.

"You must get back to Violet, no matter what the cost," she continued, catching my eyes. "She cannot succeed without you." She nodded, having said what she needed to say, then turned away from me and sat back down on her bed.

I wanted to ask her a million questions, but it was clear she was dismissing me. Leaving her to her own devices, I tried to get comfortable on the sorry excuse for a mattress and stretched my legs.

Now that I was alone with my thoughts, I let them drift to Violet. Guilt raked through me as I pictured her helpless on the beach. There was no way I'd ever be able to forgive myself for not getting to her sooner. I was supposed to protect her, keep her safe, and I'd failed her again. Living through her terror as she was taken from the cabin in Yosemite had been my own personal hell. It didn't matter that Lila had sent a squad of men to keep me occupied while they ran off with her. I never should've left her side. I wanted to show her she could still have a normal life with normal friends, but that was foolish, and I knew better. I let my feelings for her cloud my judgment.

Once I get out of here, I swore to myself, I'll never leave her side again.

It wasn't going to be easy to escape without Magic, but I had to find a way. If only I could get close to Lila, I might be able to use my history with her to my advantage. She may not be the young schoolgirl I once cared for, but I knew who she was underneath all her bravado.

Granted, getting close to her was the last thing I wanted to do. I wanted to kill her for even laying a finger on Violet. But again, it was my fault she ended up here, back under her father's thumb. If I hadn't left things so badly with her, then maybe she wouldn't have crawled back to Aiden. I would have to tread very lightly if I was going to pull this off.

Exhaustion from the battle began to creep across my eyes, but there was something I had to do before I fell asleep. Thankfully, I'd observed my instructor perform this task a hundred times when he thought someone deserved to feel the pain of a broken nose rather than just heal it with Magic. This was going to be unpleasant.

Taking a few deep breaths, I put my fingers on each side of my nose and snapped it back into place. Ripples of pain radiated across my face and hammered behind my eyes. I tried to breathe through my nose, but it was too swollen for any air to pass through. *My throat's going to be dry in the morning,* I thought as I closed my eyes and settled into my temporary quarters.

ENJOY THIS BOOK? YOU CAN MAKE A BIG DIFFERENCE

Reviews are the most powerful tool in my arsenal when it comes to getting attention for my books. It's reader like you, who share their love for a story that helps, authors like me get their stories out into the world.

Only about 1% of readers actually leave a review, good or bad. So all I ask, is that you join the 1% of readers who have already left reviews and share your thoughts with other readers!

Curious what others wrote, check it out below and get inspired to write your own Magical review!

"Soothsayer is an amazing gem of a story!"

"The writing style and setting of the novel was so addicting!"

"If you are looking for a new series THIS IS IT!!"

ACKNOWLEDGMENTS

First and foremost, I must thank my family and friends for their support on this journey. Without their encouragement and love, *Soothsayer* may not have ever seen the light of day.

Jessica, thank you for being the first person to ever read a word of *Soothsayer*. While that very first version no longer exists, your notes helped shaped the book into what it is today. You're enthusiasm for Violet and Robert kept me motivated and I'm so glad that you were by my side on this crazy ride.

Mom, you read several drafts of the book and were happy to do so each time. I couldn't have made it this far without your excitement. I'll never forget when you ran down the hall, yelling about Violet being attacked. Thank you so much for all your support over the years. I never dreamed that this could be possible and I have you and Dad to thank for that.

Now I must thank, my ever practical Dad. Thank you for proofreading *Soothsayer* and always giving me your honest opinion and advice. I know you want me to get out there and get a 'real job' but your support in making my dreams come true has meant the world to me.

Eric, I dedicated this book to you because without you *Sooth-sayer* would definitely still be sitting on the shelf. Your passion and drive to make your own dreams come true, pushed me to go after mine. I couldn't ask for a better partner in crime and I am tremendously grateful for your never ending patience, love and support. Living with a writer can't always be easy, but I know I can always count on you to help me through whatever new adventure lies ahead of us. Love you to pieces and thank you so much for helping me make my dreams come true!

Ashley, I know fantasy isn't really your thing, so it was amazing to hear how much you loved *Soothsayer*. I am so lucky to have a friend like you, who supports me. No matter how much time passes or where we're living in the world, I'll always be thankful to have you in my life.

Ginger and Craig, you've both been so amazing to me and encouraging of my dream to become a published author. I am so grateful to have you both in my life. G-snap, I can't thank you enough for not only being one of my beta readers, but also my proofreader.

I have to give a big THANK YOU to my editor David Hammons. I truly feel like I struck gold. You helped me make *Soothsayer* into the beautiful novel it is today. Your edits were always thoughtful and more than a few times, your notes and changes had me laughing. I cannot thank you enough for all your hard work.

Now I know we're not supposed to judge a book by its cover, but how can you not when my cover is so beautiful! Thank you Alessio for designing a stunning cover. You brought everything I wanted to life, with little direction and you were a pleasure to work with. I can't wait to get the rest of the series covers done by you!

The list goes on and on, but I need to make sure all my beta readers know how truly grateful I am that they took time out of their lives to read my novel and give me their notes. From the bottom of my heart thank you!

And last but certainly not least, thank you Christina Hoppe. I count my lucky stars that I had you as my 12th grade English teacher. Your passion for the written word helped set me on this path. I'll never forget how encouraging you were to me as a student and I thank you so much for teaching me the beauty of writing.

ABOUT THE AUTHOR

Allison Sipe lives in Southern California with her husband and two dogs. She has a degree from California State University Northridge in English Literature and is very proud to have gone to school for something she loves.

When she's not writing or spending hours obsessing over other books with friends, she loves to travel the world, go to Disneyland, and look for Magic is ordinary places.

www.allisonsipe.com
allison.sipe@gmail.com